The Repulse Chronicles
Book Five

The Race against Time

by
Chris James

www.chrisjamesauthor.net

Also by Chris James

Repulse: Europe at War 2062–2064
Time Is the Only God
Dystopia Descending
The Repulse Chronicles, Book One: Onslaught
The Repulse Chronicles, Book Two: Invasion
The Repulse Chronicles, Book Three: The Battle for Europe
The Repulse Chronicles, Book Four: The Endgame
The Repulse Chronicles, Book Six: Operation Repulse

Available as Kindle e-books and paperbacks from Amazon

Copyright © Chris James, 2022. All rights reserved.
Chris James asserts his moral right to be identified as the author of this work. All characters and events portrayed in this novel are a figment of the author's imagination.

ISBN: 9798809219846

Chapter 1

16.56 Thursday 31 August 2062

The Englishman buried his face in the pillow and tensed his body. A fizzing prickle of electrical charge ran over his naked skin. The shock of waking to such pain caused a wave of panic to shudder through his strained muscles.

A harried male voice introduced himself: "We're from maintenance. Don't move—we've only got seconds to fix this."

The Englishman's fear subsided and his spirits rose at the sound of a familiar English accent: not too estuary, not too received pronunciation, but the perfect formulation of vowels and consonants that he'd not heard for so very long.

A second voice, female, flat, somewhere from Middlesex or perhaps Sussex, said, "We can't be certain the MSS can't see what we're doing in real time."

"Relax," the man responded. "If they could, we'd be getting evac signals."

"Unless they can block them."

"Jesus," the man said in exasperation, "stop being picky and just get on with the job."

The Englishman half-turned his head to be able to speak, but otherwise kept his body rigid. He asked: "Evac? Are you extracting me?"

Two mirthless chuckles greeted his question. "You want to be extracted?" the man asked. "You really want to go back to Blighty, do you, mate?"

Confusion swamped the Englishman at the man's rhetorical tone. He knew about the fighting and the Caliphate's failed invasions. But what little the Chinese media reported had intimated that the British Isles remained sufficiently well defended.

The man continued, "We're hanging on like a drunk praying there's one more drop left in the bottle."

"You've got it good here, sir," the woman added. "You would be better to count your blessings."

The Englishman groaned at her asinine observation.

"Approaching ninety-eight percent," the man said.

"We've still got some time before their super AI cycles round and their bots will be missed for sure," the woman responded.

The Englishman sensed the tension in the silence that followed. He said rather than asked, "Enough of the enemy bots have degraded and you're using a temporary block to remould them, right?"

One of the pair attending to him mumbled confirmation and the woman said, "We can fix these bots, sir, and as long as the MSS don't physically pick you up and soak you again, you'll pass the relays and scans."

The Englishman groaned once more. "How the hell am I supposed to stop myself getting picked up? One false echo and they'll grab me and the game will be over."

He thought he sensed a sliver of empathy for an instant, and then the man said, "So bluff it. Aren't you undercover sorts supposed to be trained in that kind of thing?"

The foulest curse the Englishman could think of stuck in his throat.

"All done," the woman said. She began counting down: "We've got fifteen, fourteen, thirteen…"

The man leaned closer to the Englishman and hissed: "Listen: new protocol. When you file a report, do *not* mention or describe the weather. If you get compromised again, begin your report with any reference to the weather, got it?"

"… ten, nine, eight…"

"Sure, but I'm not in a good position to—"

"Don't worry, you will be. NATO has plans. Big plans. But we need to know if and when these bastard Chinks find out about them, got it?"

"… three, two, one, zero."

"Got it," the Englishman said. "But what plans?"

"That's it," the man said.

The pain vanished and the Englishman felt a friendly shove on the back of his shoulder.

There came a hurried shuffle behind him. Velcro straps tore open before hands patted material down. Muffled footsteps retreated from his bedroom and he heard the familiar click of his apartment door close.

The Englishman counted four seconds for each inhalation, paused and held his breath for four, and then exhaled for four. Whatever those two maintenance operatives had done to the Chinese nanobots in his body, they would still track and note unusual reactions in his vital signs, now that the pair had finished their work and the temporary smothering had ended. But the operatives' adjustments afforded him something of the old freedom he used to enjoy.

He reflected how battlefields used to be vast, open spaces where the opposing forces attacked each other with old-fashioned cannons and infantry employed in advances and redoubts and counterattacks. Now, battlefields could be measured in microns inside relatively vaster spaces such as a human body.

His body.

He strained to recall a paper he'd read months earlier, but the memory eluded him, merely offering a snippet of the range and abilities of nanobots that scientists could now deploy. He remembered an observation about a correlation between levels of operational complexity and lifespan in individual bots, which left certain types vulnerable after mere weeks. Another recollection surfaced that this shortcoming could be mitigated by bots working in unison. He sighed and abandoned that train of thought.

He had to plan. He decided to accept the maintenance team's assertions as fact—he had little choice, in any case—and his spirit lifted again at having regained some of his old freedom to report back to his beloved England. The Chinese bots that that vicious little bitch had put in him the previous June would still report back his movements, but they would be broken and sporadic. Chinese intelligence would, sooner or later, realise what was happening, but it was a huge organisation involving thousands of operatives overseen by hundreds of pseudo-military 'officers', and a super AI that might not be wholly independent. On top of that, Chinese intelligence had countless subjects like him under observation in Beijing and throughout the country. The sheer size of their operations meant it was possible to slip under the metaphorical radar.

How long would his luck hold out this time? And what could he find out while it did? He'd been neutered for more than two months, living a subdued existence in the ambassador's residence attending dull, third-tier diplomatic soirees while making the most tedious of small talk with equally dull people.

    He lifted his head off the crumpled pillow and flexed his neck and shoulder muscles, physical power returning with a renewed sense of elation. Old appetites began to gnaw. At last, he could sate his lusts properly again—even if it might be for the last time.

Chapter 2

08.11 Monday 4 September 2062

English Prime Minister Dahra Napier glanced at her director of communications, Crispin Webb, and said, "You look exhausted. Why don't you take some time off? You could go north. Take a few days, swim in a Scottish loch while the water's still warm. Monica and Sylvia will be able to cope while you're away."

Crispin shook his head. "Thank you, boss," he replied in a guarded tone. "I'll think about it, for sure."

Dahra blew across the foam of her coffee before sipping, the exhalation expelling a fraction of the fatigue that twisted around the top of her spine and dragged her shoulder blades down. She stood, paced around the expansive living space in the apartment above Ten Downing Street, and asked, "What does today's agenda hold?"

Crispin's eye twitched. "Regional civil directors' meeting first. We've got three hours scheduled but we might need longer."

"Why?"

"South of the Humber, the army are taking everything not nailed down, including the replica—"

"And the regional civil directors think I can do anything about it? I thought the message that I won't tread on the field marshal's toes might have got around by now."

"It'll likely be the usual exercise in listening to them let off some steam. If you want, I can postp—"

"No," Dahra broke in, "perhaps it will help them—like you say—to have someone higher up to complain to. And I assume there'll be that hermaphrodite from the West Country with the nasal whine who always moans about the refugees and seems to think I can fix everything if I only clicked my fingers a little more crisply."

Crispin's eyebrows rose. "You can always replace any or all of them."

"No, thanks. People like that somehow help keep me grounded."

Crispin nodded. "After that, you are booked at the daily NATO sitrep at—"

"Won't Terry be at this evening's COBRA?" Dahra asked, knowing that the field marshal would brief her and her ministers on any important developments then.

"No, he has meetings with the US military in the early evening. So, he prefers the NATO sitrep as it's earlier. He's got into the habit recently of grabbing the Yanks midmorning stateside to keep shoring up support for us."

"The plucky little Home Countries, yes?"

Crispin nodded.

There came a pause. Dahra thought a flicker of acknowledgement flashed across Crispin's face. She asked a simple question loaded with unspoken meaning, "Any developments?"

"Not overnight, no." He heaved a sigh. "But this really is sword-of-Damocles levels of stress, boss. If the Yanks announce, in public, that they'll stop supplying us with arms and other kit we can't replica—"

"Don't," Dahra said, putting her free hand out to stop him. "That bloody woman can't, won't—mustn't—announce anything publicly. I've got Charles doing all he can with the Department of Defense. Terry is, I think, having some success with certain commanders in their military—"

"Sure. But it's not their military who actually take the decisions. It's Coll."

Dahra met her aide's gaze and said flatly, "I am aware of that, Crispin."

His face dropped in apparent realisation he might've overstepped his position.

Dahra allowed the pause between them to settle like an autumnal leaf drifting to the ground. The fear of the Americans abandoning England and the Home Countries dominated her concerns now the fighting had reached a deadlock. She spoke her thoughts aloud, "The impasse won't last another day if Coll publicly announces American withdrawal from NATO." She gulped more coffee.

"Perhaps that's one benefit of the world's attention drifting, now the violence in the English Channel has wound down?"

"Oh?"

"Tomorrow's the fifth of September, boss. It's twenty years since China faced the Yanks down and retook Taiwan. The global media will be marking the anniversary and showing the celebrations—"

"Celebrations?" Dahra queried. "Shouldn't that be 'commemorations'?"

Crispin shook his head. "Not for the Chinese and other south Asian countries. Most of the dead during the fighting were Taiwanese and no one knows how many rebels were disappeared afterwards."

"I recall. I'd not been in parliament that long, still very much on the backbenches. The more senior MPs were so outraged... and," she added, grim-faced, "so impotent. And scared."

Crispin shrugged. "There were precedents. Vietnam, Afghanistan. It's not like the Yanks had never lost a foreign war. And those early Chinese ACAs... thuggish, but they certainly got the job done. The defenders were smashed to bits."

"I remember the older sketch writers at the time calling it 'the Americans' Suez'."

"I thought the Chinese knew the Yanks had come to regard Taiwan more as a liability?"

"No," Dahra said, "that's not quite right. "The Americans couldn't afford to antagonise them. The Chinese had already dumped enough US government bonds to force the dollar down so much the Americans were printing money like mad to shore up their economy."

"And when push came to shove—"

"The Americans had to back down and look on as the Chinese took Taiwan over."

Crispin made no sound.

"At that time," Dahra continued, tucking a strand of auburn hair behind her ear, "the fear was palpable. We were all terrified the Americans would go to war over Taiwan, even though we also knew, then, that they'd be bound to lose if they did."

She heard a grunt of confirmation, but Crispin's presence faded as the comparisons grew keener. She went on, "But now? Look at these last six months. Europe destroyed, without warning, without a chance. And us, still here only because of the Falarete."

"Boss," Crispin began, "we need to keep moving forwards, day by day. You said so yourself, remember?"

"Obviously. But if the Americans abandon us, then what will the point of our resistance have been?"

A dark silence settled over the room, and Dahra tutted in an odd sense of satisfaction at Crispin's inability to respond. She said, "I feel like we're on the edge of disaster and time has stopped, or, rather, slowed almost to imperceptible forward motion." She glanced up to see a familiar consternation on Crispin's face, but continued: "I have this recurring dream. I'm in a car approaching a building in front of me. As the car gets closer, the building explodes, it comes crashing down towards me. The car can't do anything to help. I order it, I scream at it, but it just ignores me, something no super AI has ever done to me in my life."

She paused, sipped her coffee again and went on, "As the rubble falls, the motion slows. I can make out every piece, bigger chunks and smaller pieces, but the closer they all get, the slower they move."

"Boss," Crispin began in a tone of growing impatience that Dahra recognised, "the meeting will begin soon, you might want to—"

"Yes, yes," she interrupted, suddenly angry at the effeminate whine in his voice. "Let's keep on like nothing will happen, when in reality 'nothing' is precisely the amount of influence we can exert on our soon-to-be-former allies."

Chapter 3

13.44 Thursday 7 September 2062

Field Marshal Sir Terry Tidbury focused on the face in the screen in front of him and fought to control his anger. The expression of exasperation on General Studs Stevens' face failed to mollify Terry to the least degree. He told himself to remember he was SACEUR—Supreme Allied Commander, Europe—and the most senior soldier in what, he felt certain, were the final death-throes of the world's last democracies.

"Earl," Stevens said, "you gotta understand how bad this split between the military and Washington is. I don't think there's a lot anyone here can do about it."

"If the US abandons NATO," Terry said with care, "an organisation of which you have been a member and main contributor for well over a century—and I don't for a moment doubt the political will to do so does exist—all you will achieve will be to set yourselves up as the next target for the enemy." A distant part of Terry's spirit nodded in approval at the poetic justice of what he'd pointed out. He added, with absolute conviction, "Once we are dispatched, the continental United

States will be next. And you will not last a great deal longer than Europe, even despite—"

"Don't bet on it, Ea—"

"I very much 'bet on it', Suds," Terry said, straining to keep the anger from his voice. Feelings of friendship and support melted away as the looming disaster assumed greater definition. Terry went on: "Europe has been the training ground for the Caliph's warriors. Correct?"

"The Third Caliph has got much tastier targets closer to home, including Asian territories packed with Muslims. He's not interested in the Americas beyond how much we're helping you guys."

"But it's not Muslims he wants to assimilate; it's infidels he wants to exterminate."

"No shit, field marshal. Got any other nuggets of wisdom you feel like sharing with us 'damnable colonials'?"

Terry said, "Don't make the same mistake that Europe made. Before all this chaos began in February, our so-called super artificial intelligence gave a likelihood of just eight percent of exactly this scenario happening."

"Sure, but that was then, and this is n—"

"Now," Terry broke in with an energetic nod, unable to stop his voice rising. "What do your computers tell you—*now*—about what will happen if you pull out of NATO and the war?"

"I don't have access to all of the data, but around the chow halls I'm seeing on inspections, I'm getting feedback that the continental US is not—I repeat, *not*—at substantial risk whether or not we quit."

Terry's chest tightened in certainty that Suds had evaded the question, but he chose not to push at the risk of embarrassing the airman. It was possible that Suds might indeed be restricted from knowing a depth of data that Terry took for granted.

"Isolationism has never gotten the United States too far, ever" Suds said. "I'm still hoping our commander-in-chief might get... wiser counsel on her course of action?"

Terry decided he'd done all he could for now. "I also hope she does. At least one democracy should survive into the next century, somewhere in this world, if it can. But keep me posted if any of those Republicans finally find a sense of loyalty."

"Loyalty to the flag is not the problem Republicans have, Earl," Suds shot back, "which is something everyone outside the US always gets wrong."

"Oh?"

"What matters is business. Republicans struggle to believe other countries can put something other than economic metrics at the—"

"Not interested in politics," Terry said, raising a hand to silence the airman.

Stevens' shoulders sagged. "Economics ain't politics. Do you have any idea how—"

"No. And I have more than enough on my plate right now. Just tell me when your politicians wake up over there and acknowledge the unstoppable tide of enemy violence that will come their way around about five minutes after they walk away from NATO."

Studs answered with a half-sneer: "You may be waiting awhile, Earl."

Terry ended the connection without ceremony and Suds' image vanished. He regulated his breathing before standing and exiting the small office.

On entering the expansive main War Room, he barked, "Squonk?" and noted slight flinches in the personnel at the stations. "Central display. Show current strength of all British armed forces."

The space above the circular table in the middle of the room came to holographic life with an outline of the coastline of England and Wales. Pinpricks of light resolved, dotted across the entire image, but denser in the south.

"And would someone please get me a cup of tea?" Terry asked the room, aware his adjutant Simms would not be on duty until the afternoon.

The super artificial intelligence asked, "Combat-ready troops or all units?"

"Everyone," Terry answered.

More pinpricks flashed into life over the map. Terry changed his mind: "No, show only combat-ready units." He watched as digital text resolved next to the map: three British corps and one foreign, each made up of a broad array of divisions. The text listed the names of each division's constituent battalions and their specialisations. Within those, many now consisted of regiments and other units reactivated decades after they were disbanded or merged.

He stared at the image for some time. "Current total number of combat-ready troops?" he asked, unable to identify the figure in the display.

"One million, one hundred thousand," the computer replied.

"Exactly?" Terry said, surprised by Squonk's lack of precision.

"Negative. The precise number is—"

"No, that's good enough," Terry broke in.

There came an embarrassed cough and Terry turned to see the flaxen-haired operative proffer a white-China mug of tea. "Thank you," he said, taking it by the rim, switching his grip to the handle, and blowing the steam that rose from it. Glancing back at the image, a slight shudder rippled across his shoulder blades: at the beginning of 2062, the entire British Army had consisted of just thirty-six thousand personnel. In nine months, it had increased by more than thirty times. Although many of the divisions in the European Integrated Corps were the remnants of European armies, as well as some Americans and others who had decided to join, the vast majority of recruits were from the Home Countries.

"List each corps' command structure."

The digital outline of England expanded and rose high above Terry, dominating the War Room. Terry took a step back. Red and blue highlights reflected from the stations. Names of the corps and their constituent divisions resolved. Terry sipped his tea and let it soothe his concern at the shortcomings in the military behemoth facing him. As the commander-in-chief, he had to manage the ever-increasing requirements for leaders, men and women who had to be selected, trained, promoted, and mentored by their superiors.

In peacetime, an officer who excelled might not be promoted any higher than brigadier or major general before retirement. Now, the war's casualties and military expansion unseen for a century and a half obliged Terry to ensure that the newly formed battalions and divisions were led by troops with appropriate leadership skills. As the Falarete defences around England thickened in density and the stalemate showed little sign of an immediate resolution, managing his growing forces took up a greater share of his time.

"Display summary of supply logistics, both arms and support."

New indications flashed in and around the image, pinpointing the locations of key dumps and other support elements. Terry shook his head in wonder at the volume and complexity of the operation he headed. All units enjoyed replicators that supplied the troops with uniforms and other kit. Mess halls relied primarily on old food replicators. Sourcing fresh fruit and vegetables presented a challenge that grew with the number of soldiers.

Terry took a longer pull on the hot tea and acknowledged that he now oversaw an army of hordes, trained and armed... to do what? The development of new NATO weapons proceeded, for all the urgency of survival, with what seemed to him to be glacial slowness. And if the enemy developed and deployed superior weaponry before NATO forces were ready, what difference would an army even ten million strong make?

Chapter 4

14.42 Tuesday 12 September 2062

Professor Duncan Seekings stifled a yawn. The meeting he attended virtually from his office at the Porton Down research facility had become bogged down in a pedantic issue for which he had little time, mainly because the solution was obvious. And if that was the case, what benefit could there possibly be in prolonging the debate further?

However, some of the attendees appeared to be engrossed in the redundant toing and froing. Duncan wondered if the cause could be ascribed to this issue being the last on the agenda, and the attendees not wishing to let the presentation end and allow the team to retire. Frenchie—Duncan always struggled to recall the little Frenchman's name—sat moody and apparently disinterested at the end of an oblong table, while other members of his development team fielded questions and described the internal defence system of NATO's next generation of weapons—the arms on which any counterattack would depend.

Duncan muttered to himself in response to his own consideration: "Assuming we can last long enough and those buggers don't beat us by developing better weapons sooner." Then, his memory extracted the name of the team leader: Reyer.

A large, severe man a couple of rows in front of Duncan joined the fray, speaking in accented English: "We are placing too much trust in the simulations. We should go back to reassessing the structure of the MCPU. We can find savings there to help increase the output of the—"

"No, we will not," Reyer said, sitting up straight.

Opposite him, a thin, young lady intoned in English imperiousness: "The 8C Muon-Catalyst Power Unit is shortly to begin final testing and, beyond finetuning, is an established design. Which is as you and all of us were informed at last night's briefing, I would like to add."

"But the axial-flux motors can be narrowed to allow more space for larger cryo-magnets," the severe man protested. "With only a few microns' adju—"

"Then you should have submitted your suggestions in the correct channels," the woman shot back.

"I did." The man threw his arms in the air. "But they were rejected."

Reyer held out a bony hand and said, in similarly accented English, "Professor Molina, your work on this project has been very important. However, we are discussing issues around the new weapons' shielding, not their manoeuvrability."

Duncan self-consciously rechecked he was still on mute before muttering, "Exactly. Why are we wasting time going around in circles like this? This fellow is the third speaker to make the same point, for goodness' sake."

Professor Molina said, his tone veering from complaining to pleading, "But they are related, connected issues. And many agree. We can have stronger shielding—"

"At the cost of aerial manoeuvrability," Reyer interrupted in a tone of exhausted repetition.

The woman tossed her head. "We worked through many thousands of variations that the super AI came up with." She dabbed her fingers on the surface of the table and added: "Yes, Professor Molina, your preferences match those suggested by the propulsion subcommittee."

"Thank you," Molina said with a trace of apparent mollification.

"And which were then rejected by this committee," she added.

Reyer leaned forward. "We must provide what the military have asked us for. Manoeuvrability, the new weapons' dexterity, has to have priority. Then, they must carry the new armaments. Like with the power unit, the armaments are also ready for final testing." He broke off to smother a cough and then continued: "Of course, we can discuss differences of microns as though we had all of the time in the world. But we do not. I would like, very much indeed, for our cooperation to be as open as possible. But, dear colleagues, Europe is subjugated and England remains in great danger, so we must make our best decisions and continue."

The woman next to Reyer interlinked her slender fingers. "So, thank you everyone for attending this presentation and asking such a wide range of questions. We will provide more in-depth test results at the next update conference slated for this Friday—"

Duncan whipped the glasses from his eyes, thus leaving the meeting. He pushed himself off the couch in his office-cum-living quarters. "Finally. As if we have time to waste on this kind of frivolity. Yes, yes. I am quite sure you will, my dear. But what about the snags, eh? The 8C is in fine fettle, all sorted out..."

He kept muttering as he entered the small kitchenette. He stabbed a button to activate the kettle, reached for his mug, and grabbed a teabag from the jar.

The super AI announced, "Professor, you are overdue for your periodical medical. Please place any digit on the pad at your earliest convenience."

Duncan ignored the instruction and went on: "However, I foresee issues with power drain. Assuming we actually survive long enough and those new machines actually go into battle, their time is going to be limited. And that, most definitely, is a snag." As the kettle began to judder with boiling water, a notification arrived in his lens. He twitched an eye muscle to accept it. A thumbnail of a dark-skinned man with thick eyebrows appeared in the corner of his vision. Duncan asked, "Well, there you are, Mr English. And what did you make of that, eh?"

Graham said, "Those youngsters can be frightfully timid sometimes, can't they?"

Duncan poured water into the mug. "I think they have a great deal on their shoulders. I expect Reyer and his team worry if they have chosen the correct route with these new machines."

"They are doing their best to give the military what they want. Although time is against them, I suppose," Graham said.

Duncan let his tea brew for a moment before flicking the teabag in the sink.

"I called because," Graham went on, "I must confess, the question of duration once in combat did cross my mind, and I wondered if you'd had the same thought."

Duncan smiled, left the kitchenette, and returned to the worn and very comfortable couch in the main living area. "Funnily enough, I had. Shall we compare notes?"

"Absolutely."

"Good."

Over the next hour, the two friends reviewed the available designs and documents, and discussed the wisdom of giving the least importance to the strength of the new weapons' shielding in favour of enhanced agility. They speculated over the existence of more detailed designs to which they might not have access and, if they existed, what solutions they might contain.

Duncan appreciated the return of their friendship to its more reserved footing now Graham had ceased insisting Duncan run away to America. In turn, Duncan had decided to give his friend the benefit of the doubt regarding Graham's decision to leave England in its hour of greatest need; that, perhaps, it hadn't been cowardice after all.

Graham concluded, "There remain many variables—especially in the 8C's power output—that could affect the unit's ability to defend itself, but even the most optimistic suggest that if it came under sustained attack, the shielding would not last as long as perhaps it should."

Duncan murmured his agreement. "Yes, but what else can they do? If they lowered the aerial dexterity to increase shielding duration, its overall anticipated endurance would be more subject to external variables like terrain and weather conditions."

"Indeed, but as we noted earlier, old chap, the military need a certain—what did they call it—'minimum level of battlefield performance'?"

"Yes, yes," Duncan said, suddenly wishing he were considering the problem alone. He had decided to conclude the discussion when Graham did it for him.

"Anyway, I have another meeting in a few minutes, dear fellow, so I must bring our chat to an end. I must say, it has been a pleasure."

"Likewise," Duncan answered automatically, his mind focusing on refining a potential compromise that might also increase shielding duration.

"Ah," Graham said, "I recognise that tone. But before I go, I did want to ask you about one thing."

"Yes? What is it? Er, I mean of course."

"You know contact was lost last month with the subterranean resistances in Paris, Berlin and Warsaw?"

Duncan struggled to recall, irritated at his friend derailing his train of thought. "I believe so. Horrid situation. I doubt they are—"

"Quite. The rumour over here is that it must have involved a very powerful chemical agent. I was wondering if you'd heard anything, given that you work in—"

"No, I have not heard a thing."

"But Porton Down used to be the main chemical—"

"That's right," Duncan broke in, wishing the conversation were over, "but the last chemical weapons stored here were made safe over twenty years ago. Those areas are all devoted to research now."

"I know that. I was only wondering if perhaps—oh, never mind. I have to go. Until next time, Professor Seekings."

"Indeed. Goodbye, Mr English. I hope a frame or two of snooker is not too far in the future."

The connection ended. Duncan let out a sigh and, in his lens, called up the schematics of NATO's next generation of autonomous combat aircraft.

The super AI interrupted his thoughts, "Professor, you are overdue for your periodical medical. Please place a digit on the pad at your earliest convenience."

Duncan tutted and said, "Really? I'm rather busy at the moment. Remind me later."

"This is your twenty-fifth reminder. A notification will now be sent to the Ministry of Defence that you are actively avoiding your responsibility to—"

"Oh, for Pete's sake," Duncan said in frustration. He stood up and walked to the front door. On the wall to the left of it was a small pad. Duncan told himself that the check-up really wasn't such an inconvenience, but it still rankled that the super AI wouldn't let him be. He placed his left thumb on the pad to allow the nanobots into his bloodstream.

The super AI said, "Thank you."

"Now, let me concentrate." Duncan returned to his couch.

However, three minutes later the computer interrupted his thoughts once again, "Attention: diagnostic bots have discovered mutated cells in your upper thalamus."

"So?" Duncan tutted. "Can't they deal with the problem?"

"Negative. You need to go to the medical facility in the south wing and be treated with a full GenoFluid pack."

Duncan sighed and threw his hands in the air. "Really," he said, "this had better be important. There isn't any time to waste."

Chapter 5

06.40 Saturday 23 September 2062

Colonel Trudy Pearce slowed to a walk at the end of her morning run. The rising sun behind her threw a grey shadow out on the dusty ground ahead. The air tasted dry and bitter, like her memories.

She passed rows of vehicles on her right, all covered with camouflage netting, autonomous troop and equipment transports giving way to American Abrahams. She slowed and admired the giant, four-wheeled tanks. Between each front pair of wheels—as high as her—she glimpsed the curved metal ellipsoid body that held each tank's pulsar laser. The thick armour protected the pulsar until needed, when the upper plate rotated under the body to allow the pulsar to rise and fire.

Her breathing slowed. A notification flashed in her lens informing her that the new adjutant had arrived. "Damn," she muttered, not expecting the woman to be so early. "Squonk, tell the adjutant to wait outside my office."

"Confirmed."

Trudy accelerated to a fast trot, turning north when she reached the furthermost tank. The slight incline up to the barracks obliged her to exert more effort, and by the time she arrived at the block containing her quarters, sinews in her chest and behind her shoulder blades ached with the exertion. She smiled when she recalled that she'd been off the vodkas and tonic for ten days straight, a personal best. She wondered if her new-found self-control stemmed from her experiences in the attempted invasions the previous month, or from the field marshal's smart—and unexpectedly honest—compromise at her bending the rules of engagement. In any case, the relentless swelling of the number of troops under her command itself caused the realisation that she played a role in events that extended far beyond her own personal dramas, however much they meant to her.

She entered her cramped billet, showered and changed, and then made her way east to the newly expanded command centre. The low autumn sun stung her eyes while the arid air took the moisture from her damp hair.

As Trudy approached the command post, a figure standing next to the entrance became distinct: slight and narrow with shoulders that fell away from her neck, and tufts of unruly brown hair that stuck out at odd angles. The woman advanced onto the dusty road, stood to attention, and saluted.

"Captain Marta Woodward reporting for duty, ma'am," she announced in a reedy yet determined voice.

Trudy stopped a few paces in front of the captain and put her hands on her hips. "Welcome to Crowhurst field barracks, Captain Woodward. At ease. Good journey this morning?"

Captain Woodward clasped her hands behind her back, face beaming. "Yes, thank you, colonel. And thank you for selecting me to be your adjutant."

Trudy shrugged and walked towards the woman. "To be frank, I am surprised I need an adjutant. But I liked your analytical test scores."

"Thank you, ma'am."

"Come on, I'll introduce you to Pierre." Trudy led Woodward to the command post. She turned her head back. "Our construction replicator put up this and all those stores you passed on the way in the last week."

"When you assigned me," Woodward said, "you mentioned that you weren't happy with Squonk—"

"It's not about being happy. When thinking about strategy, Squonk doesn't always give enough weight to what I regard as more natural factors."

"Uh-huh. The second attempted invasion last month."

"Exactly." Trudy opened the door and entered first, pleased that the adjutant had done her homework. When Woodward followed, Trudy said: "This is Master Sergeant Pierre LaRue, on secondment from the French 7th Brigade. And over there is his number two, Sergeant Lyon."

Woodward nodded hellos.

"Help yourself to tea." Trudy indicated a tall, narrow food replicator in one corner of the room. Then she asked Pierre: "Can we sort the captain out with a desk and chair, maybe over there?" She pointed to the wall next to Lyon.

"Yes, madame."

"Good. Are the new recruits on time?"

"They are."

"Right," Trudy said. She fixed Woodward with a stare and stuck an arm out. "My office?"

The adjutant grasped her mug of tea and nodded. Both women entered Trudy's office. Once inside, Trudy shut the door. "Wall. Plan of barracks."

A white screen on the doorway wall came to life with a series of lines in the shapes of squares and oblongs that denoted the various areas of the base seen from overhead.

Trudy leaned back on the front of her desk, looked at the screen and said, "I think I'll call you 'Marta', as that's easier than 'Woodward'."

"Very well, ma'am,"

Trudy noted with approval Marta's indifferent tone. "That's a Polish name, isn't it?"

Marta nodded. "Maternal grandfather came over at the turn of the century."

Trudy indicated the plan on the wall, "That's the current outline of this base. Squonk, add in projected expansion for the next six months."

The image shrank to one-quarter its original size and new lines resolved, extending outwards to cover much more land.

"We're due to go from three thousand troops to twenty thousand over the next nine months, assuming no surprises."

Marta nodded and Trudy held down the urge to ask the young woman why she didn't control her hair. Trudy went on, "Now, our biggest problem is going to be fat."

"Ma'am?"

"You'll see exactly what I mean when the next batch of green squaddies arrives. Recruitment parameters have been loosened to encourage as many civilians as possible to join up. Although you might not know that because you're a captain."

"Right," Marta said.

"We're now allowing applicants with greater-than-forty-percent body fat."

Marta dipped her head in apparent consideration. "But they would still have to be able to pass the BFT, yes?"

Trudy scoffed. "The basic fitness test has been made even easier, I think to let them pass. My God, it was ridiculously easy when I joined up nearly twenty years ago. Me and a couple of friends walked and chatted for half of the run and we still got to the finish line well within the time limit."

Marta smiled. "So, you have an idea to do something about it. Yes, ma'am?"

"I do," Trudy replied, noting with approval her adjutant driving the discussion forward. "I want you to design a fitness regime. Use Squonk's suggestions if you think they're good, but I want an element of randomness involved, and perhaps some competition between units and regiments."

"Yes, ma'am."

"Also, work out a pattern of integration. It's been seven weeks since the enemy tried their last invasion, and many of the troops stationed here saw combat. In the last few weeks, there's been some... friction as new recruits have arrived and units have expanded. I want suggestions how to diffuse that. I don't want fights breaking out among lower ranks, that will require harsher discipline."

"As you wish, ma'am."

"Pierre and Lyon will help you; just ask them. But our priority, Marta, for as long as this stalemate lasts, is to deal with the fat. We've only got basic food replicators which produce shit, for the most part. Fresh fruit and veg will only be delivered once, perhaps twice, a week, and likely in insufficient quantities to feed everyone. Thus, movement will have to burn up all the fat and empty calories in the replicated food and make them fit."

"Yes, ma'am."

A notification flashed in Trudy's view confirming the arrival of the first autonomous transports bearing their cargoes. She didn't need to give any orders as Squonk would instruct the regimental sergeant majors and commissioned ranks to attend.

"Will you address the new arrivals?" Marta asked.

"Yes."

"In that case, I'll go and introduce myself to the unit commanders. With your permission, ma'am?"

Trudy nodded. When Marta left and the door closed behind her, Trudy paced over to the diagram on the wall and folded her arms. A quiet voice in her head reminded her that she'd been dry for ten days. Had the reason for her sobriety really been this unexpected stalemate? Seven short weeks ago, the enemy had tried and failed to invade England for, so far, the last time. Now, all of NATO's computers suggested another invasion would be highly unlikely until new weapons became available.

The digital lines in front of her set out the proposed expansion of the base—her base. As thousands of new NATO troops passed out and arrived, the command structure would swell. As in every war, field promotions accelerated. Trudy questioned again what had happened to make her see a future she used to believe didn't exist: the certainty of promotion for her and her top-performing subordinates, as NATO forces continued to expand? The field marshal's adroit pep talk? Or, perhaps, the deeply satisfying act of killing the enemy, the same enemy who had taken Dan and her parents from her?

Trudy sighed as she placed her left thumb in her right palm and kneaded the flesh and bones in the middle of her hand. The vodkas and tonic would never bring back the people she'd lost, but now she understood that alcohol could impact her performance negatively. Before this war, it hadn't mattered. Peacetime soldiering in NATO could be as bland as working in any other top-heavy corporation, with nothing more than silly metrics to toy with and arbitrary deadlines for pretend projects to be met.

She acknowledged the irony that her musing revealed to her: losing Dan and her parents might have driven her to drink too much, but now the war that had taken them stirred passions and desires for revenge that made her appreciate the martial power she would enjoy as the battalions under her command expanded.

But if this stalemate persisted, what would all these troops be used for?

A notification flashed in her lens to announce that the new arrivals had been formed up on the open, arid space to the north that passed for a parade ground. Trudy turned away from the map on the wall, left her office, and exited the command post. The autumn sun had yet to lose a significant portion of its summer heat, but the humidity had increased and the warm, clammy air clung to her exposed forearms. Further away, the sound of hissing and clanking drifted over the single-storey huts as the construction replicators completed the barracks that would billet the new troops.

As soon as she emerged on the parade ground, a sergeant major out of sight yelled and five hundred pairs of boots shuffled together as the arrivals saluted their new commanding officer. Trudy mounted the few wooden steps of a bland podium that elevated her enough to see over the sea of uniformed heads, arranged in two phalanxes of roughly equal size. She allowed the pause to lengthen as she scanned the troops. The bright faces shone back at her: young men with chins jutting in what might have been arrogance or pride or determination; feminine cheekbones framed with fuller hair surrounding faces that beamed in what could've been trepidation or anticipation.

She repeated the message she'd given Marta only moments before, with an added embellishment: "Welcome to Crowhurst field barracks. For those of you who might not know who I am, my name is Colonel Pearce, spelt B-I-T-C-H." She paused to see a range of reactions from the troops in front of her, from grimaces to smiles. "Good," she said, dismounting the small platform.

She strode to the front, then turned and walked between the two phalanxes. None of the new soldiers looked anywhere other than straight ahead. She chose her words with care and projected her voice in the warm, still air: "In addition to building on your basic training and learning more about your specialisations, here at Crowhurst you will also learn the value of losing the excess weight I can see that many of you labour under."

She hoped to see a flash of offence taken, but all eyes remained fixed forwards.

Trudy continued: "Excess body fat is the soldier's worst enemy. It will slow down your thinking as well as your speed and agility. If you are injured, it will lessen your chances of survival."

Someone in the ranks coughed.

"And, of course, how can you help your team, for example by carrying an injured comrade to safety, if your strength is already taken up heaving around enough spare blubber to plug up the Solent's flood defences?"

She reached the last row of troops, spun on her heel, and retraced her steps back towards the podium. "So get ready, troops. Via your Squitches, each of you will undertake a proper fitness course; something a little more substantial than what you wobbled through during your basic training. If the Home Countries can hold out long enough, you will find yourselves becoming proper soldiers, the kind of combat troops of which your family and friends can be justifiably proud.

"I expect that some of you worry about what the future holds. Will the enemy try to invade us again? Will they attack us with new and better ACAs? Well, those issues are no longer your concern. Your priorities now only need focus on your teams, your platoons, your sections, and your battalions."

She reached the head of the body of soldiers and remounted the small podium. "There is no time to lose. The enemy could invade again, and sooner than we realise. We might have months, weeks, or even only days. Therefore, your new health regime begins right now. And remember one very important thing: this is the British Army, and no senior officer will order you to do something that he or she could not also do." Trudy paused to let the message sink in. She wanted the troops under her command to know that the pain of getting fit would not be due to any sadism on the part of their superior officers.

"And to prove my point," she said, holding back a satisfied smile, "you may now go and drop your kit in your billets, and form back up here again in twenty minutes. We will start with a gentle ten-K forced march, no kit, which I will lead." She enjoyed seeing some of the faces flicker in trepidation before she added: "It's best we begin as we mean to go on, especially before the morning gets too hot. Dismissed."

Chapter 6

08.22 Friday 29 September 2062

Colour Sergeant Rory Moore stared unseeing out of the window of the autonomous transport vehicle, trying not to throw up. The grey sky cast a foreboding gloom over the long, redbrick building the vehicle rolled past. He'd been here before, some vague time ago he struggled to remember.

From next to him came the familiar voice of Sergeant Heaton. "You best buck up, laddie. You might've been one of Doyle's favourites a few months ago, but you're nay going to see him now for another promotion. You're in the shit in a big way."

Rory tried to recall why he should be about to see the commanding officer of the Royal Engineers. He wished the windows would stop resetting themselves in his vision every couple of seconds. Each time he tried to focus, they seemed to judder unreasonably.

"And whatever you do," Heaton said, "don't chunder all over the colonel's shoes, got that?"

"I not… I'm not gonna chunder," Rory answered, also wishing it were easier to pronounce words.

"Come on, we're here."

The vehicle stopped and the doors opened. The rush of fresh air carried a twang of burnt grass that stuck on Rory's dry tongue. He stepped out of the ATV and pulled himself upright. He felt his upper body sway in uncertainty.

"Can you manage?" Heaton asked.

"Yeah, yeah, course I can mana—" Rory stopped talking when the pea shingle ground seemed to come up at him. He swore and suddenly found himself crouched on all fours.

"Aye, course you can," Heaton said, gripping Rory's armpits and pulling the younger man upright again.

Rory put his hand on the side of the ATV and paused, unable to focus.

"I thought I'd made you drink enough water afore we left."

"Shit," was all Rory could mutter.

"Aye, you're in that all right, and no mistake."

Rory staggered with care next to his fellow sergeant as they entered the imposing, redbrick Victorian building. The smell of weathered stone on the floor triggered a memory in Rory, of being in this building a few months before. What had happened then?

"Come on, laddie," Heaton urged. "Up the stairs and on the right to the colonel's office."

Rory placed a booted foot on the first tread of the matured oak staircase and recalled taking this route with Pip, when they finally returned home from their struggle to escape the continent. So that's what Grandad Heaton had meant about promotion. The last time Rory had been here, he'd—

"Take it easy." Heaton's arm clamped around Rory to prevent him from stumbling.

They reached the first floor of the building and Rory tried to force some semblance of sobriety into his body. But he still could not recall why they were going to see Colonel Doyle.

"Here we are."

Rory sucked in a deep breath in the vain hope more oxygen might stabilise his limbs. He looked at Heaton, whose frowning expression also seemed to judder, and said, "Shit, do I really have to see him like this?"

"Aye. Do you think you can salute?"

Rory giggled, finding the question ridiculous, and said, "Er, nope."

Heaton muttered a curse and pushed the panelled door open.

"There you are," Colonel Doyle said, already halfway to the door.

Rory squinted in order to focus on his CO's grim expression and the notion came to him that he might be in some kind of trouble.

"Aye, Sir," Heaton said.

The colonel eyed both men in apparent disdain. "Sit down over there, both of you." He slammed the door shut.

Abrupt concern forced a beginning of stability into Rory's limbs. With it came painful memories. He collapsed into a chair in front of Doyle's expansive desk. He felt rather than saw Heaton sit in a chair next to him.

Doyle took up position on the other side of the desk and remained standing, silhouetted by the bright morning sunshine outside. The colonel looked at Heaton and asked: "Is he always this bad?"

"He has been a bit, lately—"

"I'm not 'bad'," Rory broke in, "just a bit, y'know..."

"Just a bit, what, colour sergeant? Eh?" the colonel demanded.

39

Rory felt his head loll and a sudden wave of exhaustion swept over him. "I don't know. I don't want to—"

"I think it's a personal issue, sir," Heaton offered.

"I don't care if it is 'personal'. If it wasn't for his notoriety in the regiment, he'd be in far worse trouble than he already is."

"Aye," Heaton said, "and I expect that's why you gave us almost no notice, sir."

The colonel's tone darkened, "Indeed. I wanted to see for myself if the rumours were true."

Anger sparked inside Rory. "Bollocks to the rumours."

"Steady on, laddie," Heaton cautioned.

Rory fixed his uncertain gaze on his shocked CO's face. "George is dead," he said, adding with a sneer, "sir."

"George who?" the colonel asked.

"And I got her killed," Rory went on, ignoring the question. "She's dead and it was my fault." The agony of admitting the fact aloud cut into the base of Rory's throat again.

"Squonk?" the colonel barked, "to whom is Colour Sergeant Moore referring?"

The super AI responded: "Insufficient data."

"Sir," Heaton said, "she was his new squeeze, a nice filly—"

"Fuck off," Rory hissed. "She wasn't a fucking 'squeeze', she was—"

"I won't have you using that language in my office, sergeant," Doyle broke in.

"Bollocks," Rory said. "I don't give a shit, in case you hadn't noticed… sir."

There came a moment's silence and Rory imagined what his court martial might be like.

In a conciliatory tone, Heaton said, "He went to the Advanced Medical Research Establishment down the road—"

"Yes, I do know," Doyle said in irritation. "I got him in there."

"Seems he began a relationship with one of the assistants."

Rory spoke, "And I told her to join the army. I told her she... she..." but his constricting throat prevented him from saying anything more.

"She was involved in an accident," Heaton said.

"What?" Doyle asked. "How is that even possible?"

"Aye," Heaton explained, "but there was some kind of emergency with the flood defences on the Humber a couple of weeks ago. They put out an appeal and she volunteered—"

"She'd just started her basic training," Rory said in misery.

"So," Heaton went on, "they flew out over the estuary where a construction replicator had broken down."

The colonel glanced from Heaton to Rory and back. "And?"

"She fell out of the AAT and drowned in some rapids before they could find her," Rory said.

In the following silence, Rory's breathing accelerated. He hated talking or thinking about what had happened to George. He stared at his CO's steely, unmoved face, waiting for the inevitable sanction for his drunkenness.

Doyle shook his head. "And is this the first time you've lost someone you know in this war, is it, sergeant?"

A sense of having been insulted grew inside Rory. "What did you say?" he asked in drunken confrontation, pulling himself up in his chair.

Doyle stroked his moustache with a forefinger and thumb and repeated, "I said, is this the first time—"

"I heard the fucking question, sir," Rory replied, his voice rising, blood flooding his vision.

"Careful, laddie," Heaton said.

Rory locked eyes with his CO, and through his inebriation he thought he recognised a desire for conflict in Doyle's face. Rory said, "Do you know what they call her at that base where she took off from? 'Ten-minute Georgie', that's what. Because she got there, got in the AAT, and she was dead ten minutes later."

Doyle folded his arms and repeated, "And is this the first time you've lost someone you know in this war, sergeant?"

Rory's anger surged. He wanted to scream, to run, to escape. At the same time, he knew he could do none of those things. His strength deserted him. He broke eye-contact, suddenly sick of the confrontation.

Doyle barked: "Ten-shun!"

Rory's legs acted independently at the order and he rose, aided by Heaton on his left, steadying him by again grasping his upper arm. Rory staggered but managed to salute. Bile clawed at the back of his throat.

"Colour Sergeant Moore," Colonel Doyle said, "your recent conduct falls far below that expected of a non-commissioned officer in the Royal Engineers."

Rory sagged and waited for the inevitable.

"However, given your conduct to date during the war and the importance of your knowledge of the enemy, I am inclined to overlook this incident solely on this occasion and on the clear understanding that you accept the added presence of nanobots inside your body to prevent a repeat of this shameful performance. Do you agree?"

"Yes, sir. I agree."

"Furthermore, I am placing Sergeant Heaton in charge of ensuring your compliance with this order."

"Yes, sir," Heaton said.

"Squonk? Notify the regimental doctor's office of Sergeants Moore and Heaton's imminent arrival."

The super AI replied: "Confirmed."

Colonel Doyle glanced at Rory. "You are dismissed. Go to the doctor and get the nanobots." He left his desk and strode to the door, his boots squeaking on the parquet floor.

Heaton still gripped Rory's upper arm and now propelled him towards the exit.

"Thank you, sir," Heaton said as he grasped the doorknob with his free hand. He pulled the door but Doyle stopped him.

Doyle looked at Heaton and said: "Let's try to be discreet about this, understood, sergeant?"

"Aye, sir."

"This man," Doyle said, jabbing a finger at Rory, "brought a great deal of credit on the regiment, which is, in all honesty, the only reason he's still in it."

"Aye, sir," Heaton repeated.

Rory's skin prickled at the colonel's bluntness but he said nothing, sobriety gaining more ground inside him, reminding him that, once again, his position was precarious and he should act with care.

Doyle turned his attention to Rory. "And you, colour sergeant, need to bear in mind that you are not responsible for the losses in this war. No matter how much this young lady might have meant to you personally, what happened to her was not down to you. I'm sure you saw much worse at the beginning of this war, when you were in Spain, yet you did not personally consider the loss of each NATO soldier and Spanish civilian to be your fault. The situation here is the same. Now, get to the doctor."

Heaton opened the door, mumbled his thanks to the colonel, and steered Rory through the doorway. When the door clicked closed behind them and they were alone in the broad corridor, Heaton said: "I wish you'd learn to keep your big, fat mouth shut, you young bastard."

Fatigue once again made Rory's limbs feel leaden. "Give me a minute, will you?" he asked, and flopped down on an ornate waiting bench upholstered in plush red leather.

Heaton sighed and sat next to him.

"Christ, grandad, the last couple of weeks have been bollocks."

"Aye. But you've not made it easy on yourself, have you?"

Rory said nothing.

"And now you've dropped me in the shit as well, you big, lanky bugger."

Rory scoffed and said, "The bots will take care of me."

"You need to learn to take care of yourself, laddie."

"What for?"

"Eh?"

"What for? We're done. I was there at the start, in Spain. Those fuckers are unstoppable, fella—"

"We stopped them here, though, didn't we?"

Rory waved a hand in dismissiveness and said, "A fluke. A piece of dumb luck, nothing more. I bet right now the ragheads are readying their next-gen ACAs and they'll piss all over those Falaretes. We won't last long."

"Yeah, that's it; stay positive," Heaton replied, his voice thick with sarcasm. "You need to sober up and stop acting like a mardy bugger. I don't want to be a bloody nursemaid to a Nancy southerner like you. Come on, let's get these bots in your system so you'll chunder after one beer."

Rory's thoughts drifted to George, her smile, the care she gave him, and the path he'd set her on that had led to her pointless, unfair death. He felt his lower jaw tremble and then lock as a deep, penetrating emptiness welled at the bottom of his throat. Had Doyle been right? Or was it merely that his path deviated from Georgina's only for a brief period of time?

He felt sure that, soon enough, he would find Georgina again, in some better place. But not today.

Rory stuck out his hand. Heaton grabbed his forearm and pulled him to his feet. Rory thanked him.

"Aye," Heaton answered, "and don't you dare drop me in the shit like you did to yourself."

Chapter 7

09.13 Thursday 5 October 2062

Maria Phillips looked at the spats of dried blood on the off-white chalk rocks and bit her lip. She cast her gaze upwards and took in the cliff face.

Her friend and fellow medical orderly, Nabou Faye, said, "My lens is showing that the body lies a few metres up and to the left." She pointed with a slender hand the colour of onyx and added, "Probably beyond that ridge there."

"Yeah, mine's saying the same."

"Come on, Maz," Nabou urged, "you know the body will stiffen before long."

Maria watched Nabou's slender legs surmount large rocks with ease. She pulled her own heavier limbs up in pursuit.

After climbing for two minutes, Nabou glanced down and announced: "Got her. And she is a mess."

"Oh God," Maria muttered. She pulled herself almost level with her friend and inhaled sharply on seeing the broken body. "I wish they wouldn't do this."

Nabou shrugged her backpack off of her shoulders and undid the zip. She extracted and began unrolling a black body bag. "Can you get around the side, over there?"

Maria stepped gingerly along the uneven ridge. The potential fall appeared slight but still sufficient to cause her injury, so she gripped pointed edges of chalk as strongly as she could. She reached the other side of the outcrop on which the suicide lay.

"Okay, take hold of this and let us get her bagged," Nabou said, tossing over one end of the body bag.

Maria opened it, the sea breeze making strands of hair flap across her face. "Why do they choose this way? I do wish they wouldn't."

"Perhaps they are trying to make some kind of statement?" Nabou offered. "I wonder if this one put something on her feeds."

"I don't," Maria replied. "I mean, they've got choices. They could die at home if they wanted. Why choose a terrifying death over a painless one?"

"And make us have to clean up the mess," Nabou added.

They lowered the bag over the crumpled young lady who, less than two hours before, had walked and talked and had been like them. Once the bloodied face and torso were covered, Maria heaved in a breath and, together with Nabou, rolled the corpse over. She caught a brief glimpse of blonde hair matted with blood, but when the head moved forwards to slide into the bag, she saw a penetrating dent in the cranium.

"Looks like she didn't suffer too much after she hit the rocks, anyway," Maria said, pushing the zip to Nabou.

"Yes, only those hours and days and weeks and months that we do not know about, which finally brought her to the cliff edge all the way up there and made her decide that there was nothing left to live for."

"I find it's best not to think about that."

Maria retraced her steps around the outcrop. She pulled a lanyard from the body bag over her head and left shoulder. She felt Nabou take up the weight behind her and together they carried the suicide down to the beach. Once on the stones, they walked side by side, sharing the weight of the grim cargo. As they trudged back to the port's field hospital, Maria twitched her eye and said, "Ranny? We've retrieved the suicide."

The effeminate voice of the new orderly answered, "Roger that. Shall I put the oven on?"

Maria smiled at his euphemism. "Not yet, just the kettle for now. We could do with a brew."

"Roger that."

"Squonk," Nabou said, "do we have to do an autopsy on this one?"

The super AI replied, "Negative. Next of kin have been informed but have yet to respond."

"You'd think they could develop a kind of bot that could do autopsies by now," Maria said.

"Bots need the patient alive to be able to—"

"I know, I know," Maria said as each step seemed to suck her boots deeper into the stones on the beach.

"Do you think we could move a little more quickly, Maz?"

Maria chuckled. "Yeah, sure. But don't try breaking any Olympic records."

Maria tried to keep up with Nabou as her friend accelerated, telling herself that the exercise would do her good. The pebbled beach gave way to a concrete slipway that led to the harbour wall. Gulls cawed and mewed overhead in the warm, cloudy sky.

A few moments later, they arrived at the compact field hospital in the Port of Dover. The small chain-link wire gate opened at their approach. None of the few other military personnel and local civilian support staff in the compound took any notice of their arrival or what they carried.

"Place victim AX–7126 in cold storage," Squonk instructed.

"No contact from next of kin, then," Maria observed.

They reached the entrance to the morgue. The heavy metal door slid back and overhead lights flickered on inside. These revealed a bare, functional space lined with more metal doors the colour of magnolia. Maria said, "Come on," and they heaved the body bag inside the air-conditioned room.

"Place victim AX–7126 in tray 7B," Squonk said.

The third door on the left clicked and slid open. The appropriate tray rolled forwards.

"What about her final office?" Nabou asked.

"That will wait until confirmation from next of kin," Squonk replied.

"Yes, we know that," Maria replied testily, "but whatever happens, the next of kin are going to want to see her. So why don't we do the final office now?"

"While the probability of that request is very high," the super AI replied, "it is not certain, and final office will not be required if victim AX–7126 is to be cremated. In addition, the next module in your field-surgeon training course begins in seventeen minutes and requires your real-time participation."

"Oh," Nabou said. "I forgot about that."

They lifted the body bag and laid it on the tray.

"Poor woman," Nabou said as the tray retracted into the darkness of the cold store.

Maria took a step back at the same time as Nabou when the door slid closed and clicked again. She followed her friend into the warm morning air.

A voice called out from behind them, "There you are, ladies."

"Doctor Miller," Maria acknowledged, turning to see the large man lumber towards them.

He nodded to the mortuary and said, "That's, what, the tenth this week?"

"Yes, she was only a young woman," Nabou said.

Miller's eyebrows rose. "Hardly a novelty. Now, I want you two back on general ward Bravo." He turned away from them, evidently expecting them to follow. Maria swapped an unsurprised glance with Nabou. Miller continued, talking over his shoulder, "The passengers from the boat that arrived last week are making fair progress, but I'd like you to use a bit of 'bedside manner' because the computer is reporting a lack of expected responsiveness. You remember that elderly German couple? They're still not talking to anyone, not even each other."

"Yes, Doctor Miller," Maria answered, keeping her voice level, "as soon as our next field-surgeon training module finishes."

Miller stopped and turned. "You're still on that course?"

"The Medical Corps needs more field-surgeons, sir—"

"Yes, yes," Miller said, the fleshy chin under his jaw wobbling. "And as long as this impasse with the enemy remains, I suppose it's important we keep ourselves as occupied as possible."

A notification flashed in Maria's lens: a SkyWatcher had identified more human remains coming ashore on the west beach. She glanced at Nabou and asked, "Do you think we've got enough time to fetch that before the training?"

"Yes, I do," Nabou replied with a mischievous look.

"You can assign Ranny or one of the others if you prefer," Miller offered.

Nabou shook her head. "The SkyWatcher estimates the weight at about fifty kilograms. It will need two people to carry." She looked at Maria and asked, "Have you still got a body bag?"

Maria nodded and patted her shoulder to indicate her own backpack.

"Come on, then, Maz."

Doctor Miller turned and strode away without speaking.

Maria followed Nabou in the opposite direction. She twitched her eye and said, "Tea will have to wait, Ranny. We've got more remains to collect."

She heard a huff of frustration and Ranny said, "Very well. Let me know if you need me to put the oven on."

They exited the field hospital via the same chain-link gate through which they'd entered moments before. Maria said, "Give us the route, Squonk," and directions flashed into her vision that would take them behind the port, close to the road, and then on to the west beach.

Nabou chuckled. "Jog, run or sprint?"

"None of those things, thank you."

"Oh, come on. Time is short. We might not get back for the training module."

Maria sighed. "I don't care."

"Honestly?"

The sun emerged from behind a cloud and the heat on Maria's face increased. The sweat in her armpits began to irritate the skin there, despite the airiness of her fatigues. She fell in beside Nabou, who was merely walking quickly, and said, "This job's really starting to get me down, mate."

"We spoke about this, Maz. We need to use this downtime to recover our strength—"

"Handling corpses in various states of decomposition is not my idea of 'downtime'."

"So why did you join the Medical Corps?"

They reached the road that skirted the port's main infrastructure. Maria had to take little skips and hops to keep up with Nabou's long, elegant strides. Not for the first time, Maria felt amazement at the way her Senegalese friend could stride so effortlessly yet cover a remarkable distance with such grace.

"For the same reason you did," Maria said, "to help the living."

"And that is why we are going through the field-surgeon training course, correct?"

"Yes," Maria said in a tight voice, her friend's increased speed obliging her to take quicker breaths.

"Maz, my parents came to your country twenty years ago, when the Gambian invaders started getting help from the Chinese and the war became bad for us. So, I know what it is like only to have bad alternatives. I think that when you have been in a position where you have no choice, you must always choose to go on."

Nabou leapt up onto the thick wall that ran next to them. Maria copied her, wishing again that her heavy English limbs had half of Nabou's athleticism.

Nabou glanced back at Maria, smiled, and said, "Today there is little fighting, so we can make sure these victims will be treated with respect, whoever they were."

"And who hasn't suffered, one way or another?" Maria asked rhetorically. She unconsciously patted her thigh pocket to make sure the piece of wood from the foot of Billy the rabbit, which had sat atop the chimney of her home before it was destroyed, was still there.

"Exactly," Nabou said. "I count myself to be very fortunate compared to you."

Maria wondered if her friend could read her mind. "But, in a funny way, that's what makes it worse. During the fighting, the retreat across France and then all the drama here, we didn't have time to think. And now, I think—"

"Too much?" Nabou finished for her, stopping and turning to face her.

"Yes," Maria confirmed, relieved to stop and have a chance to catch her breath.

Nabou's brown eyes projected an infinite calm. She said, "Do not worry, Maz. If we have learned anything these last months, it is to expect unpleasant surprises wherever we are."

"And what 'unpleasant surprises' do you expect here then, mate?"

Nabou replied at once, casting her gaze towards the distant west beach where more human remains awaited them. "I do not know, not certainly. But to me the future is still dark, like when my parents took me and fled our home during that war. They said France would take us. They said France would meet her obligations. But we were too late; there were already too many Senegalese in the old colonial country. So, England took us in. But there were always problems."

"I can believe that," Maria said, recalling the low-level racism she'd witnessed during her own childhood.

Nabou jumped down from the wall and landed with a scrunch on the pebbles of the beach. She turned back and held out a slender arm.

Maria caught it for support as she landed on the stones.

"It took time," Nabou said, "but my parents overcame them. Because they had no choice."

"Yeah, but it's difficult to see a future if we don't have one."

"The chameleon changes colour to match the earth; the earth does not change colour to match the chameleon."

"What?"

"It's a saying."

"Okay," Maria said, a little nonplussed.

"Let us keep moving forward, one day at a time, Maz."

Maria eyed her friend and considered how she'd changed since their basic training. Gone was the carefree girl amazed by all of the new regulations of army life and the weapons. In her place, a more mature woman had developed after their experiences of war. But Maria said nothing, enjoying her friend's innate wisdom.

Nabou went on, "We shall become field surgeons if we can, and we will help others again."

"But not today, huh?" Maria said as they approached a heavy-looking black object that lay on the stones in front of them. Lazy waves curled and sloshed, ambivalent to the remains they had delivered onto the cold stones.

Chapter 8

21.54 Monday 9 October 2062

Captain Pip Clarke flopped on the narrow bed. A slight, cool breeze floated in through the open slit window in the wall on her right. With it came the sounds of distant talking: muttered words and phrases that, she sensed, carried tones of shock and urgency.

Exhaustion rippled through her limbs. The muscles around her neck, along her spine and down the backs of her legs, ached in relief at her finally reaching the end of a draining, unnerving day. It had begun with the usual practice drills, followed by fitness training, followed by the first shock: finding out the full extent of just how much her barracks were slated to expand over the next nine months. In the afternoon, a construction replicator broke down when its ultra-Graphene ribbon buckled. But the ensuing logistical issues gave her little time to recall that period earlier in the year—she couldn't believe it was still the same year—when replacing buckled ultra-Graphene ribbons in old construction replicators on the Humber had seemed like real soldiering.

Earlier in the evening, she'd attended a meeting at which two intel officers revealed the latest data on the enemy, extracted from the brains of injured warriors. A slew of new information had been released to officer-and-above ranks with the order that it was classified 'secret' and should not become general knowledge among all ranks. Pip realised at once that a few well-placed, juicy rumours would be enough to keep the lower ranks gossiping. Soon enough, titbits would leak and give ordinary squaddies, currently employed in physical, tactical, and weapons' training, something to chat about.

But the biggest shock came at the end of her duty period, when a quiet notification arrived in her lens that she had been placed on a shortlist for promotion to the rank of major.

Lying on her bed staring at the featureless magnolia ceiling, she twitched an eye muscle and reread the notification. She shivered. Of course, promotions happened more frequently in every war, but she was not yet twenty-two years old. She conceded that her experiences since the enemy invaded Europe did make her an exception, but at the same time, the way she'd lost battlefield discipline during the fighting on the coast in August had led her to question her fitness for command almost constantly. And now Brass thought she could make major?

"It's not as simple as that," she mumbled under her breath. "Besides, the list includes enough career officers who are way ahead of me in the pecking order. Perhaps I'm only on it to make up the numbers?"

She understood the unique imperative the British Army now found itself working under. The ranks swelled by thousands every week, so the managing hierarchy was also driven to expand up the chain of command: from corporals having squads of six troops, not four, all the way through platoons, battalions and regiments. Regarding the last of these, the most obscure regiments had been brought back into existence for the first time, in some cases, since the First World War—

An incoming comms request derailed her train of thought. She twitched her eye to raise. "Hi. How was your day?"

"Good," Forward Observer Martin Phillips said, "but since you've selected audio only, I'm assuming your day has been... heavy going?"

"Yeah, a little."

"Need someone to talk to? We could play a game of cards. Maybe that would help you relax?"

She smiled in gratitude for his concern and replied, "Thanks, but not tonight. I have some things—"

"You need to catch up on," he finished for her. "No worries," he said. "You know where I am. Just let me know."

"Thank you," she said in the instant he ended the communication. A gentle sigh escaped her lips. She wanted very much to talk to Martin, but knew she could not. His rank did not give him the same security clearance as she had, and Pip herself would play no role in disseminating such intel.

She closed her eyes and recalled the briefing and the two aspects that struck her most forcefully. First, the practical descriptions of the warriors' arms. Their main rifle had been given the NATO reporting name Goldfinch. There were interesting details on its performance, especially the parameters of the shells, which exceeded the Pickup's ranges by up to ten percent in certain directional aspects, but fell short of destructive impact by up to five percent, depending on the usual battlefield variables.

In addition, many warrior units—from platoon equivalent up to battalion level—were often armed with blades, ranging from daggers to scimitars. Warriors' memories confirmed that these blades represented a link to the region inside the Caliphate from where they came. Pip noted how the mighty New Persian Caliphate actually allowed historical elements of the tribes, if not the old nation states, that it had subsumed, to exist in its new armies.

However, these arms were all each warrior group possessed: the enemy's offensive tactics relied almost entirely on the Blackswan and its Spiders, and the Lapwing. Of course, this made perfect sense: super-artificial intelligence controlled every aspect of the enemy's advance. The warriors were ill-educated brutes whose only objective was to crush any resistance that might have escaped the attention of their ACAs.

The second aspect of the briefing caused her a greater disquiet. The objective fact of the enemy's destruction of Europe over the preceding eight months had been driven not only by more advanced weaponry, but also by men whose lives had been conditioned by depthless hatred for the 'infidel'. Pip shivered again at the recollection of the snippets of extracted memories that exemplified warrior training. The juxtaposition of mid-twenty-first-century technology used by brutes with a fourteenth century approach to conquest dried Pip's throat and left her feeling cast adrift. For her entire life, she'd taken equality between the sexes for granted.

She glanced at the open window. The voices had stopped. What had they been discussing? Yes, the one subject on which all ranks in the British Army had an opinion: would the Americans abandon NATO, and what would happen if they did? Pip believed it would make little difference. The future of England and the Home Countries now balanced precariously between the Falarete and the race to develop and deploy better weapons.

She saw the reports, daily sitreps from locations all around the English coast, of how many Blackswans and Lapwings the enemy decided to throw at them, always to no avail. Sometimes, they would send over a wing of Crakes, the larger enemy ACA whose only use was as a single, massive flying bomb, but Pip thought the enemy did that more to relieve the boredom. The consideration made her frown. Could this awful war have been reduced to boredom? Had the impasse existed for so long it had become an accepted part of life?

Her eyelids felt suddenly heavy. Her chest loosened and her breaths shallowed. Exhaustion enveloped her; the fatigues she'd been wearing for the last sixteen hours abruptly caressed rather than itched her skin. A voice in her head told her that brushing her teeth could wait until she'd rested. Somnolent comfort soothed her worried mind: no, it would not make any difference if America decided to abandon NATO and England; it would not change a thing. They were all finished anyway, just not this evening. And any concern beyond that could wait until the morning.

Chapter 9

07.55 Friday 13 October 2062

Recruit Mark Phillips, 3rd Airspace Defence, hurried along the bare, ill-lit corridor, grateful only that the motion ensured that he didn't have to worry about his hands trembling. In five minutes' time, the appointment for his ten-week appraisal meeting with his superior, Lieutenant Rose Cho, would begin. This would either see him taken into the 3rd Airspace Defence long-term—or rejected and cast adrift.

He'd heard whispers that the rejects were offered observer positions in field regiments. The prospect terrified Mark. Despite his progress, thanks to Simon's support since Mark's parents had been killed, he felt certain he would not cope in a traditional unit of the armed forces. Besides, he had come to enjoy what he did, and on the rare occasion when he spoke to Simon, his friend gave him much validation for how he was helping the war effort.

Mark also liked Lieutenant Cho. She was small in stature, like him, and one of the few people he'd ever met who didn't intimidate him. Also present at the appraisal would be

Captain Joe Shithead. Mark couldn't recall the man's real surname, but had decided right from the beginning that Captain Shithead suited him far better than any real name could.

He turned a corner into a broader space lit with bright overhead lights and lined with deep, curved alcoves. Each alcove contained a chaise lounge. Warmer air made his hands feel clammier. He passed several alcoves with figures reclining and heads obscured by VR sets. Mark appreciated their functionality to a greater degree as time passed, even if it did mean he had to get up and physically visit a toilet.

He reached his own alcove and entered. He grabbed the VR set lying on the chaise lounge and slid it on his head. He settled back into the soft upholstery and waited. He closed his eyes, even though his view was blank, and concentrated. He recalled Simon's advice, little tricks for coping with real people and the problems and stresses they caused. A sudden flash of anger threatened to make him lose control, but Mark understood this side of himself much better now—

"Hello, Recruit Phillips," said Lieutenant Rose Cho. "I am afraid this appraisal must take place in a visual environment, not only audio. Do you understand?"

Mark knew and hated having to engage his visual presence. He paused, calmed himself, and made the required adjustments to the VR controls. An office-like room resolved with bare walls the colour of vanilla ice cream. He pushed himself back further into the chaise lounge and tried to relax. The computer represented him as sitting in a chair in front of a plush mahogany desk, on the other side of which sat Lieutenant Cho and Captain Shithead.

"Thank you," Cho said with a pinched smile, "and welcome to your ten-week appraisal. The appraisal is being conducted by Captain Joe Neely and Lieutenant Rose Cho. It is being recorded."

Mark's skin crawled under Captain Shithead's cold gaze.

Shithead spoke in a flat, uninterested tone: "How would you rate your performance over these ten weeks, Recruit Phillips?"

Mark decided to feign a similar indifference. "Adequate, I believe."

"Your performance stats are above average across more than half of the metrics on which you are judged," Cho said.

A list of words and numbers resolved in the air above and to the right of the desk. Mark reflected that they could have been from an in-Universe game as easily as from the real world in a real war. The words included 'Responsiveness', 'Acuity' and 'Observation', and more than half of the percentage figures were in the high sixties and low seventies.

"Of course," Captain Shithead said, "those stats don't tell the whole story, do they?"

"Don't they?" Mark replied.

"No," Shithead said. "You don't get on very well with your colleagues, do you, Recruit Phillips?"

Mark felt his heartrate pick up. The constant questions at the end of each sentence created stress. He closed his eyes and struggled to remember Simon's advice.

Cho asked, "Do you have a problem with the other operatives here?"

"No," Mark said at once. His mind fought to find an answer, to break through the fog of frustration and confusion that interacting with other people always caused him. He stifled a yawn.

"Do you think the other operatives here have a problem with you?" Captain Shithead asked. "And if they do, where do you think the fault lies?"

The concern inside Mark expanded like a balloon, stretching until, suddenly, it popped. "Hold on, what does it matter even if they do? We work alone anyway, it's part of who we are. Each of us has their own sector to monitor and deal with if the shi—er, if trouble starts. And I've spoken to enough of the others here to realise that I am totally not unique. What about Bronco?" he asked, referencing the only operative who seemed weird even by Mark's own standards. "He got his commission, didn't he?"

Cho glanced at Captain Shithead and Mark caught a new feeling; that, perhaps, there might be some kind of problem between the two of them. However, this was a novel sensation. Mark's own concerns and frustrations usually consumed all of his own attention, and before he met Simon—before his parents were killed—he never realised the relevance of other people also interacting with each other.

Cho coughed and said, "One aspect of our current policy is to improve camaraderie among all of the operatives here. Although we have stopped the invaders for now, there may still come a time when they overwhelm our defences, and we will all need to help each other."

Mark glanced quickly at Captain Shithead and caught the slightest sneer roll across the man's mouth. Mark looked at Cho and decided at once that, even though the captain held the higher rank, he would show both of them whose side he was on, and screw the consequences. He replied, "I understand and agree completely, lieutenant."

Captain Shithead's eyebrows climbed up his narrow forehead.

"It is certainly the way forward," Mark went on, "although I also think it might be problematic for some of the team members."

The captain said, "Like you, for example?"

Mark ignored him, realising that he would probably like to see Mark kicked out.

Cho turned to the captain. "I think Recruit Phillips has demonstrated more than sufficient ability in his first ten weeks. He is clearly an asset to 3rd Airspace Defence. He should be given a full commission."

Her declaration nonplussed Mark. He suddenly saw through the praise and understood how what she'd said was actually a challenge to Shithead.

An indifferent expression formed on Shithead's face. He looked at Mark and then at Cho. In a tone that suggested he could not care in the least, the man said, "Very well. Welcome to 3rd Airspace Defence, Officer Cadet Phillips." Then, he vanished from the room.

"Is everything all right?" Mark asked.

Cho's face broke into a broad grin. "Yes, don't worry. Joe doesn't really like anyone at all. But I'm fairly confident dealing with his type."

"Right," Mark managed to utter as the realisation came to him that Cho probably saw him and Captain Shithead as very similar men. Mark wondered if that could actually be the case. He opened his mouth to ask her when she spoke first.

"Congratulations, Mark. I've been watching you closely since you arrived, and I'm very pleased you have passed your training period and earned a full commission. I think you should be very proud of yourself. You are an important part of a vital section of the defence of England. Without us, millions of people would be in very big trouble indeed."

Cho's effusive praise and reminder of the importance of their efforts derailed his personal concerns. He was, after all, doing vital work that could mean the difference between the survival or destruction of England. He concluded that Lieutenant Cho was right: he should be proud of himself and what he had achieved since Simon had steered him away from those stupid, immature gaming Universes.

"Thank you, Lieutenant Cho," he mumbled, wondering if he'd missed something in this appraisal.

"The pleasure was all mine," the woman replied with warmth in her eyes. "Now, let's get back to work, shall we?"

Chapter 10

03.51 Friday 13 October 2062

Operations Specialist Andrew Powell scratched his trimmed, white beard and paced around the large central command station on the bridge of the *USS George Washington*. He had to move to keep the tiredness at bay. Nevertheless, adrenalin would not let him sleep, at least until the watch changed. Perhaps if nothing had happened by the time morning watch began, he might let himself rest.

He caught a glance from Captain Mitch Taylor, standing, arms folded, at the station's main tactical station display, and guessed that the same thought occupied his captain's concerns: when would the enemy attack?

The US Navy aircraft carrier led its eighteenth relief convoy across the Atlantic, designation Convoy SE–117. In addition to the *George Washington*, the group consisted of seven destroyers in close formation, supported by a perimeter of twelve more destroyers protecting sixty merchant ships. Each one of the hundreds of sailors on them knew this was the most powerful carrier battle group to have crossed the Atlantic so far in this war. But they did not know why.

And with good reason, Powell thought.

Unknown to everyone in the convoy except the captains, their executive officers and specific intel operators, one ship in the fleet carried a vital consignment of europium, one of the rarest of rare-earth elements and a key component in muon-catalysed fusion power units.

Powell diverted his eyes back to the command station, sure that Taylor was thinking the same thing. They had only discussed their special cargo once, quietly in the captain's private quarters when they were docked at Norfolk. If the enemy could find and sink that consignment of europium—secured in the aft section of the most inconspicuous-looking merchantman in the convoy—it would set NATO's next-gen weapons' programme back by months.

The holographic display remained static, digital indicators showing the convoy ships at relative distances while the space around and above them remained empty.

Taylor asked, "Chester? Are the replacement shafts functioning as expected?"

The US Navy's super AI replied: "Affirmative."

"You still think the installation was inappropriately rushed, sir?" Powell said.

"Maybe. Two weeks for such a refit was damn quick."

"The sea trials were all good," Powell reminded the captain, adding, "and so far we've not had a swell greater than slight."

Mitch smiled at Powell and asked in a rhetorical tone, "What the hell are you still doing here, Andy? You were entitled to retire last month and yet here you are in the middle of the ocean at the ass-end of the middle watch."

Powell approached the command station and chuckled. "My solo voyage around the world can wait awhile, captain."

The joshing hid the real reason both men were on the bridge in the middle of the night.

Taylor clicked his tongue. "I think I'll take a break," he said, casting his eyes at the other manned stations. "You have the bridge, Andy." He turned to go.

"Aye, sir." A calmness suffused Powell's fatigue as he reflected on eighteen successful missions carrying vital supplies across the Atlantic in support of the US's NATO allies. The previous convoy, three weeks earlier, had seen the enemy make a concerted attack and had cost three destroyers while one Spider had snuck under the waves and damaged two of the *George Washington*'s four propeller shafts—

"Sir?" a young rating said, breaking into Powell's thoughts.

"Yes?" he replied, looking at the back of the blonde head that had addressed him.

"The *Bulkeley* is reporting a contact."

Powell's senses flashed into life and his tiredness vanished. He said nothing, letting the rating do his job.

A moment later, the young man said, "Confirm that. SkyWatcher one-seven-three is tracking five hun—correction, six—"

"Just give it a second, son," Powell said.

Captain Taylor returned through the portside entrance he'd left seconds earlier. He strode to the central command station and exclaimed, "Damn, I had a notion."

"Sixth sense?" Powell enquired with a mirthless smile.

The rating announced, "Tracking seven hundred and fifty enemy ACAs."

"General quarters," Taylor ordered.

The familiar klaxon sounded, reverberating off the ship's composite metal surfaces.

"Twice as many as last time," Powell muttered. "They must know."

Taylor continued, his voice measured and emotionless, "Give full tactical command over to Chester and link to the main display—"

A strong female voice at a different station called out, "Distance one thousand kilometres and closing in a straight line."

"Okay, let's go to battle stations, everyone," Taylor said. "Chester, establish comms to all ships in the convoy. Transfer all known data to the central command station. What is the current status?"

A strange wave of relief swelled inside Powell. Finally, the waiting had ended and the expected attack now commenced. His tactical mind appreciated the timing: only a few minutes before the middle watch changed to the morning watch at 04.00. However, while the humans might be at a low-energy ebb, fortunately Chester did not need to take a rest. Of greater concern was the unusually large number of attacking ACAs. A voice inside Powell insisted that intel must have leaked and the enemy knew the true importance of this convoy.

On the expansive central command station, the green shapes in the hologram that denoted the convoy shrivelled down to almost microscopic size, and then moved off to the left. At the opposite edge, there appeared red dots that grew into straight lines as the ship's super AI said, "Tracking seven-hundred-and-fifty hostile ACAs approaching at a unified Mach nine-point-two in a narrow-band altitude."

"Specify 'narrow band'," Powell instructed.

"All enemy ACAs are approaching at altitudes between one hundred and one thousand metres above sea level," Chester replied.

Taylor looked at Powell. "That's not their standard attack profile. Maybe they're using a new tactic?"

Powell raised his voice and asked, "Tactical, what about the SkyWatcher that detected this attack? Has it been destroyed?"

"Negative, sir."

"Chester, shut the klaxon off," Taylor said, and the noise stopped. He added, "That's not normal, either."

"Announcement: the wing of enemy ACAs has changed course," Chester said. "The battlespace is secure. There is no risk to the convoy."

"You've got to be kidding me," Taylor said with a hollow laugh.

Confusion smothered any sense of relief inside Powell, although he could imagine whoops of celebration among those suddenly awake on the merchantmen, at least. On the central command station in front of him, the red lines denoting the paths of the enemy ACAs veered away from the ships. Incredibly, it seemed the convoy was not their intended target.

"Chester, is this a feint?" Taylor asked.

"The probability is less than one percent."

Powell looked at the captain and asked, "So if we are not the target, who the hell is? My God, you don't think—"

Taylor instructed, "Chester, extrapolate and hypothesise: where is this force heading?"

"Its current course suggests a number of potential targets on the eastern seaboard of the United States."

"Notify all ships to ready missiles," Taylor ordered. "Plot interception courses to targets. We'll take these ACAs down anyway."

"Damn," Powell hissed, "we didn't think that bastard in Tehran had the guts—"

"Being a piece of shit doesn't take much guts," Taylor said.

Powell watched Taylor stare in supressed frustration at the holographic display as the enemy ACAs sped past them at seventy nautical miles to the south of their position.

Chester announced, "No interception courses are available."

"Jesus," Taylor exclaimed.

Powell said, "Explain." He decided it would help the bridge crew—including the captain—to have the answer spoken aloud, although he himself already knew.

Chester obliged: "The available weapons cannot cover the required distance in the available time." The super AI paused before adding: "Comms to all ships in the convoy are now established."

"Cancel that," Taylor said. "Establish comms with Norfolk HQ."

"That is against current, on-mission operating protocols—"

"Override, now," Taylor spat.

"Confirmed," the super AI replied.

Powell shook his head in impotent fury, watching the red lines denoting the attacking ACAs continue on their way past the convoy.

Chester announced: "Quantum-secure comms established."

"Attention," Taylor said. "This is Convoy SE–117. We are tracking seven-hundred-and-fifty enemy ACAs inbound to the eastern seaboard. Acknowledge, over?" There came a moment's silence. Taylor clicked his tongue and said, "Chester, confirm if that message—"

He was interrupted by a new voice: male, laconic and sharp. The man said, "Gee, no shit, Convoy SE–117."

Taylor said, "We thought you could use the heads-up. It sure does not look good from the—"

"Yeah, yeah. If you boys and girls don't mind, we've got to get our sea-defence shit together. But do reach out to us again if you suddenly discover anything else you think might help us out. You know, like last week's winning Lotto numbers?"

Chester reported: "Quantum-secure comms terminated."

Powell saw Taylor's face redden in anger. The captain opened his mouth but Powell, older and feeling a little wiser than him, offered: "Sir, they are about to face a life-changing event. We should cut them a little slack." He glanced back at the large central command station and watched as the digital representation of the New Persian Caliphate's first direct attack on the United States of America inexorably approached its target. He asked himself how on earth the enemy could have passed this convoy by. Moreover, did there now exist a real chance that the vital consignment of europium they carried would make it to Southampton in less than twenty-four hours' time?

Chapter 11

03.57 Friday 13 October 2062

Janet Bagget stubbed out the cigarette in the porcelain ashtray on the duvet next to her and snuggled further into her warm, comfortable bed. She looked at the chipped red varnish on her nails and tears began to well in the corners of her eyes. This was it: the day she'd been dreading all year: her fortieth birthday.

"Clear windows," she instructed her apartment's super AI.

The misty white on the glass, which obscured the outside world, vanished. A forest of lights twinkled outside, from her surroundings in Newark looking east all the way to Manhattan. Somewhere among those buildings stood the hotel she'd been in earlier in the night, earning her living the way she had been since before she was eighteen. The client had been undemanding, finishing in minutes. His subsequent somnolence allowed her to leave well ahead of the full hour. She touched herself to make sure the shower she'd taken on arriving back at the apartment had indeed removed every trace of the transaction.

Janet sat up on the edge of the bed to better control her breathing, upset by her emotions. She lit another cigarette and forced the smoke into the depths of her lungs. Her survivor's spirit of defiance gradually forced its way to the fore. She should be proud of herself for getting to forty—plenty of her peers from high school certainly didn't. Besides, for clients she would be able to describe herself as 'early thirties' for years yet, and then 'mid-thirties', and so on, especially as she'd been smart enough not to have kids.

A teardrop spilled over the corner of her eye and ran down the side of her nose. She sniffed. Her memory replayed all the terrible birthdays from her childhood in Millburn. October 13: she'd hated the day for as long as she could recall; that and Christmas Day, also for the same awful recollections the date provoked.

Exhaustion weighed on her shoulders, but when she heaved in another pull from her cigarette, her heart beat a little faster and a little harder. Anger flashed inside her when the teardrop ran off the top of her plump lip and soaked the paper of the cigarette in her mouth—

A communication notification flashed in the periphery of her vision. She recognised the ID: a semi-regular client from Washington. He often booked her when he was in Manhattan. Like a lot of her semi-regulars, she sensed some strange, evil emotions lurking under their dishonest affection for her. All affection between men and women was dishonest. God, what was wrong with people?

Janet rejected the communication. She stubbed the damp cigarette in the ashtray and lit another. Yeah, so much dishonesty, so much lying and betrayal—

A second notification from the same client flashed. She choked down an expletive. Her business acumen suggested he might be desperate and thus she would be able to ramp the price up. She twitched an eye muscle to accept the communication.

Landen's concerned face appeared in the top-right of her vision. His normal, toothy smile had been replaced with a scowl. "Hi, Angelique. You okay?"

Janet assumed a flirtatious demeanour, ignored his bad facial symmetry, and replied, "Hi, honey. Sure. What's the matter? Are you in town and feeling lonely? You know, I'm gonna need a little extra for a last-minute call-out—"

"Not now, sweetheart," he said with a shake of his head. "Listen, where are you? Are you in Manhattan or the Bronx or Queens?"

"Nope," she replied, wondering why any client would ask such a question.

"So where are you, for Christ's sake?"

"In my apartment in Newark, Landen. It is the middle of the goddamn night."

Landen's eyebrows rose. "Sure, but that's when you do most of your work, right?"

"Where the hell do you get off—?"

"Okay, doesn't matter. Listen to me: Angelique, you have to get to a high floor, got that?"

"What?"

"An attack is coming. Homeland Security has put out a confidential alert and it looks like New York is gonna get flooded pretty bad."

Janet paused. Landen had told her he worked in Homeland Security and that's why he was based in Washington, but he often escaped his wife by travelling to NY on official business. Sure, he could be lying—most clients did—but maybe he did know something?

"Hey? Did you hear me?" he demanded.

"Yeah, sure. Relax, my apartment's on the fourth floor. What's going on?"

"Can you see the Carter Dam from where you are?"

"Not straight on, no—"

"In about ninety seconds, it's gonna get hit by a ton of ACAs—"

"You mean the war? But that crap only happens to Europe," she said.

"Uh-huh, and now it's coming right at us. The dam is gonna break and a shit-ton of water is g—"

"But what about my fish?" Janet shrieked.

Landen's face creased in confusion. "What the actual fu—?"

"In the Passaic River," Janet shouted, angered at his apparent confusion. "I sponsor one of the farms there that's been breeding fish now the river's finally clean enough."

"Jesus," he exclaimed. "They are fish. They can swim, Angelique." He shook his head. "I gotta go. See ya."

Janet tutted in consternation when his face disappeared. She winked through news services and other networks, but found only rumours. Minimising those streams to clear her view, Janet stared southeast. The familiar forest of lights illuminated the local streets while the glittering skyscrapers of Manhattan twinkled distantly. Beyond them, on the dark horizon, the Carter Dam protected New York from the rising ocean.

A half-forgotten teenage memory recalled the dam's construction winning some kind of award. It must have been in '41 or '42, back when the world still admired what the US could do. Her very first boyfriend in high school, Jaxon, had told her with eyes lit up like Times Square how the dam would remind the world that the US was still—

A sudden bright glare caught her eye and rolled across the horizon. There came a rapid series of lesser flashes, splaying out left and right like some kind of fireworks. She twitched her eye to scan through feeds and alighted on a real-time account somewhere much closer to the Carter Dam than her. At first, nothing seemed to have changed—the night was cloudy and the ambient light around the dam dull—but abruptly the arrow-straight ridge of the dam's parapet wall crumbled. Then, the whole crest of the dam collapsed without fuss or fanfare.

The Atlantic Ocean spilled eagerly over the falling rubble. The digital feed fractured and dissolved into white noise; Janet's lens automatically switched to another close by. Water poured into Upper Bay and surged around the Statue of Liberty. The extensive base below Green Goddess held steadfast long enough that Janet thought the wave of water couldn't be that strong. Then, the base broke into pieces. The old lady pirouetted, stiff and awkward, and fell into the unstoppable surge, as though she'd finally decided to lay down after so many decades of standing.

Janet took another languid pull on her cigarette as digital activity erupted in reaction to the explosions. Her lens offered several on-the-spot feeds for her consideration, while her ears picked up a distant hissing that gained in volume. Her apartment's super AI issued a warning of the approaching disaster, but Janet felt safe. The super AI reassured her that the power of the water would dissipate sufficiently that residents from the third floor and higher were at limited risk. However, a lengthy power outage was a certainty as the building's batteries were located in the basement.

Janet glanced beyond the feeds in her lens, to the street outside and the dull, night-time outline of the Newark Museum of Art two blocks south of her apartment building. Regret surged inside her like the ocean swamping New York. That museum had often been a refuge for her after a trying night of awkward or demanding clients. The museum, like her fish in the Passaic, anchored her in a sea of lies and betrayal and fulfilling men's basest needs for the currency that allowed her to live a life of independence. The works it displayed took her to other cultures, so distant in time and space; and in return for her attention, those works gave her back some other measure of time and space, of comfort in a life of gilded pain.

The Atlantic Ocean, its level risen so much over the preceding decades, pushed and surged and slid and poured among and around the thousands of streets of the great city. In Manhattan, the taller buildings shuddered before toppling, their long-dead architects never dreaming of the need to protect their creations from such a fate.

With each crossroads, each junction, and every corner, a little of the mighty force unleashed by the New Persian Caliphate's unexpected attack dissipated. The water became, like Janet, more languid in its journey, content to push and slap the vertical surfaces in its way. It punched and smashed windows and sparks flashed from thousands of electrical contacts, announcing the cessation of their services.

After finishing her cigarette and lighting another, Janet noticed the first rivulets wending their way among the buildings in her neighbourhood. She leaned over her antique walnut credenza to get a better look as the water shoved cars and dumpsters into buildings. "Open the windows," she told the super AI, but nothing happened. She looked up and watched, fascinated, as the lights of New York vanished in orderly sections. She recalled that she had some scented candles in the kitchen cupboard above the stove.

Moments passed. She finished her cigarette and resisted the urge to light another immediately, wondering how long it would be before she would be able to get more. A shout outside drew her attention back to the street in front of her apartment block. She couldn't be sure as her eyes needed time to adjust to the darkness, but there seemed to be movement in the water coasting by outside.

A strange sense of elation enveloped Janet. She smiled at the realisation that the fish she sponsored in the Passaic River were now free. To celebrate, she reconsidered her self-imposed rationing and lit another cigarette. As it burned down to the filter, her exhaustion returned. It had been a long working day with clients she'd prefer to forget. And that water wasn't going anywhere.

Chapter 12

10.13 Friday 13 October 2062

Mark Phillips struggled to concentrate as he monitored his section of the English Channel. Lieutenant Cho's words had been repeating in his mind, causing feelings of pride and embarrassment in equal measure, when the alert went up that seven-hundred-and-fifty enemy ACAs were attacking four locations on the eastern seaboard of the United States, where it was just after four o'clock in the morning.

This occasioned a wave of urgency throughout 3rd Airspace Defence, as all operators received a message to anticipate the beginning of a multi-axis attack by the enemy. A part of Mark shared in the excitement, but he also felt certain no other attacks would be forthcoming. He'd analysed the Caliphate's methods, working backwards: from the invasion attempts in August, its progress across Europe over the spring and summer, back to its onslaught in February.

A creeping feeling distracted him, a solidifying belief that all of them were missing something. Before he could analyse the sensation further, several wings of Blackswans emerged from an area obscured by enemy jamming on the continent, speeding over the water towards the Kent coast. The enemy machines climbed and twisted and pirouetted and pitched and rolled and dived, utilising every second of every minute of every degree of three-dimensional space. Despite having seen versions of this performance many times over the previous few weeks, the breath still caught in Mark's throat at watching two competing artificial intelligences attempting to outwit each other for advantages that could be measured in hundredths of a millimetre or thousandths of a second. Mark followed the protocols he had to, despite realising at once the assault presented no serious threat. As had become the norm, very human enemy commanders must have instructed their super AI to attack NATO defences despite no chance of creating any kind of exploitable breach in them.

As he'd expected, in moments local batteries around Dover and Deal responded with ample volleys of Falaretes. Mark withdrew his view to a higher altitude to observe if any other sectors were experiencing similar attacks. Another flutter of pride rippled through him: now he'd been accepted as an officer cadet, he'd earned the right to view any sector he wanted and had access to many of 3rd Airspace Defence's other feeds.

Mark called up a line-feed of the attack on the United States and minimised it. The collapse of the Carter Dam seemed to be doing the greatest damage. The raw numbers of estimated water volume and casualties told their own story. Further up and down the vast eastern American seaboard, highly surgical strikes had breached sea defences in Philadelphia, New Haven and Providence. Mark shivered at the incredible amount of damage being done. No wonder his own bosses were flapping.

Then he noticed something else weird on this strange morning. The lower portion of his view carried rows of small numbers prefixed with identification codes. One of these flickered, catching his eye, and the number trebled. He raised it and recognised its code as seismic monitoring. Something very big and heavy must have hit the ground somewhere in the northern hemisphere. His first instinct was to write it off as connected to the destruction currently happening in America—probably several large buildings had collapsed simultaneously. But his curiosity nagged him, as it always did, to find the right source, because he had to be sure.

He paused and reconsidered: he'd only just been promoted and shouldn't do anything to piss his superiors off, especially Captain Shithead, who'd love a reason to criticise. Mark stared at the digits. The need to know precisely why that number had trebled burned inside him. As the moments passed, another realisation dawned: the number was not dropping back, as it would do in the event of some kind of huge impact that happened but then passed. Whatever had occurred in the last sixty seconds was continuing to happen.

"Earthquake?" Mark whispered to himself. "Has to be."

He rechecked the action over the English Channel. Sure enough, yet more scrap metal was being blasted from the sky and deposited into the water, and the enemy's latest sortie came to nothing. Because it was a distraction from something else. Something bigger.

"This is bullshit," Mark said. With waves of his hands, he left his sector and rose higher, up to the level of the SkyWatchers. He accessed the data and saw that a seismic event of some kind had taken place in the Atlantic Ocean. His physical fingers jabbed at thin air as he selected virtual options from his comfortable couch.

He stuck out a finger to contact the operator for that sector but stopped, a sudden, cold sweat staying his hand. Simon's oft-replayed advice that other people were not so different from Mark, and Mark should not be afraid to talk to them, seemed to ring hollow for a reason he could not articulate.

"Attention," Lieutenant Cho announced, "all operators, Foxtrot shift. We are tracking a sudden and unexpected undersea earthquake southwest of the European mainland. Once again, monitor your sectors closely, please. We're not certain this happening now is a coincidence."

His boss's tautology stuck out: why did she use "sudden" and "unexpected" at the same time like that, unless she was under serious pressure? He muttered another curse and stared only at the seismic monitoring number. "Squonk," he instructed, "extrapolate from currently available data and estimate the cause of the 'seismic event'."

The super AI answered: "You do not have sufficient security clearance."

Mark scoffed, the gamer inside him responding to the barrier like he'd faced so many challenges in the Universes. "Fine. So show me all of the data I do have access to."

His section of the English Channel faded as more lists of words and numbers resolved in his vision. His eyes flicked over them and alighted on the highest one. But there had to be a mistake—it reported a moving wave of water more than four hundred metres high, radiating out from the edge of Caliphate-jammed territory. He barked: "Enhance grid reference 878–N."

"You do not have sufficient security clearance."

"For fuck's sake," Mark cursed, "I want to know what's caused that wave."

"Excessive profanity may be reported to your commanding officer."

Mark ignored the admonishment and asked, "Why is the water so high there? How fast is that wave moving? That cannot be right." As he voiced his concern, that row of words and numbers vanished.

"This data is now restricted and classified secret."

Something big had happened and Brass didn't want the lower ranks to know about it. "Okay," he said, in the tone of having been challenged to a fight to the death, "have it your own way. Just one more thing: give me a history of all known 'undersea earthquakes' in that part of the Atlantic Ocean in recorded history." As the requested data resolved in his vision, Mark tied this 'earthquake' to the enemy attack on the eastern seaboard of the US. He didn't believe the two were a coincidence. And he hated not knowing why.

Chapter 13

09.45 Friday 13 October 2062

Terry Tidbury stood at the holographic display in the War Room underneath Whitehall and held his breath. In all of the violent precision of the enemy's merciless advance across Europe over the preceding eight months, nothing had left him as stunned as this abrupt turn of events. The soldier in him reeled in staggered amazement—bordering on the greatest respect—for an enemy that used the most extreme, outlandish tactics for no reason other than to kill, to erase as many innocent lives as possible, without resorting to nuclear weapons.

But first, he cautioned himself for believing something that had yet to be proven. Somehow, the enemy was responsible for this 'undersea earthquake', but would deny that responsibility absolutely. A rare flash of egotism sparked inside Terry: he finally felt able to predict his enemy's moves. After eight months of overseeing and trying to manage relentless reverses, Terry had learned how the man who was the Third Caliph and his forces preferred to proceed.

An hour earlier, Simms had informed him of the ACA attack on the eastern seaboard of the US while he'd been travelling from his home on the south coast into Whitehall. At once, Terry had suspected something greater, more outrageous, would follow.

The assortment of seven hundred and fifty of the enemy's ACAs represented a formidable destructive force. They would likely cause significant disruption to American civilians as well as US Navy operations. However, it would deal them a blow comparatively no worse than that which the Japanese inflicted at Pearl Harbour in 1941: more of a painful insect sting to rouse the beast rather than a powerful uppercut to cause material damage to the American war effort. No, as soon as Terry learned of the ACA attack, its strength and locations, he'd been expecting the enemy to attempt some kind of far-reaching knockout blow. The attack on the US's flood defences was the sucker punch, and the enemy—or at any rate his computers—had found some way of engineering another attack that might cause far greater damage.

In the holographic display in front of him, the digital representation of a set of vast waves in the Atlantic Ocean undulated, radiating outwards from a point somewhere just inside Caliphate-controlled waters; a movement of billions of tons of water, waves that had dropped from their peak but which still rose over three hundred metres above sea level. Forecasts already suggested atrocious inland flooding all along the eastern seaboard, down to Central America, the Caribbean and South America, which would make landfall in six to nine hours. Closer to home, the Iberian Peninsula and France's Atlantic coast would endure a punishing inundation in less than fifteen minutes, with the southern English coast due to receive waves up to a few metres high.

"Squonk," Terry said, "recalculate. Could there be a mistake?"

"Negative."

"Where will the most damage happen?"

"When the tsunami makes landfall—"

"Excuse me, sir," Simms broke in, hurrying towards the station, hands held outwards. "There's an emergency COBRA just started, with the PM, most of the ministers. Would you like to attend in person or virtually?"

Terry looked down at the digital representation of the huge waves and felt that he needed to move physically. He strode towards the door without speaking. Footsteps told him that his adjutant followed.

Once the lift doors slid closed, Terry glanced at Simms's stern, angular face and asked: "What's happening in the US right now?" He watched the taller man's eye twitch and Terry considered again if he shouldn't finally give in and get one of those damnable lenses put in his eye.

His adjutant replied, "In terms of loss of life, most damagingly the Carter Dam is completely breached, and large parts of New York will remain under water until it can be repaired."

"And militarily?"

"Norfolk has been deluged, which is certain to affect future planned supply convoys."

"Without a doubt."

Simms gave a laconic shrug and added: "Although we can assume the submarines based at the New London yard should've managed to cope a little better."

Terry let out a mirthless chuckle. "If only the subs could bring us the supplies." The field marshal exited the lift and made his way along corridors he knew well towards the COBRA meeting room. As he approached the figures around the panelled double doors, he recognised Napier's aide, Webb, managing the arrivals with a lean complacency made up of subtle nods and slight gestures with his hands.

Webb said, "Field marshal. We've got a full house this morning. It's going to be a little tight in there."

"Good morning, Mr Webb. Indeed."

People animated with concern moved through the doorway. Terry felt as though he and Simms were navigating a rush hour crush in a department store—and then had to brush aside a sudden sensation of nostalgia.

Inside Cabinet Briefing Room A, people shuffled along the walls; the worn, oblong oak table already fully occupied. Terry saw over thirty individuals were already squeezed in, and those standing obscured the screens that made up the side walls. His eyes alighted on Napier, her head tipped forward listening to Blackwood, the foreign secretary, next to her. Terry scanned the other attendees and noted ministers and their aides, the head of England's civil defence operations, as well as men and women who oversaw the key functions that held battered and broken English society together.

He leaned back towards Simms. "I assume most of the military commanders are attending from their bases?"

"Yes, sir," Simms murmured, "nearly all of those with the required clearance. Ah, and General Pakla has just joined, so that's all of the senior staff."

"Good."

The screen in the wall at the head of the conference room displayed a scene so similar it might've been a mirrored reflection. An oval table, larger and richer in colour than the English one, hosted over twenty personnel, most of them military. A small panel in the lower righthand corner stated 'Joint Chiefs of Staff Action Room'. Terry recognised Staff General Ava King by her cropped red hair. She stared at a small screen in the table in front of her, and others peered in, some in dress uniform, most in combat fatigues. None of those in the image gave any acknowledgement of the English observers.

Napier lifted her head and spoke over the whispers and mutterings, "Can we keep the noise down?"

Silence fell.

"Thank you," she said, tucking some strands of lank auburn hair behind her left ear. "The Pentagon is going to address all US and NATO allies shortly. Please remember that Washington is five hours behind us. It's barely morning there and they have had a very unpleasant night."

Terry glanced back at Simms and muttered, "That's putting it mildly."

Simms said nothing.

From the other side of the table, Defence Secretary Liam Burton twisted his head in Terry's direction. "I still can't get over the fact that a measly seven hundred and fifty enemy machines could've caused so much damage. For God's sake, we've dealt with thousands of the damn things—often dispatching them in less than an hour—and we can still hold them off when we have to. Why couldn't the Ya—er, Americans?"

Terry opened his mouth to speak, but from a chair to his left the portly Aiden Hicks said loudly, "The Falarete, of course," in a tone of obviousness.

Burton's young face looked at Hicks and then back at Terry, his eyes widening in apparent disbelief. "You mean they don't have them?"

"No, the bloody fools," Hicks said in contempt.

"Designs for all of NATO's armaments are of course available to all members," Terry offered.

Exasperation suffused Burton's voice, "But they didn't replicate and deploy them? Not even at their most important bases? Seriously?"

Hicks leaned forward at the table, the material of his white shirt stretching against the flesh on his forearms. "The Americans considered themselves beyond the Third Caliph's attentions. As is well known, Coll has only been waiting for plucky little England and the other Home Countries to collapse before—"

"That's enough, Aiden," Napier interrupted, weariness in her voice.

Terry kept his tone even, "It's worth bearing in mind that, for all its effectiveness in holding the enemy off, the Falarete is a stopgap, a temporary defensive field weapon designed only to buy us time. Those of our American allies with whom I've discussed our defences have praised the weapon, but not perhaps deemed it worthy of adopting."

"Wow," Burton said. "Bet they'll adopt it now."

Hicks let out a stifled 'harrumph' but Terry sensed general acceptance of his explanation. He preferred it when the civilian politicians reacted more like he expected his subordinate commanders to behave.

The view in the screen changed, closing in on Staff General King. When she spoke, she glanced at only those in her presence. Her bony, drawn face exuded concern and fatigue. "Okay, everyone. This is a short briefing to bring our allies up to date with current developments. So, ah, the situation is not looking too good. We have reports of an undersea earthquake that, uh, appears to have created a very large tsunami, er, here."

An image swept out from the lower righthand corner and covered the screen. An animated curved red line crossed a digital representation of the Atlantic Ocean. King said, "Here are the current estimated impact times and the height of the waves when they get here. Right now, we have a ton of variables concerning a low-pressure weather system in the mid-Atlantic and the effects it can have on the bore, and how much the waves' depth, and therefore their power, might lessen on reaching the continental shelf. Ample Annie is forecasting a wide range of potential outcomes. But, as I said, it's not looking good."

The image withdrew to show King had tipped her head forward in apparent concentration. The people around Terry in the COBRA room shuffled and a few muffled coughs broke the silence.

"Ah, right," King said, "we've got some news just in. Wait one."

Napier sighed. "God, isn't there anything they can do to stop the waves, somehow diffuse them, even a little?"

King said, "Okay, I'm going to bring Professor Chris Hill, from the US Geological Survey at our Florida station. Professor Hill is head of Seismic Monitoring, Eastern Seaboard. Go ahead, please."

A new image emerged, this time only covering the lower righthand quarter of the screen. An intense, bearded man frowned and said, "Thank you, ma'am. Our latest data shows this tsunami is not—I repeat not—caused by an undersea earthquake. We have confirmation that the northern flank of the Cumbre Vieja volcanic ridge collapsed into the sea at approximately 04.23 standard eastern."

General King put her hand on her forehead. "Thank you," she said, "but I don't think that really matters right now. Whatever the cause was, in a few hours we are going to endure the biggest natural disaster in this country's histo—"

"Excuse me, ma'am, but that's just my point," Hill said. "I have reason to believe it is not a natural disaster."

"What?" King said.

The bearded man shook his head. "Ma'am, the Cumbre Vieja ridge is well-known in the volcanic and seismic disciplines. Has been for decades. This is—or maybe it would be better to say was—a crack; actually a fault-line consisting of several cracks."

"Get to the point," King ordered in a stern voice, her face reddening like her hair.

"The last independent survey was twenty years ago, right before the Caliphate took over what were then called the Canary Islands. That survey estimated the fault-line was not a major cause for concern. The probability of the ridge collapsing, as it appears to have done, was deemed to be a one-in-one-hundred-thousand-year event. Now, right as we were being hit by the enemy's bombs, seismic stations all over the US and beyond recorded a sequence of very minor tremors that Ample Annie confirms to ninety-nine-point-whatever percent were not naturally occurring—"

"Wait a minute," King broke in. "You're talking about explosions, right? Detonations? Have I got that right?"

The skin on the back of Terry's head prickled with sweat at the confirmation of his own theory. His heartrate picked up further when he realised how the bulk of US politicians might want America to respond if the enemy could be shown to have created the tsunami—after all, they had already suffered thousands of casualties from the ACA attack. Now, they were obliged to face a disaster several magnitudes greater.

Hill nodded. "That is correct, ma'am. It looks a whole lot like the New Persian Caliphate used bombs to break Cumbre Vieja ridge free. It slid into the ocean and created the approaching tsunami."

Terry tried to imagine how Staff General King felt.

The woman tipped her head forward again and her shoulders heaved. She looked back up at the people around the conference table in Washington and exhaled. "I think we need to take this one step at a time," she said. "Thank you, Professor Hill, but we should wait on firmer evidence before claiming we know for certain that our enemy somehow caused this calamity."

Terry nodded in appreciation of King's diffusive approach.

The staff general continued, "Right now we have a set of huge waves moving across the Atlantic at—" she squinted at the surface of the table in front of her, "—about four hundred and fifty miles per hour. Obviously, all emergency protocols have been activated. It's still early here, and we can't be sure how bad this will turn out. However, this is to notify our NATO partners that US defensive capabilities may be limited for an as-yet-to-be-determined period of time—" the last word caught in King's throat. She looked down again, presumably to compose herself. She continued, "Autonomous military systems should of course not be significantly affected."

Napier put out a hand. "General, has President Coll been informed? Will she make a statement?"

"As far as I know, yes, the president has been roused and told of both the initial attack and the approaching tsunami."

"Please convey the English government's deepest sympathies at this awful turn of events."

King's eyebrows rose. "Yeah, sure. Er, thanks." She gathered herself and concluded, "Okay, we need to end this announcement meeting for our allies. We hope to be able to hold regular update meetings in due course. Please consult your super artificial intelligence for more details. Thank you for attending."

The screen flickered and the English government's portcullis placeholder appeared.

Terry watched the attendees look at each other in stunned shock and worried concern, but he had little time for such sentiments given the gravity and urgency of this new disaster. "Squonk," he barked, "display a graphic on the main screen of the Cumbre Vieja ridge on the island formally known as La Palma. Use available current data to show how the flank fell—or was made to fall—into the Atlantic Ocean."

"Confirmed," Squonk answered.

The portcullis was replaced with a three-dimensional image of the island in green, surrounded by weak blue representing the ocean. Squonk said, "Caution. Your location shows you are in the company of persons who do not have sufficient security clearance."

Terry scoffed at the computer adhering so closely to established protocol. He bit his lip before asking Napier, "With your permission, PM?"

"Of course," she replied with a nod.

Terry said, "Override that restriction. Authorisation Tidbury, Sir Terry, field marshal. Confirm."

"Confirmed."

The image rotated and zoomed towards the island, whose shape reminded Terry of a prehistoric flint dagger that stone age people were often depicted using to cut fur skins and suchlike. A red, jagged line helpfully bisected the island, indicating the Cumbre Vieja ridge, which Terry only now realised had been in the centre of the island. If all of the land west of the ridge had collapsed—

Squonk said, "Approximately five hundred and seventy-four cubic kilometres of rock and vegetation has collapsed into the Atlantic Ocean."

On the screen, the part of the island Terry feared had fallen did indeed separate and descend into the light blue that represented the water. A huge dome of water rose up in reaction to the huge chunk of island sliding into it. At the top edge of the screen, a timer showed the minutes and seconds accelerating faster than real time. The dome of water collapsed into a series of waves that began to radiate outwards. Part of Terry felt compelled to admire the geometric beauty, despite the destructive implications.

Squonk went on, "This has led to the creation of a train of waves that exceeded six hundred metres in height at their outset."

Gasps of shock and mumbled epithets rippled around the conference room.

The image in the screen withdrew to bring the outlines of Europe and Africa into view. Squonk said, "The first waves inundated the other local islands and have caused significant flooding along the Iberian Peninsula and Africa's Atlantic coast. Here are the waves' current locations in real time."

The image flickered and more numbers resolved around the depiction of the wave train.

Terry asked: "How high will those waves be once they've crossed the Atlantic Ocean, and when will they hit America?"

The super AI replied: "The tsunami will make landfall between Florida and Newfoundland in from six to nine hours. Current modelling suggests initial wave height on landfall of between thirty and fifty metres, subject to the following variables: a developing low-pressure system mid-ocean; the continental shelf dampening the waves' power, and therefore lowering height, as the waves approach land—"

"That's enough," Terry barked.

The mutterings of shock around the table increased, and Terry began to wish he was questioning the computer in the more military surroundings of the War Rooms.

Someone behind him said: "The Yanks are going to get one hell of a bath this afternoon," which elicited a few mirthless chuckles.

Terry bit down a reprimand, understanding a very human need for levity in the face of disaster. "Speculate cause," he ordered, not taking his eyes off the image in the screen.

The view zoomed once more until the island—whole again as it had been before the collapse—covered the screen. The red line identifying the ridge returned, but now it sprouted numerous smaller squiggles that descended deep into the island.

Squonk said, "Seismic stations in north America recorded over two hundred distinct events in the fifteen minutes before the collapse. These were almost certainly detonations of conventional explosives." The view rotated ninety degrees to the left as indicators blinked to denote explosions around and inside the island.

Terry, thinking ahead to what the next few hours and days might bring, asked: "What else could have caused these 'tremors' leading to the collapse? If, for example, someone wanted to claim this as a natural event and not artificial explosions, how could they?"

Squonk replied: "There is no data to support such a position."

"Expand on that," Terry ordered.

"The detonations of conventional explosive must have been artificially planned and executed to ensure the greatest volume of island-mass broke away. Volcanic islands invariably shed mass as they expand over time, however such events rarely generate highly damaging tsunamis. At some point in the next one hundred thousand years, the Cumbre Vieja ridge was certain to collapse. But it is much more probable such collapse would have been substantially smaller, happening in stages over a far longer period of time than a few minutes."

Terry said, "I've seen enough." He addressed Napier, "If you don't mind, PM, I need to talk to NATO colleagues in the US."

"Yes," Napier replied, a quaver in her voice. "After this, the rest of the agenda is routine, civilian concerns. Makes our current predicament seem quite bland, somehow."

"Thank you," Terry said. He turned for the door and only then noticed every pair of eyes in the room on him. He avoided their gazes, wondering why the civilians still seemed surprised by how quickly and suddenly events could turn. During a war, events invariably changed rapidly. But civilians always seemed to struggle to keep up.

Once outside, Terry strode ahead in urgency. He turned his head back and said, "Do keep up, Simms."

"Yes, sir," his adjutant replied, extending his stride.

When Simms drew alongside him, Terry said, "I want to speak to General Stevens first."

"Very good, Sir. Shall I see if he is avail—?"

"Yes, please," Terry said. They turned a corner and approached the lift. Terry could almost feel the static electricity building up in his boots as he walked on the thick, heavy carpet. Next to the lift sat one of those pieces of furniture his wife Maureen called an 'occasional table', a pointless thing too small to be of any use, with legs like curved matchsticks that looked as though they'd snap under the weight of a bowl of fruit.

They entered the lift. When the doors closed, Terry asked: "Well?"

"General Stevens is currently engaged but his adjutant has assured me she will pass the request to him."

"Good," Terry replied. "What do you think will happen next, Simms?"

"I think many Americans are going to have to endure a taste of what Europe has been bearing for the last eight months, sir," the adjutant replied in a tone of circumspection.

"Yes, yes," Terry said in irritation. "But what then? How do you think they will react?"

"I believe their hands are tied, sir."

"How so?"

The lift doors opened. Terry strode out, keen to return to his own domain.

Simms said: "They have no options open to them. A counterattack is out of the question until the new weapons are ready."

"Indeed," Terry said. "But what concerns me is the fact that not having options is, in general, anathema to Americans."

They entered the War Rooms.

Terry welcomed the familiarity of the grey steel and colourful screens and muted chatter. He turned to Simms and said: "Have a look over things here. I want to know if there is even the slightest hint the enemy might also pull another trick out of the bag today. I'll be in my office."

"Very good, sir," Simms replied with a nod. "Tea?"

"Yes, thank you," Terry said. He turned and entered his office, formulating his thoughts as he closed the door gently. "Squonk, open a private comms link to General Studs Stevens, USAF." Terry sat at his desk.

"Confirmed. General Stevens will be available directly."

Terry cast his gaze around the other data the screen offered, concern that he could be missing something scratching at the back of his throat like rising stomach acid.

Minutes passed. Simms delivered a steaming mug of tea and Terry voiced his thoughts to his adjutant again. Simms confirmed Terry's observation that no other attack seemed to be in progress, and then left.

Terry sipped his tea. The lean, angular face of General Studs Stevens resolved in the screen. Without preamble, Terry asked: "How many of your politicians are demanding the US responds to the tsunami?"

Stevens frowned. "Take it easy, Earl. We've got enough going on here that I don't think any kind of response is at the top of the agenda right now. Do you know what's happening at Norfolk? We've got cruisers sitting on top of admin blocks—"

"And that's another thing. Why the hell didn't you deploy Falaretes? I cannot believe you failed to take such an obvious defensive measure."

"Not my decision. There's a whole ocean separating you and us. I guess the folks in Homeland Security thought we didn't—"

"But Pulsars and missiles were never going to be enough to defend you against an enemy ACA attack, Suds. Did you all really think the enemy would never trouble you? The Third Caliph even said he was thinking about having a go at you in his—"

"Goddamn, Earl," Stevens broke in, anger deepening the scar above his right eye. "That is not the most important issue right now. In a few hours, the eastern seaboard will be hit by waves that might be as high as a five-storey building. And those waves are going to push inland and drown everyone who can't get out of the way."

Terry realised he was talking to his friend as though Suds were a subordinate. His fears had to be getting the better of him. He asked, "What are your computers telling you? How many people will you be able to save?"

Stevens visibly calmed down. "We've got a ton of protocols activated, but we're getting reports of a lot of panic, especially outside autonomous vehicle zones. I'm pretty sure I remember wargaming something like this a few years ago, Earl. But that was mainly based on terrorists taking out the Carter Dam—hell, we've even got dormant construction replicators on the bed of the Hudson ready to go in just this scenario."

"You're kidding," Terry said in shock.

"No way. When they finished the dam back in the 2040s, they tried to plan for every contingency. Those replicators are huge and were slated to be able to remain operable for a minimum hundred years without replacement. They're designed so that if the dam was ever damaged real bad—like it just was—they could rebuild it enough from under the seabed up to start pumping water back out into the ocean within a few days."

Terry shook his head. "I had no idea."

"You shouldn't have—that was top secret. But the goddamn enemy must've known. I'm certain that's why that tsunami is headed our way."

"But after the tsunami has passed, the replicators will still be able to reconstruct the dam, yes?"

"I guess that depends on the power of the waves, and neither of us are experts on that. Ample Annie says it's fifty-fifty: the replicators might survive and be able to rebuild the dam, they might not."

"Look, Suds," Terry said, "I think our main concern now is your politicians."

"Uh-huh," Stevens agreed. "Media's already going crazy with Republican rednecks saying we should nuke the Caliphate."

"That's what I feared. They have to be stopped."

"Coll won't listen to them. They're mostly loud-mouthed freaks from the rustbelt, anyhow."

Suds' dismissal unnerved Terry further. He pushed: "Might they not convince her otherwise? Could they claim they now have some advantage—for example, using the SHF burner corridors—that would allow US's nuclear weapons to succeed where the Israelis failed? You know how those extremists can take the slightest half-truth and twist it."

Stevens paused before replying, "They could try, I guess, but reprisal is something that's going to have to wait anyways, Earl. Today's gonna be bad enough as it is, and Coll and the rest of the government have got way more to deal with."

"I understand. I know what's happening over there doesn't strictly involve me as SACEUR, but I'm going to request further admission to the Joint Chiefs Action Room."

Stevens shrugged and answered, "Sure, but don't get offended if you don't get access. And if you do, for God's sake lay off the lectures. Okay, I gotta go."

"Good luck over there."

Stevens' face disappeared, replaced with a real-time image of the situation over the English Channel. Terry stared at it absentmindedly, a part of him noting the minimal activity, but being more aware of a creeping sense of being trapped overtaking him. NATO and the democracies were forced always to react to the enemy, never able to take the initiative. He thought back to his initial estimation of this unexpected attack on the United States and wondered if his first notion—that this was an insect sting more likely to rouse the beast—did in fact contain a grain of truth. Or would the approaching tsunami carry enough power to deliver a knockout blow?

He sat back in his chair with a sigh and gulped down the hot tea, resigned again to being a spectator to the enemy's next action. NATO's next-gen weapons remained months from mass production, and would in any case rely on the enemy not deploying his own superior weapons. In the meantime, Terry felt as though the whole of the forces at his command; indeed, the British Isles themselves, were like a trapped antelope, staring in impotent dismay as the lion of the New Persian Caliphate chomped down and slowly consumed its fresh kill of Europe.

Chapter 14

11.57 Friday 13 October 2062

Janet Bagget sipped her coffee with one hand and reached for her new packet of cigarettes with the other. Sleep hadn't fully left her, but the next smoke should see to that. She put the coffee down on the nightstand, sat up higher in her bed, stuck the filter-tip in the corner of her mouth and lit it with her gold furnace lighter.

With a quick huff she discarded the initial drag, and then drew the poisonous smoke as deeply into her lungs as she could, twitching her eye muscles to rotate around news feeds, social sites, and local New York authority services that were trying to manage a disaster which had become unmanageable. She reflected how the sounds seemed more frightening than the images, because sometimes she could not be sure whether a shriek, shout or gunshot came from a feed in her lens or from the street outside her fourth-floor apartment in Newark.

The building's super AI notified her that five minutes remained and she should get to the roof of the apartment block.

"At least," she mused aloud, "I know my fortieth birthday is gonna be my last."

Confusion had given way to a familiar sense of unfairness, an extension of the unfairness that had dogged her for her entire life. When she'd fallen asleep, the Carter Dam had been destroyed and she faced days without power or any easy way to leave her apartment block. Now, she'd woken a few hours later to find that a massive wave was heading across the ocean to swamp New York with even more water.

She kicked her legs out from under the soft duvet and stood in her sheer silk nightgown. She recalled a pleasant memory before she fell asleep, of finding an emergency cache of ten packets of cigarettes she'd stashed at the back of a grocery cupboard. But this was tempered by the relentless scenes of chaos that New York—still the greatest city on Earth, despite what those goddamn Chinese thought—endured as its people tried to cope with the collapse of the Carter Dam, the resulting flooding, and the foreknowledge of approaching catastrophe.

She blinked to minimise the feeds in her lens and strode to the windows looking out over Newark and towards Manhattan. The morning sun shone bright and warm in a turquoise sky of chilled autumnal clarity: there really was nothing as pure as an endless, empty New York sky in October.

But then she raised the city's emergency feed and saw the approaching wave. Apparently, it was called a 'tsunami' and it was coming towards New York at over two hundred and fifty miles an hour and rose more than hundred-and-twenty feet high. The mayor was pleading with city residents to give the weak and injured priority for evacuation inland. He said that if you were healthy, you should wait while the emergency services got those in greater need out. But there seemed to be a problem with autonomous vehicles clogging the roads.

Down in the street below, she estimated the water to be about four feet deep. People struggled to wade through it, some holding things aloft: belongings, pets, babies, guns. The scene looked somehow familiar but she struggled to recall. Then she realised that her street looked just like the streets in all those news reports of flooding elsewhere around the world, news of constant inundations with which she'd grown up. It seemed strange that New York could or should suffer in the same way as so many lesser places in cities like Africa and Asia.

She noticed a new number appear in the top-left of her view: a countdown. She twitched her eye muscle and the rest of the view suddenly zoomed, to be filled by the onrushing giant wave. The countdown, provided courtesy of her building's super AI via the New York City Emergency Management Department, dipped below four minutes. Janet drew on her cigarette. Memories tumbled through her mind like piano notes tinkling down the scales in endless repetition. After all the disappointments, all the let-downs, all the lies, she felt unexpectedly sanguine about the approaching waves.

She glanced through her fourth-floor window at the street below. People stranded there were yelling and calling to each other. Then she noticed the water receding. She caught her breath and nearly choked on the smoke that became trapped in her throat. When the coughing subsided, she heard cheers waft up from below. The dirty road was visible once more, albeit coated in mud and muck and debris. A pang of concern made Janet gasp when she realised the sudden lowering of the water level might hurt her beloved fish that must have escaped from the special farm on the Passaic River during the initial flood. She disregarded the feeling when she realised that now she'd never find out.

She leaned her head close to the glass of the window to peer at the Museum of Art two blocks south. Water dribbled from its broken lower floors, gurgling out of windows and doorways and sloshing down the metal fire escape. She could hear gushing and dripping all along the street.

The countdown dropped to less than one minute. Janet shut off the feeds in her lens and refocused her eyes to observe the first distant, shimmering wave advancing towards the city with the kind of resolute grace and majesty she once dreamed she might possess. God, where had it all gone? Had she really needed to spend the best years of her life working like this, earning good money from men she hated, men who thought they could own her for a night or even an hour. The money, the silk nightgowns, the satin bedsheets—had it really been worth it?

Something large and black flashed past the window, landing with a thump on the street below. Shouts rose up to greet her as she saw the person who fell had now become a body.

"Idiots," she mumbled, knowing that roofs would be overloaded with people trying to save themselves. And even if they survived the dozen or more waves, what then?

A gentle tremor began in the pane of glass against which her face rested. The first wave drew closer. The buildings of Manhattan that remained standing after the dam burst were swamped, a vast white curtain of sea spray surging out from around each one as the wave hit it. The majesty and power of nature tempered the hope deep in her soul that those remaining skyscrapers might break the wave, perhaps absorb its energy and lessen the impact. But the wall of water kept coming towards her, covering everything in its path.

Janet Bagget turned from the window and flicked her cigarette from between her index finger and thumb. It spun through the air to land on the parquet floor on the opposite side of the bed, where the curl of the smoke told her it had begun to burn the floor. She grabbed the packet from the bedside table, slid out another, and held the gold furnace lighter to it, ready to light the cigarette. She looked at her hand. It trembled. She wondered if she were scared. But her arm trembled, and then her whole body shook. Her instinct urged her to turn, to see the water coming on and smashing everything in its path, so that she might take some kind of evasive action, however futile.

Instead, she lit her last cigarette, knowing she would never inhale its wonderful smoke.

Chapter 15

18.00 Friday 13 October 2062

Aggression surged through Mark Phillips. He whispered, "Come on," as he scanned his sector of the English Channel for enemy activity. He knew, along with everyone else in 3rd Airspace Defence, that a train of giant waves was rolling over Atlantic coastal regions from South America all the way up to Canada.

Mark would've preferred to observe the destruction, for tens of thousands of people were broadcasting the view of the event on their own feeds. The most respected news aggregators struggled to report the tsunami with impartiality, giving some kind of equal weight to each affected country and region, but as the chaos grew, Mark forced himself to focus on his duty to spot and react to the enemy's next attack.

However, the one variable that super artificial intelligence could not dominate in this war remained atmospheric conditions. While the ACAs themselves were sufficiently fast, powerful and agile to be unaffected by a wide range of forecastable weather types, occasionally a rarer combination of the elements might offer a moment's tactical advantage, and if and when that happened, events could move very quickly indeed.

But as Mark stared at Sector 129, which encompassed a slice of English coastal area and the adjacent English Channel, the airspace remained stubbornly empty. The gamer's instinct in him circled and then centred on strategy—the enemy's strategy. A new idea came to him: the enemy had to make today's events look good. To do so, there could be no increased ACA activity because the collapse had to look natural, not part of a wider attack. Once the idea had revealed itself, Mark relaxed, certain that no significant enemy activity would be forthcoming.

The hours passed. Mark stole surreptitious glances at news feeds in his view. Although this was against the letter of the regulations, the scenes of chaos became irresistible as they worsened. The banality of the loss of life struck him with the most force. In games, deaths were always somehow dramatic, or designed to elicit emotion. But now, the news feeds carried images of people simply sinking beneath the water.

The end of Mark's duty period arrived, and with some relief he handed over responsibility for his sector to another operative. He removed and stowed his headset, and left the monitoring room, padding softly past other reclined figures who also monitored England's defences. He made his way back to his quarters, trying to predict the next move in the enemy's strategy. Rogue thoughts of his siblings trespassed on his concentration, and he had to push them aside. Whatever else was going on, his older brother Martin and his younger sister Maria would certainly be doing something he'd find impossibly dull.

His quarters consisted of a small, windowless room, one of many that lined three parallel corridors one floor below the monitoring level. Mark slid the door closed. At once an unpleasant feeling began inside him. The walls of the small and confined room seemed to close in on him. He controlled his breathing in the manner Simon had shown him.

He untied and kicked off his boots, and sat on the single bunk, his back against the wall. Opposite him, a screen came to life with the regiment's emblem: a grid surrounded by a cluster of leaves he couldn't name, with arrows pointing to the centre. He twitched his eye to scroll through the feeds in his lens, curiosity increasing. The death tolls in numerous cities, states and countries had reached the thousands.

Mark's eye alighted on one feed that he transferred to the larger screen. Oblong roofs surrounded by dirty, moving water shone white in the sunlight. Little specks that Mark realised were people, emerged from tiny doorways. The caption at the bottom of the screen read: 'LIVE: Windsor, Virginia'. Autonomous aircraft arrived from the sky and descended. The view also came down and closed in on the people, who appeared frightened.

Suddenly, a red-level comms notification flashed in the top-right corner of the screen. Mark raised it and the image of evacuation was replaced with the picture of a dark-skinned young man sitting at an old-fashioned newsreader's desk. Over his right shoulder rested the crest of the New Persian Caliphate.

The man opened his mouth and spoke a series of liquid sounds interspersed with guttural exclamations and short pauses. An English translation scrolled across the bottom of the screen. It read: "An historic day has arrived. Allah has acted to punish the infidel! The illustrious Third Caliph, leader and protector of the Persian Caliphate, celebrates Allah's wise decision to make the Old Summit in the Atlantic Ocean collapse."

Mark used his lens to establish that 'Old Summit' was the English translation of 'Cumbre Vieja'.

The young man went on, "The illustrious Third Caliph beseeched Allah for His assistance. The illustrious Third Caliph lit the touchpaper by destroying the infidel's protection against the rising seas—rising seas caused by five hundred years of the infidel's greed! And Allah answered. He responded by causing a massive undersea earthquake to make the Old Summit fall into the ocean. In turn, this created waves that travelled across the seas to visit a just punishment upon the infidel."

Mark mumbled: "Bull-fucking-shit, Allah did."

"Now, the illustrious Third Caliph wishes it to be known that he advises the infidel to accept the punishment meted out to him on this day. The infidel of today must pay the price for the wrongs and injustices committed by his forefathers for the last five hundred years. This is a heavy price to pay. Furthermore, it would be unwise in the extreme to question Allah's will in this matter. Infidels driven to insanity by this punishment must accept wiser council before believing they have any right to act against the Persian Caliphate."

Mark pulled himself further up the mattress and said: "Are you seriously—?"

"From tomorrow, there will be three days of celebrations throughout the entire Persian Caliphate to acknowledge this taming of the infidel. This day will be remembered for all history as proof of Allah's limitless justice and mercy. The wrongs of centuries past have been righted on this day. The righteous among us have had to wait centuries, but Allah, in his wisdom, did not desert us. And we shall celebrate His justice. God is great."

The transmission ended. The image on the screen reverted to the autonomous air transports conducting the evacuation in Virginia. Mark got off his bunk and paced back and forth in his tiny quarters. He whispered: "There is no way the island fell into the sea by itself. The enemy did it. If so, how?" He sat back on his bunk, heaved in a deep breath and decided, "There must be evidence, somewhere. But how to find it?"

Chapter 16

18.53 Friday 13 October 2062

Crispin Webb ran through the corridor that led to Napier's flat on the third floor of Ten Downing Street. He hated days that turned to rat-shit when he least expected it. He told himself he should be used to it by now, but as the weeks turned into months and England continued in this stalemate, the constant low-level stress ground everyone down. Even a few of the less important cabinet members—the cowards, as he thought of them—had returned from across the Atlantic for reasons he could not fathom: did they really think that there could be any other outcome to this bloody war than that which the army had merely managed to postpone?

However, the returnees included the boss's husband and her children, although even this transpired to be a double-edged sword. On the one hand, her family's presence tended to keep her booze consumption a bit more under control. On the other, she'd begun delegating more of the meetings to the cabinet members she valued. Now, if only they could find a way to rebuild her relationship with that idiot-vamp Coll in the White House?

Then, this morning, the Caliphate had attacked the US, confirming finally that its ACAs could in fact reach that far. Crispin felt little more than indifference to the Americans getting a taste of what Europe had been suffering, but just when he began to get used to that event, a part of an island in the Atlantic fell into the sea. Sometimes, he wondered if the bad news would ever stop.

Barely breaking his stride, he arrived at the heavy oak-panelled door, grasped the handle and pushed it open.

"Ow," exclaimed Monica, the boss's PA. "You nearly hit me, yeah?"

Crispin strode past her and on towards the main living area. "Sorry," he muttered insincerely.

She spoke from behind him, "I was coming to get you. We're trying to organise—"

"Yes, my lens is working, thank you." Crispin stopped and faced her.

Monica's narrow eyes drew closer together under her frown. "A lot of Americans are talking about trying to nuke the Caliphate."

Crispin scoffed. "Let them. Do you think they've already forgotten what happened to the Jews?" He strode on and arrived at the main living area. "Where is everyone?" he demanded. "I thought I was the one running late."

"Dahra is on her way, the others should—"

She broke off as the door on the opposite side of the living area opened.

Defence Secretary Liam Burton swept in, buttoning his sports jacket. The young man glanced at each of them and said, "The others are right behind me. Can't believe the Chief Raghead is claiming the tsunami was an act of their rather bloody God." He nodded towards the elegant sideboard furnished with several bottles. "I'll help myself, if you don't mind."

Monica shrugged. "Go ahead."

Burton crossed the expansive room, strode past the windows and marble fireplace, and reached the sideboard with the drinks.

Crispin checked the feeds in his lens and said, "Good, they're here."

The door swung open again and Crispin stopped a grimace forming as the rotund Aiden Hicks wobbled into the room. Crispin wondered just how much weight the home secretary had put on since the attempted invasions. He supposed that all of them needed their crutches.

Foreign Secretary Charles Blackwood followed and closed the door. He flashed the room one of his gorgeous smiles and asked: "PM not here yet?"

"Apparently not," Hicks said, wheezing as he bent over to lower himself into one corner of the plush two-seater settee. He looked left and right, sighed, and addressed Monica: "Young lady, would you be kind enough to save me the bother of having to get up again and get me a glass of wine?"

Monica stood and asked, "Red or white?"

"Red, please."

Crispin noted all of the men's eyes at once stray to her slim legs, probably the most attractive thing about her.

Moving towards the fireplace to allow Monica to reach the sideboard, Burton said, "I assume we're all here because the Yanks are losing their sh—, er, minds over the tsunami, yes?" He took a tight sip from his scotch.

"Not sure what the PM thinks we can do about it," Blackwood said, waiting for Monica to finish pouring Hicks's wine. "My God, have you seen some of those feeds? I've always thought drowning must absolutely be the worst way to go."

Monica passed the glass to the home secretary. He took it with a nod and said: "Thank you, dear." Then he addressed the room, his nasal tone more pronounced, "Yes, but it all rather works in our favour, wouldn't you say?"

Blackwood took the top off a cut-glass decanter and brandy the colour of walnut glugged into a low tumbler. "Not sure what you mean by that, Aiden."

Hicks gave a mischievous smile and replied, "It's only seven and you're already on the brandy, foreign secretary? I think you know exactly what I mean."

There came a moment's silence. Crispin abruptly sensed a new mood in the men around the room.

Blackwood sipped his brandy and said, "I'm not sure I do. It's not at all clear what the Terror of Tehran—to use your preferred phrase—thinks he's going to achieve with this destruction. If the Americans get sufficiently hot-headed to lose their senses and try to hit the Caliphate with nuclear weapons, presumably he'll have to send swarms of his ACAs to burn them like he did with Israel. Only that's obviously going to be logistically impossible, even for him."

Burton wandered past Crispin and lowered himself into an armchair on the other side of the large, glass-topped coffee table. He also addressed Hicks, "I swear any 'advantage' you see for us in this debacle—if there is one—is by accident and not design. What that madman is after is world dominance, plain and sim—"

Dahra Napier arrived from the same corridor as Crispin and Monica. "Right, good you're here," she breathed. "Monica, a glass, if you would, please."

Crispin noted her more positive bearing with approval. Mr Napier's and the little Napiers' return seemed to be having a positive effect.

The boss turned to him and asked, "Are the arrangements in hand?"

Crispin selected the appropriate feed in his lens, analysed the data there, and replied, "Yes, boss."

"Good," Napier said, adding, "Thank you," when Monica handed her a glass of white wine. Napier sat on the right of the three-seater couch facing the fireplace.

Hicks cleared his throat, which made his chins wobble, and asked, "What is the latest with the rest of the cabinet? Now we seem to have reached this impasse, are we going to encourage them to return to Blighty?"

Napier took a sip from her glass and said, "No. I prefer the current arrangements. If any of them are desperate to return, say for personal reasons, they can, of course. But I think the situation we have now is optimum. Besides, I've decided to keep those portfolios mothballed. It's not as though the ministers for the environment or the leader of the house have much urgent business on. I assume none of you minds?"

A pang of distant familiarity rolled through Crispin as he eyed the other ministers for the slightest sign of dissent. They all acquiesced with grunts or nods, and he wished things could be how they were, when gossip, tittle-tattle and the potential for back-stabbing were not only the most important things he had deal with, but also the most entertaining.

"Good," the boss repeated. "Are you all up to speed?" she asked, glancing around the room.

Blackwood let out a hollow laugh. "As if it's possible to keep up with this. I think I shall be glad when today is over." He threw down a gulp of brandy.

"Indeed," Napier said.

Liam Burton leaned forward. "Have you been in touch with Coll? Do we know how the Americans are coping, apart from what we can see for ourselves?"

Napier tutted and replied, "No, I think, understandably, it's all a bit chaotic over there. I did talk briefly with Secretary Bradon to offer any assistance we could, but that unsurprisingly fell on deaf ears."

Blackwood said, "I also had a conversation with him a couple of hours ago, PM, and he did ask me to pass on his thanks. But now the issue is how the Americans can respond. I tried to tap him on the likelihood of them giving in to their emotions and employing their—still extensive—nuclear arsenal."

"Really? And?" Hicks asked.

Blackwood frowned. "He thinks the risk went up with the Third Caliph spinning the line that the tsunami was exclusively the work of Allah."

"But can it be proved?" Burton asked.

"That's what I asked you all here for."

Crispin watched the men look at the boss. Blackwood's handsome face creased in interest; he put his glass down and tugged a cufflink to the correct length beyond his jacket sleeve. Hicks's round face carried a slightly bemused look, as though he was more concerned with asking Monica for a refill, while the young blade of a defence secretary appeared pensive, hanging on the boss's every word.

Crispin waited for a glance from the boss to proceed. She gave it with an added nod, and Crispin began. He said, "We're going to be advised by the English Geological Survey. At their HQ in Nottingham, a Doctor Hannah Jeffreys is waiting to describe—" Crispin stopped when a red-level comms notification arrived. His breath stopped in anticipation of what new problem would present itself.

"Well," Burton said, "that has to be the least surprising thing to happen today."

The others gestured their agreement, except for Blackwood. He coughed in apparent discomfort and said, "Erm, I don't have my lens in. Would one of you mind telling me what's happened?"

"Crispin, put it on there," Napier instructed with a nod towards the fireplace.

The screen above the fireplace came to life with the familiar portcullis placeholder. This flickered and text and an image resolved.

Blackwood read what was there and exclaimed: "My God, have the Chinese ever been so explicit? They cannot suggest that the Third Caliph is telling the truth and that the tsunami really was an act of God."

Hicks said, "I don't want to sound like a historical bore, but the Caliphate is a very peculiar Chinese creation. They have to support their mad, flabby, Middle-Eastern bastard, if you think about it."

With cynicism Napier said, "But to publish false seismic records? That is a fabrication without precedent. Unbelievable."

Blackwood shrugged and said, "On the surface, it seems pretty convincing. There really was a series of tremors that made that island fall into the ocean. How nice of the Chinese to release evidence in support of the enemy."

"It can't be true," Burton said, flopping back into the armchair.

"Of course, it's not true," Napier replied. She turned her head back and said: "Crispin? Let's get on with what we're here to discuss, please."

"Yes, boss," he replied, making the necessary adjustments.

A new image resolved in the screen of a woman with skin that appeared pasty in the washed-out light. Lank blonde hair hung down both sides of her pensive face from a straight parting that showed darkening roots.

"Doctor Jeffreys?" Napier asked.

The woman's eyes widened. She said, "Wow, the actual prime minister. Hello there."

"You're working late tonight, aren't you?" Napier said with, Crispin thought, a trace of her old, pre-war charm she employed to put strangers at ease.

Jeffreys shrugged. "Aren't we all?"

Napier smiled and asked, "What happened today, to that island in the Atlantic? Was it as our enemy has claimed?"

Jeffreys scoffed and said, "Hardly. Judging by what our instruments recorded, the tremors that made the Cumbre Vieja collapse were created artificially."

"You mean it was blown up?" Burton queried.

"More or less," Jeffreys replied. "You know, I'm only a seismologist. I can give you the data and tell you that it was definitely not caused by naturally occurring forces, unless they were naturally occurring forces never before witnessed in nature."

Napier smiled and said, "We don't mind you speculating a little. How can you be sure the cause was certainly not an earthquake?"

"Well, to keep it as simple as possible, earthquake tremors vibrate through solids—like rock—and liquids—like seawater—in very specific patterns. By studying those vibrations, we can work out where an earthquake originated, how strong it was in several places, whether and how much magma was involved, and so on. But this morning, our monitoring stations recorded what turned out to be... how to put it? A series of little pops? The pattern of vibrations meant that whatever caused them at the source could not have been naturally occurring."

Standing to the side of the fireplace, Blackwood asked, "Is it really that simple?"

Jeffreys lifted a mug by its handle and drank from it. Clearly visible on the side were the words, 'Fuck the Chief Raghead' under which was a picture of a generic Muslim with a large, red 'X' over it. She repeated, "More or less."

Hicks asked: "So how can the Terror of Tehran claim it was an act of God and expect such claim to be taken seriously?"

"Because he can say that pressure under the cracks that were already in the rock was released, and so the collapse occurred naturally."

Blackwood pointed at the screen and said: "But you just explained—proved, even—that the collapse was artificial."

"Yes," Jeffreys replied, "but false seismic records can be created, fairly easily, I should think. And the one indisputable fact is that the Cumbre Vieja was already pretty riddled with cracks, which means it was bound to fall quite soon, geologically speaking."

The boss asked: "And what is 'quite soon' geologically speaking exactly?"

Jeffreys' forehead creased and she replied, "Any time within the next hundred thousand years."

"But you are certain," Napier pushed, putting her hand out flat, "that the collapse was caused artificially, yes?"

Jeffreys replied, "According to my data, absolutely. I did my doctorate on the new cracks in Hekla—well, ten years ago they were new—on Iceland. It's more or less the same thing: the cracks can bring the whole south face down maybe next week or maybe not for twenty millennia. But if it fell next week, it would be due to magma pressure behind those cracks being released in an earthquake, thus pushing the rock free. Now, if Cumbre Vieja had fallen because of magma build-up, the seismic readings would be different than what I've been analysing since this morn—"

"But different readings could be manufactured to falsely show that magma was there and there was an earthquake, when in fact it was something else," Napier broke in.

"Yes," Jeffreys said, "but the readings at other seismic monitoring stations around the world will all point to the same conclusions, so if false ones are created, it won't change a great deal unless you get all of those hundreds of monitoring stations all over the world to report the same false data."

Napier said, "Very well. Could you do something for us, doctor?"

Jeffreys' head moved back in surprise. "Sure, what?"

"Have you seen the 'evidence' the Chinese government's press office has just put out, supporting the enemy's claim that the collapse did occur naturally?"

"I was just starting on it when your gofer contacted me and we began our conversation."

Crispin bristled at being called a 'gofer' for the first time in his life.

"Good," Napier replied, smiling. "Could you create a comparison showing the differences between those two data sets that explicitly says the enemy's is false and why?"

"Sure, when do you need it by?"

"More or less?" Napier asked, and Crispin smothered a sudden laugh at the boss using Jeffreys' preferred idiom.

Jeffreys considered and said, "Half an hour to an hour… more or less?"

Napier smiled and replied, "That will do. Thank you for your time, Doctor Jeffreys."

"Sure, my pleasure."

The portcullis placeholder returned to the screen.

"I don't mean to pry, PM," Blackwood said, "but what use do you hope to get from such a 'comparison'?"

Napier replied in consideration: "I'm not entirely sure, yet."

Burton tutted and leaned forward in his chair. "I think we need to find stronger evidence. What would actually prove that the Caliphate hit that island with ACAs?"

"We'd need some proof of them in flight at the time, I suppose," Blackwood offered.

Napier said, "I need to speak to Terry."

A new notification flashed in Crispin's eye from Sir John Speake, the English ambassador to the US. Given that only a few weeks ago, the boss had used the information he gave her in confidence to burn the diplomatic relationship between the two countries almost to a crisp, his initial reaction was to postpone it, but he reconsidered. He recalled that the two of them had spoken since, and as Sir John was still in post, the boss must have smoothed things over. "Excuse me, boss. I've got Ambassador Speake asking if you're available. Should I put him off until you're alone?"

"Oh, no, not at all."

In the screen above the fireplace appeared the severe face of Sir John Speake. His eyes darted and light glistened off his trimmed brown beard. "Hello, PM? Is that a full-on COBRA or a cabinet meeting?"

Napier said, "Good to see you, Sir John. How are things unfolding in Washington?"

Sir John shook his head. "Desperate. No exaggeration to say one of the worst days in American history."

"Yes," Napier said, "but how are they actually coping?"

"I suppose there are some interesting things behind the raw numbers. For example, some districts are managing far better than others. If I may?"

Napier turned to Crispin and nodded her consent.

Crispin twitched an eye muscle and said, "Our screen is all yours, Sir John."

"Thank you."

The image of Sir John vanished, replaced by a map of the US eastern seaboard overlaid with hundreds of coloured lines, some of which streaked from east to west while others curved and meandered around every point of the compass. The map centred on Washington.

Sir John spoke: "To start with, here in Washington things haven't been too bad. We got a huge swell up the Potomac but that's already receding. For the life of me, I can't understand why the attackers took out some dams but not others. The Carter Dam protecting New York was smashed up, as was the Reagan Dam in front of Philadelphia just north of here. But for reasons best known to themselves, their flying bombs didn't bother with the Clinton dam, which has left Washington relatively unscathed."

The map withdrew to reveal more of the coastline as Sir John continued, "The Carolinas appear to have coped the best as geography worked in their favour—many coastal regions have been depopulated over the last twenty years anyway, given the Atlantic's gradual rise. But the entire United States has come to the rescue. There's a little-known clause in the Super Artificial Intelligence Act that lets US Homeland Security requisition autonomous aircraft in certain specific events, one of which is a catastrophic failure of one or more of the Atlantic Dams. Thus, thousands of vehicles were flown in from all over the country. As you can imagine, super AI organised and prioritised rescues, and established recovery and triage centres on the nearest higher ground."

Napier said, "We're still hearing about countless casualties, Sir John."

"Oh, yes, the final death toll is sure to be in the tens of thousands. And God alone knows how long it will take the Americans to rebuild those dams. But the number of stranded and at-risk people being saved here is a marvel of super-AI organisation. However, I did not contact you merely to update you on how the situation looks stateside."

Napier tucked a strand of auburn hair behind her ear and said, "Your on-the-spot assessment is nevertheless very welcome."

Crispin caught the placatory tone in the boss's voice and wondered what she might be afraid of the ambassador mentioning. Could it be something to do with Coll?

Sir John scratched his beard and said, "There's a great deal of speculation going around here, some of it quite… crazed?"

"Conspiracy theories? That's only to be expected," Napier said.

Crispin saw the faces of the other ministers drop in what might have been anticipation or concern.

"Apart from that section of American politicians that we might refer to as the 'Rabid Republicans', there are utterances from others that… well, if I am to be frank—"

"I wish you would be," Napier said.

"That we English might have had a hand in the creation of this tsunami."

Crispin felt the mood in the room collapse in a manner not dissimilar to what had happened to Cumbre Vieja.

The boss's jaw fell open. "What?" she said, aghast.

Sir John's eyebrows rose as he said, "I'm surprised you seem so shocked. Have you not been following domestic American politics at all recently? The pressure on the government here to withdraw from supporting Europe has been growing since those Marines got cut to pieces on the English coast in August."

Napier stammered, "Yes, of course, we have been urging the Americans to continue supporting us…"

The boss's words trailed off. Crispin's eyes darted around the room as the sudden implications of what the ambassador said became apparent. He knew at once that the ludicrousness of the suggestion would not be sufficient to deflect its cause. And if any of the cabinet decided the real fault lay with the boss, Crispin would have to defend her.

"Well," Sir John said, "given how bad relations between you and President Coll have become over recent weeks, it is perhaps not such a surprise that some commentators here in the Washington bubble are pointing a finger across the Atlantic."

Blackwood put his glass on the mantle below the screen, took a step back, and said, "Now steady on, Sir John. We realise you're much closer to the action over there, but you must appreciate the ridiculousness of the very idea, as if we could have any influence whatsoever—"

"It is not about 'influence', foreign minister," Sir John broke in, "it is about the very real fact that England, the Home Countries and by extension Europe are finished without American support. You need to keep America in the war. And today's events should go some way to doing precisely that."

"But we're allies," Burton said in a mix of confusion and exasperation.

"And in any case," Blackwood said, his face a mask of fury that Crispin found incredibly attractive, "I think you'll find our defences are holding up pretty well, all round. Pity the Atlantic Dams were not protected by batteries of Falaretes, even though they could've been. If they had, perhaps the Americans wouldn't have so many corpses to count?"

"Thank you, Charles," Napier said. She addressed the screen, "Sir John, I expect you to ensure that such outlandish accusations are given the shortest shrift. You are to treat them with the contempt they deserve, understood?"

Sir John replied, "That goes without saying, PM. I only contacted you to give you advance notice of what may very well cause you unwanted and, clearly I can see now, unexpected problems. Please be advised that a significant and growing section of the American body politic is pushing harder for disentanglement from the European quagmire. And they are leaping on today's twin disasters to push even more strongly for America's exit."

"Thank you, Sir John," Napier said. "Please contact us again at any time if you hear anything more, before our next catch-up."

The bearded face on the screen nodded before the portcullis placeholder reappeared.

Napier let out a sigh, turned behind her and addressed Monica, "Please, my dear, would you get me a G&T?"

Monica rose with a nod of confirmation and went to the elaborate sideboard.

From the two-seater couch, Hicks said: "Absolutely preposterous, even to suggest such an asinine thing."

Napier said, "I suppose it was good of him to warn us, really. I think what he is driving at is how convenient it looks."

Blackwood said, "But PM, you can't actually be suggesting—"

She stopped him with a wave of her hand. "I'm not; of course, I'm not. But look at what's already happening. If the Chinese are prepared to release conflicting seismic records, what else might they like to put out?"

"Ah, right," Blackwood conceded.

Napier suggested, "How about some kind of false intel trail that 'proved' we had advance warning that the Caliphate were preparing to attack the United States, but sat on it because we needed them to stay in the war?"

Crispin's sense of feeling crestfallen was reflected back at him in the faces of the other men in the room.

Monica handed the tumbler containing gin and tonic water to Napier, who thanked her.

Napier took a sip and went on, "Of course it would all be lies, but it would delight those Americans who oppose the war. Bloody cowards that they are notwithstanding."

Crispin glanced at the boss, recognising the tone in her voice. He readied himself for another vocal outburst.

Napier stared at the clear liquid in her glass, a thin slice of lemon giving it a splash of colour. Her shoulders sagged and she said, "In addition, I should be honest here: this is partly my fault." She stood, walked around the back of the couch, and gulped her drink.

As she spoke, Crispin eyed the ministers for a trace of any of them spying an opportunity for power.

"The irony is," she said after drinking, "that that was indeed my initial thought: first the dams, then the tsunami, and the Americans would be hell-bent on revenge. And that would give us a bit more certainty of being able to hold on. But now?" she seemed to ask no one in particular. "Another vicious act by that awful man in Tehran and England remains in the same stalemate."

"I think," Blackwood said, his right hand brushing imaginary dust from his left sleeve, "that when things settle, or perhaps I should say, 'when the waters recede', today's events will in fact keep the US with us."

Crispin noted that no one even smiled at the foreign secretary's black humour.

Burton leaned forward in the armchair and said, "We should remember the strategic issues here. The Third Caliph clearly wanted to hurt America and perhaps was even hoping to provoke a nuclear response—"

"We still don't know that he hasn't," Hicks cautioned.

Burton waved a hand in dismissiveness and said, "Not going to happen, I reckon. Too many American Jews are still crying over Israel's fate last February—they'll make the rednecks see sense. I believe he doesn't really care one way or another if the US abandons what's left of Europe."

Blackwood's eyebrows rose as he said, "You sound quite certain."

The defence secretary glanced up at the foreign secretary, shook his head and replied: "Don't you see? It's not about us. He's showing the rest of the world what his forces can do."

Hicks murmured an indifferent agreement but said nothing. Crispin watched Blackwood stare at Burton with the faintest pang of jealousy, wishing Blackwood would look at him with similar intensity.

From his chair, Burton addressed the boss: "We should consider the broader picture here, PM. All other potential enemies of the Caliphate are either dictatorships or autocracies. I know from our pre-war wargaming strategies how difficult it was to estimate the military strengths of those potential enemies—"

"And of the one enemy our computers never saw coming," Hicks interjected unhelpfully.

"Right," Burton said in apparent irritation. "We know China has the largest and best-equipped military in the world. But India and Brazil are also very much top-tier. Now, India and China have that little agreement no one's supposed to mention in public: where India does what it likes in Kashmir and China has similar latitude in Tibet, and they both cover for each other—"

The boss broke in: "That's not news, Liam. Spheres of influence are as old as the—"

"Yes, but, look, sorry to interrupt, PM, my point is the Caliphate's arrival on the world stage as a serious military player. This upends everything those powers had assumed until now."

"Okay," Napier said.

"What's happened today forces China, India, Brazil and probably Russia—not to mention a number of second-tier powers all over the globe like Argentina, Indonesia, the Philippines and so on—to acknowledge that the Third Caliph can pretty much strike wherever, whenever, and with whatever he wants. He really, really wants to show the top players that this previously benign Caliphate—a bastion of Islamic peacefulness—is ready and able to take any of them on."

"Hmm," Blackwood mused. "I'm not convinced, Liam. So what does he want, global domination? He's not going to reach that objective in fifty years. And why show your potential enemies how good or bad your forces are?"

Burton answered: "That is his whole point. Our latest wargaming intel—just last year—suggested strongly that NATO ACAs were within spitting distance in performance terms of China's and Russia's equivalents. The Third Caliph is totally glorifying in how much better his ACAs are than anything anyone else has got."

Napier pointed out: "Then, as far as those other countries are concerned, all he does is start an arms race."

"Absolutely," Burton agreed with enthusiasm. "But he has the edge today. Now. And that's the real reason behind this attack on the US and his deliberate collapse of the island. Sometimes, however much we are directly at risk, we also need to see the strategic picture."

"Rubbish," Hicks blurted out from his seat.

"Oh?" Burton queried, looking at the home secretary.

"Yes," Hicks said. "If that is truly the case and the Terror of Tehran is engaging in some serious willie-waving—oh, no offence, PM—"

"None taken," the boss said with a smile.

"Then why," Hicks continued with a wave of his pudgy hand, "is China offering up these false seismic 'records' to support his damnable lies that this was all an act of God, eh?"

Burton's brow furrowed and he said, "I'm not a hundred percent but I'd guess the long game."

"What?" Hicks said.

"Come on, Aiden. You know the Chinese," Burton said in frustration. "They're not thinking in terms of next week or next year, that's not their style. What was it that awful Chinese defence secretary said a few years ago? About China thinking in terms of millennia?"

"Yes, but," Blackwood cautioned, "he also claimed that the twenty-first century was China's century."

Napier asked the men, "And what impact would our western methods of counting years have from the Chinese perspective?"

Crispin hid a smile at the way her observation stopped the others in their tracks.

She went on, "China has been the economically strongest country in the world for decades and will likely remain so for the foreseeable future. Why their 'scientists' are releasing false seismic records to try to legitimise today's atrocity probably has more to do with their ridiculous ideas of 'saving face' given that most of the world still perceives the Caliphate as a Chinese creation."

Hicks nodded. "Agreed. That's absolutely correct, PM."

"In any case," the boss concluded, "our position does not seem to have changed a great deal." She looked at the men and said: "We have to begin a charm offensive to keep the Americans on our side and convince them not to believe the propaganda." Holding onto the back of the couch with one hand, with the other she drained the last of her G&T.

Blackwood asked, "Are you going to talk directly to Coll?"

Napier scoffed and replied, "Only if our objective were to get the Americans to abandon us. No, fortunately I have my reliable cabinet to support me."

Crispin noted the smiles of relief on the men, and he agreed with them. Finally, it seemed the boss was becoming sufficiently self-aware to understand how important her inactivity could be.

Chapter 17

16.08 Sunday 15 October 2062

Serena Rizzi stared through the first-floor window down at Father's children as they ran around the ornate fountain in the courtyard outside. Bare branches on the orange trees twisted like dancers' arms frozen in mid-pirouette, while shouts and giggles from the two young girls carried innocence on the hot air. Father sat on one of the stone benches, his kind face suffused with affection.

From above, she watched a scene of domesticity that seemed utterly alien yet which caused a certain sensation deep inside her. Memories flashed into her mind's eye from so many years ago, of playing with her brother Max in their home in one of the southern *municipos* in Rome—she caught her breath and stopped the recollections, burying them as deeply as she could, and remembering who and where she now was. Father and his children existed in a different realm, in an alternate reality into which a Caliphate warrior had dragged her; into which one of the Caliphate's vast autonomous aircraft had flown her. In her body floated an implant that allowed her to be killed in an instant for any infraction of their real or imagined 'laws'.

The young sisters, miniatures of their mother, flicked water from the fountain at each other and giggled, their burnished teak skin shining in the hot sunlight. Father said something to them and they stopped for an instant before continuing again, this time running towards him and flicking water at his face. He pretended to cower, laughing, and Serena realised she had never seen Father smile before.

"What are you doing?"

Serena spun round at the sound of Ahmed's brittle voice. Anger welled but she fought to control it. She spoke in her own language, too furious to call up her growing knowledge of the enemy's tongue: "I am on my way back to the kitchen."

Ahmed muttered in aggression and the translated words resolved in the air next to him: "Why are you not there now?"

"Mother asked for my help with unpacking—"

"Enough," Ahmed said in a quiet voice but with a raised hand. "Go back to your chores. In a few hours, we will have guests. The cook will arrive and there will be much to do."

Serena gave a slight bow of her head, mentally readying herself for another evening and night of relentless work.

"In addition, I have also arranged some extra help."

Serena could hardly believe her ears: Ahmed treated her and Liliana with contempt, and now he seemed to be offering something? She kept her eyes down and mouth closed.

Ahmed went on, "The guests this evening are very important and I will not allow even one mistake. If anything should go even slightly wrong, there will be only one punishment. Do you understand?"

A new wave of fear resolved inside Serena. She nodded.

"Good. Now go."

Without looking up, Serena gathered the folds of her *abaya* and hurried away. She reached the north side and entered the cool interior of the house. Pain began next to her left temple. She trotted down the wooden stairs to the ground floor, opened the door on her right, and then trod down the stone stairs into the basement.

She arrived at the main kitchen and, once inside, automatically checked that equipment was in its correct place. The surfaces and floor smelled of the usual weak cleaning fluid. She crossed the flagstone floor and reached the pantry. She turned the metal lever and the wooden door squeaked open. In the dimness she made out Liliana's waifish form. The young girl sat slumped on a chair, leaning against shelves on which rested bags of pulses. As she watched, Liliana came to, scrunching up her face and squinting against the light.

"Come along, sister," Serena said, relieved as always to speak Italian to the only other person for thousands of kilometres who would understand her. "We need to appear ready to work."

"What has happened?" Liliana asked, stretching her thin arms.

"Ahmed told me the cook is coming here. There is a big dinner for important guests this evening."

Liliana's face changed, her blue eyes widening in surprise. "The cook?" she exclaimed. "We are not simply going to prepare the usual meals?"

Serena shook her head. "No," she replied. "So, we would do well to make sure everything is ready. Come on."

The two women left the small pantry. They cleaned the large double sink at which Serena spent most of her day, and then wiped down the surfaces and tidied the jars of spices.

Serena rechecked the most elegant serving dishes, although she knew they were clean. She didn't care who the guests were or the significance of their importance; she only hoped there would be no mistakes, or if there were, Ahmed would deem it more trouble to replace her than it—

The door swung open with a squeak. Ahmed stood there, looking even slighter in the doorway's frame. He grasped the folds of his black *kandora* and glanced with a certain disdain around the kitchen. He entered and spoke. Serena struggled to follow his words in his language and again had to rely on the translation that resolved in the air close to him: "The cook will arrive in half an hour. Make sure everything in here is spotless. The cook is highly regarded and does Father's house much honour by coming to prepare the food for our exalted guests."

Serena again said nothing, merely bowing her head in meek acceptance of his commands.

There came a pathetic sniff from the doorway. Serena looked up to see a young woman staring back at her. With a shove from behind, she stumbled into the kitchen.

Ahmed said, "As I mentioned to you upstairs, I have acquired another member of the staff. This one has the same implant as you two, and is aware of what will happen to her if she makes any mistakes. I expect you to introduce her to the rules of the house and train her to help. Now, clean this filthy room." He turned and disappeared into the dimness beyond the doorway.

The woman lifted her head and looked at Serena. Her round, pale eyes exuded fear and confusion. Her waist seemed pinched under the threadbare dress she wore, but her shoulders and arms carried more weight. Serena almost shocked herself at the novel thought that this new arrival was more strongly built than either she or Liliana, and might therefore be of use.

"Hello," Serena said. "What is your name?"

The girl cleared her throat and said: "Tiphanie."

"You are French, yes?"

The girl nodded. A tear ran out from her eye and her body trembled.

"Sister," Serena said to Liliana, "fetch some water."

Liliana went to the sink.

Serena approached Tiphanie and said, "Come and sit down." She led Tiphanie to the broad table in the middle of the kitchen. "How long have you been here?"

The girl shook her head and replied in French, "I don't recall."

"Do you need a doctor? We have some supplies here you can use."

Tiphanie mumbled, "Thank you."

Serena put her hand over Tiphanie's. The girl flinched. Serena said, "You don't have to be so afraid now."

Liliana set down a glass of water in front of Tiphanie. The new arrival lifted it and took a sip with her free hand. At once, some colour came back into her face. She turned to Serena and asked: "Where am I?"

Serena replied, "You have arrived at the House of Badr Shakir al-Sayyab. I am Serena and this is Liliana. We were abducted from Italy."

Tiphanie nodded in comprehension. She said, "Do you know they can kill... us? Can they do the same to y—?"

"Yes, yes," Serena murmured, willing the girl to stay calm. "But you're not in as much danger here. Do you understand?"

Tiphanie stared at Serena but made no answer.

Serena went on, "All you must do is work, all right? If you work and do as you are told, you will receive food and you will have a bed with us in the servants' lodgings."

Liliana whispered, "You really are fortunate. We have been here for months and have hardly been mistreated. The owner—we call him 'Father'—is not a bad man, although Ahmed, the man who brought you here, most certainly is."

Tiphanie looked from Liliana to Serena and back again, but said nothing. She sipped more water.

Serena felt time passing. The cook would arrive soon, and this evening promised to be more stressful than usual if Ahmed were to be believed regarding the importance of the guests. She decided that if this Tiphanie could not be cajoled into helping, she could be left out of the way in their sleeping quarters, and Serena and Liliana would have to manage. But deep inside, a surge of enthusiasm buoyed Serena. For now, she had gained another ally, another person who, in time, would be able to support her and Liliana. Serena stared at Tiphanie's confused, lost and damaged face, silently thanking God above for sending her more help.

Chapter 18

14.54 Wednesday 18 October 2062

After travelling for most of the day, Maria Phillips finally reached her home town of East Grinstead. An air transport had been taking supplies across country from Dover to a large depot to the west of Crawley, and in the back, an uncomfortable fold-down seat had allowed her just enough room to squeeze in. The fifteen minutes of discomfort left her legs numb, but now, as she strode along the road into town, the pins and needles vanished and her anticipation grew.

She passed damaged and destroyed houses set back from the road, which stood out among the verdant shrubs and trees. The destruction seemed arbitrary. At one property, manual efforts had been made to try to rebuild something habitable, while the next house along remained untouched. A few steps on and she passed a close of bungalows that sat undamaged, followed by two streets of terraced houses where only the ground floors remained.

The cooler breeze of an English autumn afternoon blew past her face, but in its wake the summer's residual heat wafted up from the ground, dragging up memories of the worst year of her life.

At length, she reached her own neighbourhood. Two male figures stood at the end of her street. They both walked towards her, smiling.

"Hello, Maz," Martin said.

"Hello, sister," Mark said.

Warmth and relief surged through Maria on seeing her brothers again for the first time in months. She hugged the oldest, Martin, reaching up to enclose her arms around his broad shoulders, then Mark, her arms easily encircling his slight frame. She asked, "Have you already been inside the house?"

Martin nodded and replied. "It's not the same, you know?"

She looked along the row of rebuilt houses and said: "I wouldn't expect it to be."

"Come on," Martin said.

They walked along the pavement until they reached the rebuilt family home. Maria looked up to see if Billy the wooden rabbit had been reconstructed, but the ridge of the roof was bare. "Where's the chimney stack?" she asked.

Martin glanced at her and replied, "It's the most straightforward design, Maz. The replicators were in big demand—they still are—so they only have time to put the buildings back to new minimum standards."

"You've still got that piece of Billy's toe that I saved for you, haven't you?" Mark asked.

Maria smiled and replied, "Yes, of course. I never let that out of my sight."

Martin nodded at the house and said, "Nothing's decorated, but the bathroom and kitchen are plumbed in and we pretty much have the same number of power transmitters."

Maria looked at her brothers and asked, "So, do we agree?"

Martin shrugged and said, "Why not? We're all in barracks for the foreseeable."

Mark nodded agreement and said, "My quarters at 3rd Airspace Defence are small but okay. I really like it there."

Maria still struggled to accept the changes in Mark since their home had been destroyed and they lost their parents, but she took comfort that he'd finally found a role in the real world. She said, "Okay, we'll make the house available for homeless refugees."

Maria twitched her eye muscle to call up the relevant acceptance protocol that would be notified to the local authority. Beyond the digital details in her immediate view, she noted her brothers' eyes flickering as they took the same steps. Neither of their parents had made wills—and they certainly hadn't been anticipating their lives to end in such sudden and violent circumstances—so each of the children had a one-third share in their estate.

Martin said, "We could easily have done all this without coming here."

"Yes," Mark said, "but I thought it was important that we should meet up if we could. We still don't know what will happen next."

"I agree," Maria said at once. "Let's go to the café on the high street and have a brew."

As they began walking, Mark asked: "Are your Squitches off?"

"Mine is," Martin said.

Maria mumbled her confirmation.

Mark said, "Amazing what the Chief Raghead did to America, don't you think?"

"Incredible that he claimed it was an act of God that brought that island down and started the tsunami," Maria said.

"Clever thing is," Martin pointed out, "that there's no real proof. There's a load of controversy in the media between all the earthquake records, but nothing certain one way or another. He can claim it was an act of God, NATO and the West can say he bombed it, but without certain proof one way or the other, the enemy wins the media war over it and a billion Muslims think he's telling the truth and Allah really did punish the Yanks."

"There is proof," Mark said in a determined voice.

"How do you know?" Maria asked.

Mark frowned and replied, "I don't, for certain. But I am convinced it's there and I only need to find it. And I will."

They crossed a traffic junction in silence and then entered the high street, lined with old buildings made up of dirty glass frontages and weathered stone facades.

"Have you heard about the big plan?" Martin asked.

"They're just rumours," Maria said. "I'm sure it's more about keeping up morale."

"You both know what I do," Mark said, abruptly sounding assertive. "I don't believe there is any big plan. You don't know how close it is. We are in a real knife-edge stalemate over the English Channel."

"So how close is it, really?" Martin asked.

Mark lowered his voice as they passed civilians on the path, but his words took on a tone of urgency. "They attack all the time. My CO thinks it's just probing and harassment, but many people seem to have forgotten that if their super AI can find and exploit another breach, they will be ready to try and invade again."

"But we've got enough defences all over the place now," Martin said.

The three siblings fell into silence on entering the small café. Maria ordered tea for them. Martin insisted on a bacon sandwich with brown sauce while Mark sat at one of the small tables when it became free.

When all three were seated, Mark went on, "Whatever anyone else says, I can't see the way out of this—and in the Universes, I was able to find my way out of almost any situation."

Martin tutted and complained, "For God's sake, brother, this is not the Univer—"

But Maria broke in, "I think Mark means that he doesn't believe the rumours of any big plans."

Mark's forehead creased and he nodded.

Martin said, "There is a big plan. I know it's true."

Maria asked, "How?"

Martin folded half of the bacon sandwich over and jammed it in his mouth. He chewed while staring out of the window. Across the street, orange sunlight reflected in the windows of a municipal building. Martin swallowed some tea and spoke: "I know an officer at my base. She's well known in the regiment. She was in Europe when the invasion started back in February and has survived the whole thing."

"Wow," Maria said. "Hang on, is she the same one who came into Dover injured in the summer? What was her name, Clarke?"

Martin looked at Maria and said, "Yes. Anyway, I think she's really well-connected—"

"She would be if she's a career soldier," Maria said.

"My point is," Martin said, "Brass would not be recruiting so many new squaddies if they didn't know what they were going to do with them."

"I think you just explained your own reasoning," Maria said before sipping her tea. "Remember, all the recruitment last spring was to fight against the invasion when it reached England, right? But instead, they got the Falarete to postpone the inevitable. Now, the British Army has got thousands more soldiers and nothing for them to do."

Mark looked suspicious. He said, "So why not just be open about it, if they do have a plan? It's not like the enemy has any spies in England, is it?"

Maria caught Martin's glance. He wiped the residue of brown sauce from his mouth with a paper napkin and said, "It's not as simple as that. Other countries are involved, for example China. Did you hear about what happened to the American marines in Hastings?"

Mark shrugged and said, "Only that their exoskeletons didn't work. They got trapped in them, didn't they?"

Martin explained: "The ragheads knew about the exoskeletons and had specially designed ammo to take them out. And they found out thanks to the Chinese."

A brief look of confrontation formed on Mark's face. Maria waited for her brother to begin arguing, but Mark's expression changed and he only said, "Oh, I didn't know that."

"Right," Martin said. "So, secrecy still counts for a lot."

Maria said, "At the same time, Brass doesn't want two million, or however many it is, newly trained squaddies wondering what's to be done with them, and with this situation."

"Oh, okay," Mark said.

Martin said, "So I think we should keep our mouths shut."

Mark asked his brother: "So how much do you know about it, then?"

Martin shrugged and replied, "Nothing. Only that it exists."

A notification flashed in Maria's lens informing her that she needed to be at the station in half an hour to begin her return journey to Dover.

Mark coughed and said, "Look, I know things were difficult before. You know, before the war and before, well, everything." He lifted a pack of playing cards up and placed them in the middle of the rickety table. "Only," he began, "I've studied the rules and I thought it would be a good idea. And I thought maybe we could have a game of forecast whist before we all went back to our units."

"No, Mark," Maria said without hesitation. "That was something we did with mum and dad. And I'm not ready for that, not yet."

She watched her brother consider her words and a pang of regret flashed through her.

Martin leaned forward and said, "Mark, it was a kind thought, thanks. But now's not the right time."

Mark frowned and said, "Yeah, okay."

"Look," Martin said, "We've got done what we came here to sort out. Let's get back to our units and stay in touch."

Maria looked at her brothers and said, "It's been good to see the pair of you."

Chapter 19

07.50 Monday 23 October 2062

Terry Tidbury slowed to a fast walk as he entered the beach at Ferring on England's south coast. Low and vast tubes of grey cloud hung over the sea, bunched together all the way to the horizon. Waves crashed onto the stony beach, followed by a loud whoosh as the stones rolled over each other when the water retreated. The strong wind blew fast across his skin, making him feel more alive. His boots sank into the stones, requiring extra effort to make progress.

He rued days gone by, when, as a paratrooper, a ten-mile run was more of a light trot, the monotony of exercising a young man's body offering him the space to think and consider. Today, his fifty-three-year-old muscle and bone didn't have the same endless durability he'd enjoyed from his twenties to his forties. As he trudged through the heavy stones, a light stabbing pain came from behind his knees. His left hip joint clicked annoyingly, and some upper-disc compression in his spine made his shoulders ache.

But still he had a lightness in his step. For the first time since the war began, Terry felt as though he had a measure of influence on events. The seemingly endless days and weeks and months during which he'd believed his true job had simply been to manage the final destruction of NATO, were over. Certainty was a rare commodity in this war—indeed, he reflected that thus far there'd been no certainty at all, apart from that of approaching defeat.

Now, Terry took pleasure knowing he could rely on several certainties. Firstly, preparations for Operation Repulse proceeded as fast as super artificial intelligence and the limits of replication technology would allow. The power units for the next generation of NATO ACAs were already in advanced testing and refinement, and designs for weapons were developing apace—weapons that had to leapfrog the enemy: powerful enough not only to dominate the battlefield, but to best any new weapons the enemy brought to the war.

Secondly, America had declared its commitment to remain in support of NATO and the defence of the British Isles. Cooler heads seemed to have prevailed after the destruction wrought by the enemy's attack and following tsunami. Demands to throw America's ageing nuclear arsenal at the enemy had been criticised for their idiocy, while the ridiculous accusations that England had somehow had a hand in creating, or had previous knowledge of, the tsunami also faded in the bright light of common sense.

Terry had scored a victory with the American's decision to support Operation Repulse, with Terry leading it. The key meeting with the joint chiefs of staff had become fractious when the commandant of the marine corps tried to insist that an American should take over command of Repulse. Terry pointed out that he would have to be relieved of his post as SACEUR to make way for his successor, something to which he declared Napier would never agree. Although the

Americans conceded, Terry had made a note to identify and promote the more able American commanders as Repulse developed. In addition, Terry suspected the commandant of the marine corps was still smarting over the marines' punishment at the enemy's hands in August, and would've preferred an American in charge to ensure appropriate retribution, but that was hardly Terry's concern.

A pair of grey gulls squealed and cried overhead. Aided by a powerful gust, they swooped towards one of the long, wooden breakers and settled next to a dozen of their fellows, any further noise lost on the wind.

Additionally, the data coming from the *Institut Neuropsi* was exceeding expectations, proving far more insightful than the best conventional methods of gathering intelligence about the enemy. Terry had intentionally kept his anticipation in check; he was no scientist and found the concept of extracting a person's entire memories like some kind of film that could be watched, more than a little fantastic. It took the computers comparatively long periods of time to review years' worth of data and extrapolate that which might be of use.

By the time the aggregated and filtered data reached Terry and other members of the NATO hierarchy, it was helpfully cross-referenced by subtopic. More and more often, Terry found himself absorbed, reading late into the night about the enemy: how the New Persian Caliphate was in fact divided into thousands of subunits organised and run by a small army of civil servants using super artificial intelligence. These were overseen by an elite cadre of men from the Third Caliph's own region in the northeast of the vast Middle-Eastern land mass, who answered directly to him and, as it transpired, his two brothers. NATO did not yet have the brothers' names, but Terry knew they would in time.

However, the most shocking revelation by far had been the role modern technology played in the creation and control of this essentially medieval society. The extracted memories of captured warriors revealed networks of thousands of villages and towns connected by massive highways and monorails built by Chinese construction replicators. Water replicators obviated the need for wells and the problems of living in ever-more arid deserts: even warriors from the meanest villages far from any major conurbations enjoyed the security of a government-provided water replicator. The Third Caliph used his 'largesse' in supplying this advanced equipment as a means to ensure support and loyalty at the level of district and area authority. Elders and tribal leaders who, some of the data suggested, had no love for the Third Caliph nevertheless acquiesced simply because it made sense to do so. With the minimum of fuss, violence could be avoided and headmen's villages could continue the simple existences they had led for centuries—if they preferred—with all risk of herd loss or crop failure removed.

In larger towns and cities, what used to be the luxuries of the ultra-wealthy, like air-conditioning and fresh fruit and vegetables, became available to almost all of the Caliphate's subjects as a result of its economy's management by super artificial intelligence. Of course, this progress was presented to the Caliphate's subjects as a consequence of the Third Caliph's genius that was itself a gift bestowed by Allah.

Terry's stomach rumbled. He continued stomping through the stones that seemed to suck his boots into them. A young child's laugh carried on the breeze as he or she ran up the beach ahead of an especially large wave. Terry spied the old, whitewashed café that served all manner of breakfasts, where the beach narrowed, turned to a rocky outcrop, and became impassable. He glanced to his right. Beyond the vehicle park there ran a narrow canal that would take him up the low hill where, a few short miles beyond, he would find his home. And there, he would make himself and his wife

Maureen poached eggs on toast for breakfast. He trudged to the end of the beach and readied himself to recommence running once his boots where back on concrete and free of those stones that seemed to have a power similar to quicksand.

Nevertheless, the most significant fact that the *Institut Neuropsi* had revealed was the level of automated ACA production. Extracted memories from wounded warriors from specific districts inside the Caliphate had yielded tiny snippets—often no more than an overheard conversation in childhood or a stolen glimpse over forbidden fences—that revealed the locations of the enemy's primary weapons' production facilities. Once this data was assessed by NATO's own super AI, it quickly became clear how the enemy had been able to all-but-destroy resistance to its onslaught against Europe.

Terry shivered at the thought of what might have happened if the enemy's forces had been commanded by an even remotely competent officer, instead of a cadre of semi-trained sycophants who had merely followed their computer's instructions with neither initiative nor question. He even doubted that the enemy had followed its computers' suggestions: sufficient enemy forces must have been ready days before NATO could deploy enough Falaretes to repel the attempted invasions of England. Without that brief pause by the enemy—for reasons unknown—England and the Home Countries would've been wholly occupied by now.

The slate in his thigh pocket vibrated. He sighed and pulled at the Velcro flap on his fatigues, wondering what this new problem might be. He discounted any security issues: high above him a SkyWatcher monitored his location, ready to bring in all available NATO defences if the enemy made even the slightest effort to approach this part of the English coast. But when he spun his slate open, a message resolved from his wife Maureen. It read: "Do you want me put the water on to boil?"

Terry let out a guffaw, which elicited an amused glance from a passing young father and his daughter. He retracted his slate, slipped it back into the pocket, and stepped up onto the concrete path. When he recommenced running, his thoughts returned fully to Operation Repulse. The next months—and what an incredible luxury to realise that they did still probably have months—would see plans progress even further in anticipation of its commencement on 1 October next year. Despite apparently having so much time, Terry picked up his pace, eager to return home, and then to work after those poached eggs.

Chapter 20

13.03 Thursday 14 December 2062

Terry strode into the officers' mess beneath the War Rooms. He stopped by the large mess table with its bowls of fruit and large, ornate silver candlesticks, and cast his gaze around the smaller tables. At one, the elderly waiter finished topping up the glasses of two patrons, put the bottle back on the table, and paced with understated elegance towards Terry.

"Good afternoon, field marshal," he intoned with a bow from the neck. "Your guest has arrived and is seated. Please follow me."

Terry did so as the man led him deeper into the mess, to a table in one of the many discreet alcoves. As he approached, a man stood, tall and slim with a pencil moustache. He stepped out from the table and offered his hand.

Terry grasped it and with warmth in his voice said, "Welcome to the War Rooms, General Hastings. I'm sorry for being late."

Hastings tilted his head. "Ah, I believe I may have also been a little too prompt, field marshal."

The man's outward diffidence hadn't changed in over twenty years, and Terry hoped it still concealed the steely determination that he recalled from their officer training course in the early 2040s.

The waiter gave a slight cough. "Something to drink before ordering, field marshal?" he asked.

"Just water, thank you."

The waiter retreated and the two soldiers sat opposite each other.

Terry spoke while opening the leatherbound menu, "I was delayed on a sitrep regarding our latest intel from the US."

Hastings clasped his hands together on the table, slender fingers interlinked. "Remarkable what that technology has allowed us to find out. From the limited conclusions I've seen, our total knowledge of the enemy must be quite extensive now."

"Yes," Terry replied. "It's similar to that psychological trick about being afraid of the dark. The more we find out about the enemy—his strengths, weaknesses and tactics—the less threatening he seems."

"Pity the scanning process kills the subjects."

"We'd hardly send prisoners of war back to the Caliphate. Although, fortunately, the politicians have somewhat let that issue drop."

Hastings said, "I never would've thought it would be a problem, to be honest with you, sir. I don't want to suggest I speak for the general public, but I'm fairly sure not many citizens have a problem with wounded enemy being put to such use to gain intelligence we have no other way of finding out."

"I agree, but we shouldn't disregard the moral dimension entirely. Look at the Americans in the early part of the century, using extrajudicial execution as though they were killing beetles. Not surprising they lost authority. Besides, it's a subject close to the PM's heart, and I like to keep her on-side if I can."

The waiter arrived with a glass jug of water and a glass. "Are you ready to order, gentlemen?"

Terry put the menu down and glanced at Hastings, eyebrow raised in query.

The general said, "I looked at the menu before you arrived."

Terry addressed the waiter, "The Beef Wellington, please."

Hastings said, "I'll have the same."

The waiter gave a stiff bow and left.

"Anyway, how are things up at Kendrew?"

Hastings nodded in approval "Very good, all round. I assume you review the summary reports from all barracks, sir?"

"Of course, but I like to speak to my generals in person when I can, especially those with whom I was on the same officer training course."

Hastings smiled. "Good of you to remember."

"I haven't forgotten you beat me on the navigation challenge," Terry said with a smile, enjoying the recollection.

"Ah, I think that might have been more luck than judgement," Hastings replied diplomatically.

"Rubbish. So tell me, how are things in the barracks?"

"Good," Hastings repeated. "Those construction replicators are useful, allowing us to accommodate hundreds more recruits. We keep them busy with fire drill, among other things—we're training the frontline troops on how to regroup in the event of a total comms breakdown on the battlefield."

"Difficult to imagine how wars were fought before replicators, isn't it?"

"Indeed."

Terry paused and eyed Hastings. They were acquaintances, not friends, and Terry was Hastings' commanding officer. Terry said, "As you can imagine, preparations for Operation Repulse continue to proceed as forecasted." The look in the general's eye changed and Terry recognised a certain relief that perhaps now they would get to the point of the meeting.

"I don't doubt it, sir," Hastings said. "There's talk among the lower ranks concerning what's to be done with an army approaching two million strong. Although in the Anglian we do keep them busy."

"However," Terry said, "there is one particular objective, a special, unique requirement upon which the entire operation depends."

The waiter arrived with a younger man. Each lowered a plate down on which generous slices of Beef Wellington sat and steamed, surrounded by vegetables. They left the two soldiers.

Hastings said with a smile, "My curiosity is piqued, field marshal."

"Perhaps we should eat first?"

"My appetite currently lies elsewhere, if you'll forgive me."

"Very well," Terry said. "We've found out that the enemy has a number of ACA manufacturing plants scattered throughout his extensive territory. However, only two are significant. Each of these plants is responsible for producing thousands of Blackswans and Lapwings per week. For Repulse to succeed; that is, for our troops to make progress across the European mainland, at least one of those two plants has to be disabled."

Terry watched Hastings stare back at him. The general stroked his pencil moustache with the knuckle of his index finger but remained silent. Terry went on, "By disabled, I mean we need to reduce it to rubble so that the enemy's construction replicators will take weeks to bring it back into production. The most likely range of forecasts indicate that such a depletion will allow NATO forces to gain enough ground that Repulse will not be able to be reversed."

"Could the enemy not simply increase production at his other sites?" Hastings asked.

"Oh, certainly, but not by enough, and not quickly enough, either. I am of course assuming we do enjoy an element of surprise. When we aggregate the probabilities, the destruction of this plant yields the greatest advantage. And without its destruction, Repulse would be almost certain to be... repulsed? And we will only get one chance at this. If the enemy defeats us on the mainland again, we won't get a second opportunity for many years."

"And where exactly is this production facility?"

"It's at a place called Tazirbu in North Africa. It used to be an oasis, nothing more, but now it is linked by a multi-lane highway to all of the enemy's major cities. It is itself the size of a small city now. The weapons' production facility lies to the west of the built-up area. Tazirbu is about six hundred kilometres south from the Mediterranean coast of North Africa."

"So," Hastings said, "you are tasking me with a finding a way to get inside enemy territory, travel to one of his most important military facilities, destroy it to the point where it is out of action for at least several weeks, and then come back, correct?"

Terry nodded, taking pleasure in seeing that Hastings was not in the least fazed by the objective. Terry said, "You have my full authority to requisition, sequester for yourself, and otherwise draw on any military or governmental resources that you might need. You decide how to proceed using anyone you need."

"Very well."

"General," Terry said, "I don't wish to sound unnecessarily dramatic, but the problem of what to do about Tazirbu is a great unfathomable to me. I need an answer, and your record suggests you might be the person to find that answer."

Hastings picked up his knife and fork, smiled at Terry and said: "Of course, field marshal. Leave it with me."

Chapter 21

22.34 Sunday 24 December 2062

Serena Rizzi lifted another ivory pawn from the ornamental chessboard, collected a sheet of paper by the side, wrapped the pawn up, and placed it with care in the shallow box on the floor. The chess set was only one of at least a hundred ornaments scattered around Father's house that she was responsible for packing. While Serena worked in the library, downstairs on the ground floor, Liliana packed the ornaments in the main living area, including gilded plates, figurines and placemats. Tiphanie should have been finishing cleaning the kitchen.

Serena lifted up a knight and admired the artwork in the carving; the outsized horse's head sat atop a Persian tower that reminded her of Pisa in her distant home. From all of the furnishings and decorations in the house, only this chess set offered her any comfort of the familiar. But even that was limited, for the sixty-four black and white squares were set in an octagonal board and surrounded with Middle-Eastern artistic flourishes of horsemen waving sabres above their heads.

She wrapped the knight and placed it inside the box on the floor. One of the pair of doors creaked. She looked up and caught her breath.

Father stood there, silhouetted by the light from the hall behind him. He swept in, holding the folds of his cream *kandora*. The wooden floorboards creaked under his heavy steps. He said, "You are working very late, child. Is this necessary?"

Serena pointed her head at the floor in supplication and fought to compose herself. Not only had Badr Shakir al-Sayyab surprised her, she'd been lost in thought. She replied: "Yes, Father. We must pack all of these things in boxes by tomorrow night."

"Look at me," he instructed.

She raised her head.

His kind face offered a calming half-smile. "Ahmed speaks well of you when I question him. But I think that, perhaps, you are afraid to ask for help when there is much to do, yes?"

As the translation of Father's words finished resolving in her vision, Serena bit down on a flash of anger. She wanted to scream that she feared no man, not after all that had happened to her. But she knew she had to bide her time. She wanted very much to kill Ahmed, and hoped she would one glorious day. But for now, she had to continue the pretence. She whined: "I think Ahmed would like me to execute my duties with the minimum of trouble, Father."

"But look," Father said, waving his arms around the library, "there are hundreds of books in addition to the decorations."

Serena said nothing.

"I will speak with Ahmed—"

"No, please. He will be angry at me—"

Father raised his hand to stop her. "Fear not, child. Ahmed answers to me and will do as he is told. Today there is far too much to do for him to play silly games with you servants."

"Yes, Father," Serena intoned, bristling at her designation.

"Child," he said, "much will change in the next few days. The Third Caliph himself has blessed this house. We are all to move closer to him, to play a role in the running and organisation of this great Caliphate."

Serena nodded.

"Our house will grow. We will move to a much grander residence. We will entertain high functionaries. If you and the other two slaves behave and work as well you do now, I undertake to ensure you will remain safe here. As my property, you will enjoy protection."

Serena looked up into his eyes and certainty that he spoke the truth suffused her. "Thank you, Father," she mumbled.

"Now," he said with a clap of his hands, "finish with those trinkets and go and rest. We all have a busy day tomorrow."

Serena said nothing as Father turned and left through the double doors. She glanced back at the elaborate chess set. What had happened to cause Father's sudden elevation in the Caliphate's hierarchy? Then, suddenly, the answer came to her. Like a knight jumping over a pawn and landing one row to the left, the reason for Father's advancement became plain. The realisation hit her like a physical blow.

She staggered backwards and collapsed onto a reading couch, a combination of chaise lounge and settee. She began to hyperventilate. She put a hand to her chest as if trying to force the breaths to slow, even a little.

The tsunami. The flood wrought by Allah Himself. What had the Third Caliph claimed? Allah had made an island collapse into the sea to send a giant wave to drown the American infidels as punishment for helping Europe? But there had been few details of the cause, only pictures of the destruction meted out to American cities, and then the joyous celebrations inside the Caliphate.

Serena recalled the day she'd seen Father's screen, months before. She'd had to clean up spilt tea and a broken glass. She wracked her memory for the name of the island... La Palma. The image of the island on his screen had been divided up into sections, she thought for administrative purposes.

Her breathing began to slow. She kept her eyes fixed on the doors, half-expecting Ahmed to burst in with more demands and criticism. The doors did not move. She understood now why the family would enjoy such an elevated status. Father must have had a hand in creating the tsunami, and the new house closer to the seat of power was his reward.

Should she tell her sisters? She asked herself why—this knowledge did not change anything for them, apart from the benefit of better protection. On the other hand, a voice in her head argued, would Europeans like her and Liliana and Tiphanie be safe if they were closer to the centre of the Caliphate, or actually in more danger? Serena didn't believe European slaves would be allowed anywhere near high-ranking Caliphate subjects.

That didn't matter now, she told herself. She cast one more glance at the beautiful chess set and decided she would finish packing it first thing in the morning. She padded quietly out of the library, along the hall and down the broad wooden staircase. She entered the main living area to find Liliana slumped in an armchair. A flash of concern vanished quickly when Liliana let out a snore.

Serena woke the girl and together they made their way to the kitchen at the back of the house. As soon as she pushed the door open, the warm scent of fresh baking assailed Serena's senses. They entered and Serena pushed the door closed.

"There you are," Tiphanie said with a half-smile.

"I thought you were cleaning the kitchen?" Serena said.

A sheepish look crossed Tiphanie's face. "I did… but then, I thought. Here, why not see?"

Serena and Liliana walked the length of the kitchen. Tiphanie lifted a plate on which sat a pile of small, golden cakes.

"Please," Tiphanie offered.

Serena and Liliana swapped a glance. Serena took a cake and bit into it. A light, buttery orange flavour melted into her taste buds and she looked at Tiphanie in awe.

Tiphanie said, "They are called 'Madeleines'. We have them at home every Christmas." She shrugged and her lower lip trembled. "I am, I am sorry. I think we should celebrate, although there is nothing to celebrate… Happy Christmas."

A tear welled and slid down Serena's cheek. She swallowed the cake and said, "Thank you, Tiphanie. But we can at least celebrate being together."

The three women hugged, cried, and ate all of the Madeleines.

Chapter 22

10.34 Monday 9 January 2063

Fatigue suffused the limbs of Professor Duncan Seekings. He lay slumped on the couch in the living area in his office-cum-living quarters in the Porton Down research facility. His entire life seemed to revolve around repeated visits to the medical wing to lie on a bed for hours at a time with a GenoFluid pack for a pillow. The bots entered through the skin on the back of his neck and went to work fighting new growths that sprouted in his brain: alien, unwelcome, and, however reluctant he was to admit it, quite draining.

The treatment had been going on for months. Porton Down had some of the best doctors in the British Army, and they assured him the bots would keep the tumours under control permanently, provided they did not mutate in certain, highly specific, ways. Nevertheless, they could not resolve or even alleviate all of the related symptoms.

"That's because of the snags," Duncan muttered, deciding that, super-cancers be damned, he would get up and make himself a decent cup of tea. He'd learned the necessity to rest properly and concentrate before attempting to stand, so he closed his eyes and regulated his breathing in anticipation of the effort. But when he did so, a comms notification arrived in his lens.

"Good morning, Mr English," he said.

"Good morning, Professor Seekings," his friend replied. "I'm calling because I have a tricky request for you."

"Oh?" Duncan said, curiosity energising his weak limbs. He threw his legs off the couch and pushed himself up to a sitting position. "What's happened?"

"Nothing, I'm afraid," Graham said in awkwardness, adding, "which is precisely the problem."

"What are you stuck on?"

"We have to develop a weapon—"

"Really? Is that why your department is called 'Weapons' Research'? I had been wondering about that—"

"Yes, yes, very droll, professor. Anyway, it's a conundrum and I thought the sort of thing you might find challenging."

"That's very kind of you, old boy. What is the problem?"

There came a pause as, in Duncan's vision, Graham's bushy eyebrows came together in a frown. Graham said, "I think it would be better if the requesting general explained the problem to you himself."

Then it was Duncan's turn to frown. "If you think so, of course. But I would like us to compare notes afterwards."

"Absolutely. Sending you over now."

"Right you are."

The image in front of Duncan shimmered and changed to a narrower face with a strong jawline and a pencil moustache. Next to the face, the lettering, 'General Maximilian Hastings, Royal Anglian Regiment' appeared.

The man spoke in words clipped in the traditional military style, but his voice carried an understated tone that struck Duncan as disarming. He said, "Professor, I need a particular kind of weapon and I have been told you might be able to help."

"I will if I can," Duncan answered carefully. If it was something Graham could not resolve, then Duncan did not rate his own chances especially highly.

"I need a kind of bomb. It has to be small enough to be carried by one soldier moving on foot and it must be powerful enough to destroy a building the size of, say, an aircraft hangar."

"I see," Duncan said, not at all sure that he did.

"Oh, and there's one other thing."

"Yes?"

"It absolutely must not use any modern technology that might be detected by the enemy."

"Oh, I see," Duncan repeated.

"And I may require a number of such bombs. I might wish to destroy several aircraft hangars."

"Yes," Duncan mumbled amid growing incredulity.

"And one last thing."

"Hmm?"

"It would be greatly appreciated if the bombs could not make too much noise. I might still be in the vicinity when they go off and would not wish to draw attention to myself."

"Right you are," Duncan said. "And can you give me a deadline of when you require these munitions?"

"No rush," Hastings replied. "But do please keep me updated. I would like to know as soon as you have some suggestions."

"Some?" Duncan queried, failing to keep the shock out of his voice.

Hastings frowned. "Well, whatever you can come up with, just keep me posted. Thank you."

The general's face disappeared. Duncan slumped back into his couch and waited. The fatigue crept back into his limbs. This frustrated him so he forced himself back onto his feet and into the kitchen to put the kettle on. As the water began to boil, Graham became available.

Duncan twitched his eye to raise the connection and said, "That was fun."

"Now you understand the problem."

"I am so very tempted to reply that it is not my problem at all, but rather yours, Mr English."

"But you wouldn't be that churlish… would you?"

Duncan put a teabag in his mug and poured the water in. "I suppose not. But I really don't see the answer to this one, I'm afraid. I assume atomic weapons are off the table."

"Absolutely."

"In that case, we have a conundrum."

"You enjoy those, don't you?"

"You can stop behaving quite so obsequiously now."

"Right-ho, professor."

Duncan sighed. "And when are you coming back to England so we might enjoy a frame or two of snooker?"

"If that's the cost of your assistance, I will make every effort to return as soon as possible."

Duncan chuckled. "It's hardly a cost. I shan't be billing you."

"I'll see what I can do."

"I will be in touch if and when I can come up with something."

Graham nodded his confirmation and disappeared. Duncan picked up the mug of tea and a sharp bolt of pain shot from his wrist. "Damn and blast it," he muttered. He returned to the couch and flopped back down. How on earth could he make a bomb powerful enough to destroy an aircraft hangar, small and light enough to be carried in a soldier's kitbag, quiet enough not to 'draw attention' to the bomber if he should still be in the vicinity, and which only used materials undetectable by the enemy?

He closed his eyes, automatically discounting all types of conventional explosives. This meant the device would have to be something utterly unique, never done or even attempted before. As was his way, Duncan reduced the problem to its key elements. He visualised an aircraft hangar. What in all of physics could flatten it, outside the traditional effects such as blast waves?

Suddenly, a childhood memory resurfaced: the ever-curious face of Uncle Bernard, who had been responsible for setting the young Duncan on his path into the world of science. For many years, when confronted with a knotty problem, Duncan used to ask himself what Uncle Bernard would do. But he hadn't used that hypothetical for a long time because his own abilities matched those of his uncle by the time Bernard retired. But now, a forgotten conversation from years earlier came back to him, of his uncle explaining to him the little-appreciated powers of sound waves.

Duncan let out a yelp and smothered an abrupt feeling of elation. "Remember," he cautioned himself, "about the snags. There will always be snags." He gulped down some tea and then barked: "Computer? Give me all possible options for generating ultra-low sound waves, maximum destructiveness, effective to a range of one hundred metres on all axes away from the generating unit."

Squonk replied: "Confirmed."

Chapter 23

15.55 Friday 16 February 2063

Pip Clarke pulled down and patted the Velcro pads on her kitbag. She glanced around the small room that had been her quarters for the last six months. Her left hand felt for the irregular depression in the flesh on the back of her upper-left arm.

That wasn't the only scar she was taking with her to her new deployment. Others ran down the backs of her thighs as well. She had neither the time nor the inclination to visit a beauty salon in the town to have the scars removed, for they represented evidence of her payment for still being alive—the receipts for her continued existence. How much luck did she still have in the bank? That remained the great unknown and unknowable.

The battles of the previous summer faded in her memory; some images she blocked, others made her shudder when they arose unbidden in her mind's eye. The strangeness of the passing of time provoked her curiosity. The winter was progressing in a kind of chilled stress, no one knowing if and when the enemy would deploy improved weapons to counter the Falarete's defensive abilities.

At the same time, NATO had not been idle, and Pip tried to recall how many versions of the Falarete they were up to now: eleven, twelve? Almost every conceivable use had been explored and implemented: fixed launchers covering every nook and cranny in built-up areas, autonomous mobile launchers, mobile Falarete fire teams, launchers fitted onto tanks, and mergers with existing weapons' systems.

A notification flashed in Pip's lens informing her that her autonomous air transport would leave in a few moments.

She hoisted the strap of her kitbag and slipped it over her head. She turned, grabbed her Bergan pack and left her quarters. Outside, yellow sunlight flecked the high and broken cirrocumulus clouds. Good weather for a short flight. The huge barracks hummed with activity: to the north, training units practised drills; newer recruits did physical activity to the west; air and terrain vehicles took off and landed and rolled and turned. Somewhere behind her sat the hangar in which she'd first seen Falaretes being replicated, only then everyone called them 'Tidbury's Follies'.

"Hey, Pip," a voice cried. "Wait."

She turned to see Martin Phillips running towards her. She smiled.

"I thought you were leaving later. Is that your AAT?" he asked.

She glanced ahead to see the Boeing 818 on the apron in front of her. A queue of other troops made their way up the few steps into the aircraft's fat body. "That's me, yup," she said.

"What stop are you getting off at?"

"Rochester is the fourth, I think."

"Oh, right. Well, I just wanted to say thanks for everything."

She shook her head. "I thank you."

"Look, I don't want to—"

"So don't," she broke in. "We discussed this. It was good while it lasted."

Martin looked crestfallen but appeared to recover himself under a gaze she tried to keep warm but distant. She turned and walked to the Boeing without looking back. The queue moved forward. Pip entered the cool interior, dropped her Bergan and kitbag in large wire baskets aft, then went to her allocated seat and clipped her Pickup to the wall mounting next to it. She reflected how a few months ago, she would've likely recognised most of the faces she came across, but the base had grown tenfold in acreage as well as in personnel, and when she glanced at the people sharing the flight with her, she didn't recognise a single one.

The last person boarded and seated herself. The door slid closed and the aircraft rose. It banked and through the window opposite her, Pip made out the airfield and barracks and stores, all bathed in the fading sunlight. She sent a silent thank you to Forward Observer Martin Phillips, who'd helped her so much the previous year, although in truth they'd supported each other. But mundanity is the enemy of desire, and as winter had come on, Pip returned more often to her survivor's guilt.

And now she faced a new challenge. She adjusted the view in her lens and called up the list of Rochester airfield's command personnel. Names and images scrolled by as the AAT descended to its first stop, only a little further along the coast at Deal. She tried to remember the names and faces, but gave up. She leaned back into the seat and closed her eyes. It offered the kind of discomfort only military designs could produce.

She must have dozed, for suddenly her lens shone a light of increasing brightness to alert her to the fact that the

AAT would shortly land at her destination. She looked out of the window opposite to see only darkness. A civilian blackout was in force all over the county of Kent, and in any case the super AI controlling all air and surface transport hardly required visible light to function.

With no external visual reference, Pip waited for the gentle bump of touchdown. Her Squitch told her to exit. She unclipped her Pickup and collected her kitbag and Bergan. The door slid upwards and Pip was the sole passenger to alight. She walked into the blackness, her boots feeling the resistance of concrete under them; her nose detecting a harsher, muddier coastal smell than the south coast she'd left.

"Captain Clarke?" a voice called.

Her lens enhanced her vision with an infrared hue, and she made out a figure in front of her. As she walked towards the man, his name and rank resolved in her vision. She said, "Yes, sir."

In the dimness he stuck out his hand and said: "Major Pickard. Welcome to Rochester airfield."

She shook his hand with her free hand and replied, "Thank you, sir."

"I'll show you to your quarters. Would you like a hand with your kit?"

"No, thank you, sir."

"Very well. Come along."

She followed the man, catching the faint whine of the AAT's engines as it took off behind them.

"I'm afraid our construction replicators are still engaged repairing enemy ACA damage in the town."

"Is it anything related to key infrastructure?"

"No, mostly civilian needs, schools and a leisure centre. The local council put in a request last year for more attack shelters. Bloody council leader keeps bothering me about it, but from what I can see, the locals are more than capable of digging holes in their back gardens and putting some corrugated metal sheets over the top."

Pip smiled at the major's complaint. She said, "I'll have to take the replicators back tomorrow if they're not finished."

"Really? Couldn't you wait and give them until Monday? I thought you could spend the weekend settling in, have a look around the area—Medway has a fair bit of history. Dickens lived here, and the cathedral is nearly fifteen hundred years old."

Pip considered his suggestion and, feeling tired and disinclined to argue, as well as the fact that he outranked her, acquiesced: "Of course, sir. I can give them until Monday."

They reached a narrow, long, single-storey building. A small, dim light above the door illuminated just enough of Pickard for Pip to see a handsome diamond face with dark eyebrows over penetrating eyes.

"Very good. So, here's your billet. Your Squitch will guide you to your own quarters."

"Thank you." Pip added, "I can give the construction replicators until Monday, but then I really will have to call them back, sir."

"If you must, captain," Pickard replied, with a slight emphasis on her lower rank.

Pip knew she should let it pass, but couldn't. She replied, "Yes, *Major* Pickard, I'm afraid I must. I have very limited time to ensure this airfield has sufficient infrastructure for two thousand soldiers and their battalion's supporting equipment."

"Yes, quite," Pickard said with what Pip thought might have been sneer, but she couldn't be sure in the dim light.

"With respect, major," she said, "I am a Royal Engineer. This is what I do."

Chapter 24

15.46 Monday 12 March 2063

Terry Tidbury paced around his office in the War Rooms rehearsing in his mind what he intended to say at the approaching meeting. Its significance was not lost on him. Initial plans for how Operation Repulse would commence and proceed had been finalised the previous week and sent out to those commanders who had sufficiently high security clearance. In a few moments, he would open himself up to his generals' questions and find out what they thought about how their armies and corps and battalions would begin to reclaim Europe.

Simms had suggested organising it in a larger auditorium with greater in-person attendance, but Terry decided that would be a waste of resources—too many attendees were at bases all over England and the other Home Countries, while others were in the US.

Next to the screen in his desk, steam curled up from a mug of tea Simms had thoughtfully deposited. He turned and decided to use the screen in the wall behind his desk, as he would be able to stand while addressing his subordinates. He picked up the tea and sipped it.

A comms signal flashed in the lower-right of the screen. "Accept that," he said.

"Hey, Earl," General Studs Stevens of the USAF said, his concerned face expanding in the screen. "I need to give you a heads-up before the conference starts."

"I knew you'd hardly contact me now for something trivial, Suds. What's up?"

"A lot of the high-ranking folks over here looking at the plans are making noises that the start date should be brought forward."

"No way," Terry answered. "The plans are sound. We were working on them for months before we disseminated them. Now, I'm prepared to let my generals have a say—I'm always open to other viewpoints and I certainly don't discount that either we or the computers may have missed something—but major policy changes are not on the table here."

"Sure," Suds replied in mollification. "Don't shoot the messenger."

"Yes, yes. I get it."

"They're looking at the numbers and drawing conclusions that we should not wait until October."

"And you think they'll raise this issue today?"

Suds shook his head. "Nope, because I think you enjoy a lot of respect. But it will likely go up the political chain. Defense has gotten much closer to the president since last October, and has real influence. On the other hand, I could be wrong—sure wouldn't be the first time. Watch the chief master sergeant, a guy called Carter. Anyways, I thought you ought to know."

"Thanks, Suds. I appreciate that."

Stevens let out a chuckle. "Well, I encouraged you to take this path, so now I feel kinda responsible."

Terry also laughed. "You definitely should not. Besides, I have a nice little surprise up my sleeve to make sure none of my generals gets too far out of line."

"Yeah? So now it's your turn to give me a heads-up, Earl. What's the surprise?"

"I'm afraid you'll have to wait and see."

"Damn and curse you, field marshal."

"See you later," Terry said, and Stevens' face vanished. He sipped his tea and glanced down at a page of notes he'd scribbled on a piece of paper.

Squonk announced, "Field marshal, the initial oversight meeting is about to begin."

"Onscreen and react to my comments."

"Confirmed."

A green outline map of England resolved in the screen on the wall. Pinpricks of red flashed over locations as commanders joined the meeting. From barracks and bases all over the country, the faces of brigadiers, major generals, lieutenant generals and full generals appeared in thumbnails. To the left, more images resolved of American military commanders. Terry took a moment to marvel that all of this ability and martial professionalism was under his command as SACEUR—Supreme Allied Commander, Europe.

"Welcome, everyone," he began, leaning the base of his spine against the edge of his desk. "Firstly, I would like to congratulate our American colleagues on the incredible achievement this week of completing repairs to all military facilities damaged by the tsunami some five months ago. The Atlantic convoys continue to constitute a vital part of NATO's continuing defence, and now that naval bases such as Norfolk are once again fully operational, this will allow us all to feel a sense of increased security.

"To turn to our intention for the future: three days ago, you all received outline plans for the opening and initial objectives of Operation Repulse. By necessity, these plans only contain a high-level overview, although I believe it is sufficient for each of you to understand what your objectives will be for the first thirty days of the campaign. Since you received those plans, nothing material has changed. Resources continue to accrue; personnel continue to be relocated as best suits their talents.

"To recap: our invasion will consist of two spearheads. Attack Group East will make landfall on the Franco-Belgium border in order to secure the Delta Works, which is an R-plus-one objective." Terry paused and tried a little levity: "One of many first-day objectives, naturally."

None of the faces reacted.

Images of arrows resolved on the map of Europe as Terry continued: "Attack Group South will infiltrate northern France, clearing suitable landing areas between Caen and Le Havre. As of today, the indications on the map are the objectives for the end of R-plus-one."

Like ink spilt on blotting paper, blue spread out in two spots in Belgium and France.

"As Repulse continues, Attack Group East will drive into northern Germany with supporting spearheads moving south to protect its flank. Similarly, Attack Group South will be reinforced with spearheads moving east to protect its flank."

In the screen, the 'R-plus' figure crept up, denoting the passage of the campaign. NATO forces spread out over the landmass until, when the figure reached R-plus-90, all European countries had been recovered, from Poland's eastern border south to Moldovia at the Black Sea, then southwest to the Turkish border and along the Mediterranean to the Iberian Peninsula. A creeping sense of disbelief grew inside Terry. A voice insisted it could not be so straightforward, and he thus wondered how much weight this plan would carry with those under his command. "Of course," he continued, "this is a preliminary outline to expel the enemy and take back what was taken from us. One of the most important benefits is that, with a start-date of 1 October, the latter portion of the campaign will happen during the winter, and our intel has shown that many enemy warriors find fighting in lower temperatures to be disagreeable.

"Given the stage of the plans so far, do any of you have any concerns or suggestions you'd like to voice now?"

"Field marshal, I have a question." The thumbnail of Polish General Pakla increased to cover a quarter of the screen. From all of the commanders present, Pakla had been in Terry's top five of those most likely to speak. He recalled the Polish general's support the previous August on announcing Operation Repulse, and hoped that, despite issues regarding the deployment of his Polish regiment, little had changed since then.

Pakla's Slavic forehead creased as he said, "The numbers of enemy ACAs that we think will defend our homelands are a mistake, no? We know we will have new weapons, and we have an idea of what they will be able to do, but is not the number of enemy ACAs an underestimate in these plans?"

Terry replied, "That's a good question. For Repulse to succeed, we must indeed reduce the number of enemy machines in theatre. Plans are in hand to do that, although I am not at liberty to reveal them now."

"Excuse me, sir," said General Abrio of the French 2nd Dragoon Regiment, "what account has been taken of survivors? Do we have plans to provide medical aid in theatre, or will there be evacuations? Any survivors will be suffering greatly, I expect."

"That will depend on who we find, who's left. The computers estimate that by R-plus-two, we will be able to extrapolate the numbers and extent of survivors for most of the continent. But to be frank, the enemy's behaviour to date—especially given what we've extracted from the brains of wounded warriors—leads us to believe there will not be many survivors. Our projections give a range of numbers, but they're low."

"Thank you, field marshal."

A female brigadier from a base in southern England, who Terry did not recognise, asked: "Sir, do you personally anticipate anything that might push the start-date for the operation back past 1 October. For example, if the enemy were to deploy new weapons? I have to say that among my teams, there's a lot of black humour—not to mention certain disbelief—that the enemy hasn't already hit us with new weapons."

Terry shook his head and replied: "No," wishing to appear certain. "You can see for yourself the probabilities the computers forecast, although we know how wrong they can be. All of our intel points to the fact that the enemy believes us defeated, and that the British Isles aren't worth the trouble."

"I was more concerned with your own feelings, sir, given that all of us are really depending on your expertise regarding this enemy."

Terry paused and sipped his tea. The woman's words heightened the realisation that these people were to an extent placing their faith in his judgement as their commanding officer. Terry seldom concerned himself with how his subordinates perceived him. He knew what he had to do to get the best of out of people, and the relentlessness of managing a war that might yet see the final destruction of the democracies left him little time for the niceties of self-assessment and reflection. The young brigadier's request threw the spotlight back on him. Terry responded, "My personal feelings are that, until Repulse begins, we are not under a material threat. If the enemy were intent on finishing us off and continuing on to the continental United States, he would've done so by now. The fact that he hasn't—yet—strongly suggests we maintain the advantage we need for Repulse to at least begin as we intend."

"Thank you, sir."

"I haven't finished. He will of course punish us where he can, although I believe things like attacks on the Atlantic convoys are more speculative operations by battlefield commanders than part of any defined strategy. Intel has shown that there is often conflict between the enemy's equivalent of enlisted men and the elite, pseudo-political cadre responsible for discipline. The elite might be too thinly spread, especially given the wealth they've been stealing from the mainland. And that, I suspect, is the real reason we remain at liberty here on these islands: the enemy has so much to consume having conquered the mainland that we now constitute an afterthought.

"In addition, intel has also shown that there is political instability inside the New Persian Caliphate. We don't have many details so far, although I am confident we'll have more soon, but what we do have suggests that the Third Caliph's Council of Elders does every once in a while throw up a coup attempt, usually based around a faction from one or more of the hundreds of administrative districts inside the Caliphate. Whether those are genuine attempts to overthrow the regime or falsely created to keep the rest in line, we don't know. But all this taken together is why we are where we are today."

There came a silence and Terry waited for the next question. "Very well," he said when he decided he'd allowed enough time. "All of you know where to find me if you have any additional thoughts or suggestions. But before we—"

"Er, field marshal," an Italian lieutenant-general said. "What solutions does the plan have in case of Russian aggression? Attack Group East's northern flank will be, I think we can assume, safe due to the Nordic countries. But when we will be reclaiming more and more territory, will Moscow try to interrupt?"

Terry hid a smile at the Italian's turn of phrase. "The estimates of that likelihood at this stage are low, but it is of course something we will monitor as Repulse progresses." He thought for a moment before adding, "In my opinion, I think it unlikely because their ACAs are behind NATO's in terms of manoeuvrability as well as firepower. Besides, the country is still recovering from the great leap backwards it took in the 2020s."

"Thank you, field marshal."

After allowing another moment for any other speakers, Terry said, "Very well. Although this was to be a single-issue meeting, I have one other item of importance I'd like to share."

Terry paused. In truth, it should've been Air Marshal Thomas making this announcement, but Thomas's health had been failing and there were precious few men and women of any competence in what was left of the RAF.

"As I am sure many of you will have deduced from the outline plans for Repulse you've seen, our forces' progress has been based on the performance of new weapons. I can now reveal to you what those weapons are."

In the screen, the map of Europe vanished. A broadly ellipsoid shape appeared and grew. It had slim, narrow fins fore and aft. Against a light background, the dark shape rotated to reveal serrated edges that indicated a core body divided into separate sections.

Terry announced: "This is NATO's next generation autonomous combat aircraft, called the Scythe. This leading version that you see now is the X–7, armed with a Pulsar Mark Five laser, which is nearly forty percent more powerful than the current mark three. The mark five contains its own coherence-length variation unit. The X–7 also boasts more powerful shielding that will have greater battlefield duration due to a unique threat-assessment trigger which will keep the shielding on standby until a threat materialises. At the outset, I want to publicly thank the hundreds of scientists and experts who have been working so hard since last summer to produce this ACA."

Terry admired the shape of the new aircraft. To him, it seemed to combine power and athleticism; the lines suggested something dextrous yet incredibly strong.

He continued, "The Scythe X–7 will be joined by the X–9. In essence, this is a larger version that will have its main arms' cavity stocked with either missiles or Falaretes."

In the screen, the X–7 moved to the left and a similar shape appeared, showing two more fins fore and aft than the X–7.

Terry said, "Of course, it goes without saying that these weapons will only be as effective as the super artificial intelligence controlling them. To deal with this, the SkyWatcher has been upgraded so that each will carry its own super-AI unit in the event of any electronic interference on or above the battlefield, and will boast strengthened shielding similar to the Scythes. This improved battlefield management ACA is called the SkyMaster."

Terry stopped speaking again, suddenly realising that his breaths had grown shallow in his own excitement at revealing these new weapons, on which so much depended. He scanned the faces in the thumbnails and saw mostly smiles and faces nodding in approval. Having delivered what he believed would give a definite leg-up to morale in the command ranks, he decided to close the meeting.

"Ladies and gentlemen, I think now we will leave it there for today. I know you are all cognisant of the fact, but it bears repeating: all of this is absolutely top secret. Operation Repulse will very much need the element of surprise. Despite the continuing impasse, we should nevertheless assume that the enemy's computers are working just as hard as our own to estimate what we will deploy. We cannot afford to give the enemy any advance notice. The Scythes have already begun field testing, and on achieving the required performance parameters, both the X–7 and the X–9 will go into full production. Thank you for attending, everyone, and for your comments and observations. As usual, I will update all of you at our specific, periodic meetings."

The screen went blank and Terry let out a heavy sigh. He felt sure that revealing the Scythes at this time—when the long winter of inactivity had finally relented but six months still remained before Repulse was due to kick off—would help sustain enthusiasm and thus the professionalism of his commanders. He glanced down at the mug of tea he held to see only a residue of cold, brown liquid barely covering the bottom of it.

Chapter 25

08.45 Monday 26 March 2063

David Perkins, the head of MI5, stared down at the small package on the desk in front of him. He lifted it up and tore the tag on the side of it. From within, a small cylinder no larger than an elongated marble rolled into his palm.

"So, a data-pod," he muttered aloud. "That's your game now, is it?"

He held it up between his index finger and thumb, and rolled it from side to side. He placed it in a circular port on his desk. "Computer, scan this data-pod."

The super AI replied: "Affirmative."

"And run SPI protocols." Perkins stood and walked away from his desk. Next to the panelled door sat an occasional table offering several soft drinks. He took a small tumbler and poured apple juice from a carafe. He sauntered over to the window and looked out at the bland Whitehall street. Ever since the invasion, he'd had to work from a tawdry room in the Foreign Office's premises, and it still made him bitter. He gulped down the apple juice and acid clawed back up his throat in response.

The super AI spoke: "The data-pod contains two sub-topics."

Perkins tutted. "Is it SPI-secure?"

"Affirmative."

"Play first sub-topic."

The voice of his best mole in Beijing sounded in his office. Perkins shook his head in bewilderment that the man could still be alive. He recalled that the local embassy had secured clandestine operatives to 'clean' his Chinese monitoring bots about six months ago, but since then his reports had been bland, containing no useful or useable information. Perkins surmised this may have been deliberate. But now—a data-pod?

The man said, "The Englishman, reporting from Beijing. I've decided to go traditional and use a data-pod. Given the shit-festival concerning the SPI issue, it seems using some old-fashioned tech might not be such a bad idea. Besides, I can chuck this in the diplomatic pouch and as long as our slitty-eyed overseers don't get—or don't spot—my indiscretions, this will reach its destination. Also, besides which, it's far more probable than not that my usual comms method is under constant surveillance."

"Do get on with it," Perkins muttered.

"I've split my report into two sub-topics. This is the first, and it's short: rumours have begun circulating in certain parts of the Chinese civil service that, contrary to popular wisdom, NATO isn't totally destroyed. From the pretty young things I can meet and get drunk and pile the latest narcotics down their necks, from all of the international shenanigans that the most powerful country in the world is involved with, that tiny island on the edge of Europe might be up to something. I've established 'habituals' with one or two sad little people and already have them coming back to me for more with little effort."

Perkins shook his head, knowing that the embassy would have yet more expenses to pay for all the narcotics.

"The second issue is actually far more important in the grand scheme of global political affairs. There's one pretty young thing that doesn't know if it's a boy or a girl, but despite its junior position in Beijing's foreign ministry, it comes across all kinds of comms. It graduated in Urdu—God alone knows why given super AI's abilities—and has been going on about movements along the demilitarised zone on Pakistan's north-western border with the Caliphate. This is a big deal because, since the fighting wound down in Europe and the Third Caliph declared his 'victory' last year, speculation has been rife about where he's going to go next. A lot of the smart money is on the Stans to the north, which is why the Russians are getting itchy that he's going to come up into their soft underbelly, but Pakistan and then, presumably, India, well, that's a different proposal altogether."

"Indeed it is," Perkins agreed.

"To conclude, standard comms will remain the same: either irrelevant or intentionally misleading. If anything substantial comes along, it will be delivered in a data-pod. Any response to this comm should be recorded here and posted back to the embassy—and how quaint is that? Sub-topics end."

Perkins turned from the window, smothered a curse at the mole's irreverence, and said: "Computer. Rewrite as follows: sub-topic one is irrelevant without evidence. Sub-topic two is more interesting. Treat as priority and supply evidence asap. Ends. Now quantum-encrypt."

"Encryption confirmed."

Perkins returned to his desk, lifted the data-pod from the port, and left his office to go and post it back to the embassy in Beijing.

Chapter 26

11.34 Wednesday 18 April 2063

For the first time in fourteen months, a belief solidified inside Terry Tidbury that NATO might not be finished. He stood aghast and watched as, on the opposite side of the lake, a prototype Scythe X–7 flashed overhead and destroyed a row of hastily constructed single-storey buildings. The ACA receded to a tiny black dot in the azure sky before racing back to hit the smouldering ruins with more bursts from its Pulsar laser. The noises of splitting tiles, shattering glass and collapsing masonry travelled over the smooth surface of Derwent Lake to lend an uncomfortable immediacy to the event.

Next to Terry stood General Sir Patrick Fox, whom Terry regarded as one of the British Army's most able soldiers, now in command of First Corps.

Fox, short and well-built like Terry, leaned over to him. "Looks all right to me, TT."

Terry raised an eyebrow at Fox's understatement. "All right?" he repeated. "It looks quite a bit better than 'all right', general."

Fox smiled but didn't reply.

From behind Terry, Air Chief Marshal Thomas cleared his throat. "This is the fifth day of tests, but the first time we've used the Pulsar."

"What about the X–9?" Terry asked.

Thomas replied: "That gets rolled out for its first tests next week."

Fox nodded to a group of individuals standing further along the shore of the lake. "I'm not convinced they are greatly impressed."

"I'm glad we've got them back in England and not still over in the States," Terry said. "Reyer and his people have done remarkable work the last year to get us to where we are now."

Fox turned behind him to his adjutant, a young man with an unruly quiff of blond hair. "Booth, you were talking to them earlier, weren't you?"

"Yes, sir," the young man answered. "I don't think they're very easily impressed. I spoke to one of the ladies and she explained they have a small manoeuvrability issue they're struggling to fix."

"Really?" Fox said, sounding surprised. "It seems to move quite well enough to me."

The X–7 reappeared over the distant green hills north of the local village and came swiftly down to rooftop height. With an elegant hiss it decelerated and settled into a specially built cradle on the back of an autonomous transport vehicle.

"Very well," Terry said. "I need to move on to my next appointment. Simms?"

"Yes, Sir Terry?" the adjutant said.

"Get the aircraft powered up." Terry turned to Fox and asked: "Are you sure I can't offer you and your adjutant a lift?"

"No, thank you, TT," Fox replied. "Those tech chaps have an 818 on the way and can drop me at Donnington."

"All right. Contact me if you need anything." Terry offered his hand and Fox shook it with a firm grip.

Simms said, "This way, Sir Terry."

They strode away from the edge of the lake and up a slight incline. They entered a small Airbus C440 and sat on seats that folded out from the fuselage. Tasting the metallic tang of the air inside the autonomous air transport, Terry pulled the straps over his shoulders and buckled himself in. The door slid closed and the engines whined. He watched the shore of the lake fall away as the AAT climbed into the sky, banked away from the palls of smoke from the new ACA test, and accelerated.

He leaned towards Simms and raised his voice over the noise of air rushing past the aircraft: "This thing could carry at least thirty people. Isn't it a bit of a waste on just the pair of us?"

"Quite so, sir," Simms half-shouted back. "Although I should remind you that you are the most important commander in NATO. We wouldn't want to encourage the enemy even more by including more important personnel."

"Is that why General Fox declined my offer?"

"Not at all, sir. His base is in the other direction."

"How many stops are we making today?"

"Nine more in total before we return to London."

"Good. Although it's the next one I'm most interested in."

The AAT flew on for fifteen minutes before descending into a patchwork of black and brown fields in the centre of which nestled a group of buildings. It landed with a soft bump in a designated area to the west of the entrance road to Kendrew barracks, central England.

The whine of the engines faded and the door slid up. Terry unbuckled his safety straps, stood and asked Simms: "Where is my appointment?"

Simms's eye twitched and his head dipped as if to concentrate. He replied: "Exit the AAT and on your right is a single-storey block finished in grey stone. Enter the main doors and there will be a guard."

"Thank you. Go to the mess hall and get yourself something to eat. I expect this will take the full half hour we've allotted."

"Very good, sir," Simms answered.

Terry stepped out of the aircraft into gusty fresh air. The sky shone blue and shapeless masses of cloud sped overhead. He entered the low building through doors with glass panels that reflected the daylight.

On the other side stood a young, uniformed guard. He saluted and barked: "Field marshal, sir. Welcome to Kendrew barracks, sir."

Terry returned the salute. "At ease, son. Is the general in?"

Confusion creased the young man's heavy forehead. He stammered, "Er, don't you see, sir? In your lens—"

"No," Terry broke in, "I don't have one of those confounded things in my eye."

"Ah, right you are, sir. Please follow me."

Terry trailed the guard through another doorway to the right. Spotless boots squeaked on an equally spotless floor tiled in a black and white diamond pattern.

They reached the furthest door and the young man asked: "Would you like me to show you in, sir?"

"No, thank you."

"Can I fetch you some refreshment, sir?"

"Tea, NATO standard, and let it brew."

"Very good, sir." The guard strode off back along the corridor, boots squeaking.

Terry smiled. He rapped on the panelled door, grasped the handle, and entered.

General Maximillian Hastings was already striding towards Terry, a reserved half-smile on his face. He offered his hand. "Good journey up, field marshal?"

Terry shook it. "So far it's been very useful."

"Good. Won't you take a seat?"

They walked across the expansive office. Terry glanced at some of the paintings on the walls and guessed at the historical significance of the characters depicted in them. The room reeked of Hastings' individuality. In any other army in the world, such personal stylings might cause friction, but Terry saw them only as an advantage.

"Did young Fincastle offer you a refreshment?" Hastings asked, sitting in a chair on the opposite side of the desk.

Terry smiled. "Yes, he did."

"Good. Well, I shan't beat about the bush, field marshal."

"Please don't," Terry said.

"I've considered how best to achieve the objective of disabling the enemy's ACA production plant next to the city of Tazirbu in the North African desert."

Terry kept silent, hoping that speaking to Hastings on his home ground would give the man the confidence to be blunter about the not insubstantial problems presented by the objective.

Hastings stroked his pencil moustache with the knuckle of his index finger and went on: "The way I see it, we have two options. One, we can go in with a sufficiently strong combined battlegroup, head on in an open, frontal attack. This would need three mobile battalions screened by, say, about ten thousand of the new ACAs. Unfortunately, the enemy is almost certain to deploy sufficient resources to seriously hinder such a force. In addition, all of our super AI forecasts indicate that such a force would indeed suffer one-hundred-percent casualties, although I suppose that would remove the need to include any supporting medic regiments, given that all of the soldiers involved would certainly perish. And that isn't the worst of it."

"Really?" Terry said, wondering how the annihilation of the attacking force couldn't be the worst of it.

"No," Hastings went on. "The worst of it is that, in addition to the certainty of suffering one-hundred-percent casualties, forecasts indicate that there would also be a notable probability of the attacking force being destroyed before it was, in fact, able to reach the target and carry out—or even attempt to carry out—its mission."

"So how close would it get?"

"In the best-case scenario? Not much further than about thirty kilometres inside enemy territory."

Terry dipped his head in consideration. "So, we agree the frontal attack approach is not the way to go."

Hastings nodded with enthusiasm. "Absolutely. Thus, we have to look at the alternative."

The door to the office clicked open and the young guard approached, carrying a tray.

"Ah, Fincastle. Good."

Fincastle deposited the tray on the desk. On it sat a regimental mug filled with steaming brown tea. The guard retreated and the door clicked closed behind him.

Terry asked, "And the alternative is?"

Hastings didn't miss a beat, "A dedicated, specialised and very small infiltration team. I will, of course, lead it. I have one fellow, called Dixon, who I will certainly take with me. I will select up to three other specialists, each having particular abilities and skills. I assume I can approach any soldier who might fit the bill?"

"You assume correctly," Terry said. "But if three battalions and ten thousand ACAs don't stand a chance, what hope would such a small team have?"

Hastings nodded. "Indeed. There remain a number of significant hurdles to overcome. One, we absolutely cannot take any modern equipment. If the team uses any contemporary military transport or communications devices; if it carries any kit constructed from state-of-the-art materials such as ultra-3D Graphene, the enemy's defensive systems will detect them at once and the game will be up."

"Indeed," Terry agreed.

"Furthermore, this restriction also applies to modern arms. All of NATO's current small arms and battlefield support equipment, from the Squitch to the Pickup to the water replicator, would at once give the team's presence away and absolutely cannot be used in theatre."

A sinking feeling developed inside Terry. He voiced his concern: "Forgive me, general. But it seems the mission I've tasked you to undertake may in fact be beyond the capabilities of any of us."

Hastings reacted almost with offence. "Nonsense," he declared. "Field marshal, I told you I would deal with it, and I shall. The first step in solving any problem is first identifying the precise parameters within which one has to work. The next is to seek out solutions that will allow those parameters to be... breached? For today, I can tell you that I, along with more than a little help from other experts in the British Army, have already begun finding solutions to these problems."

"Very well."

Hastings indicated the mug sitting on the tray in front of Terry. "Is the tea to your liking?"

Abruptly nonplussed, Terry lifted the mug and drank. "Yes, it is," he replied.

"Then that is a relief. Fincastle sometimes gets it wrong, but he's trying. These youngsters today rely too much on their blessed technology."

Terry turned to his left and indicated a martial portrait on the wall. "Who is that person, general?"

Hastings' face lit up. "Thank you for asking. That is one of my distant ancestors, Sir Alfred Hastings. I've never been sure how many 'greats' I need to add with any of them, to be honest. But we trace our family back to the Battle of Waterloo."

Terry stood, collected his mug of tea, and asked Hastings, "I have some time before I need to be on my way to my next appointment. Please, show me the rest of the pictures and tell me about your family's history."

Hastings leapt to his feet, his cheeks suffused with what Terry took to be pride.

Chapter 27

20.03 Wednesday 19 April 2063

Serena Rizzi held Tiphanie in her arms.
The young French woman's head nestled above Serena's right breast. Tiphanie's shoulders heaved with deep sobs.

Serena glanced up from the couch on which they sat and took in the huge bedroom that constituted their new quarters. She did not feel that they were being observed. She shushed the girl and said, "We are safe as long as we do not cause upset to the people in the house."

Tiphanie's head shook and said in French, "No. They will kill us soon. I can feel it."

When the Italian translation had resolved in her vision, Serena stroked Tiphanie's brittle brown hair and said, "Why do you have such thoughts? Has not God protected us up to now? You, me and Liliana. We were brought to this place—"

"I am scared because of this place. We are too close to the centre of power. Almost every night we have visitors. Father is now a chosen confidante of a member of the Council of Elders."

Rather than too close, Serena thought that they were not yet close enough.

Tiphanie went on: "This new cook. I do not like the way he looks at me or the things he says to me."

"Kasra is young and foolish. As are Hormoz and Aziz."

"He scares me. All of them do."

"I have Father's ear when we need it. And now I can speak to them in their own tongue, and that makes everything easier for the three of us. Shush now and gather your strength, sister." Serena placed a comforting kiss on the crown of Tiphanie's head.

Kasra the cook and his two 'apprentices' had arrived in January, within a couple of weeks of the relocation. That month had seen more staff join the household. All of them seemed to be aware that Father appreciated his European slaves and would be displeased if anything untoward happened to them, but of course there were moments when one or more of the male brutes decided to remind the European women of their lack of worth. Serena thought about her childhood in Italy, and the times she'd seen drunk Italian men shout abuse at dark-skinned female refugees. She shuddered, knowing what they must have felt then, because to be here, inside the Caliphate, with pink skin was just as dangerous.

The house to which they'd moved would be better described as a palace. To Serena it lacked sufficient furnishings, although delicate carved patterns covered many of the walls. Father and his family occupied barely a quarter of all the rooms, and the emptiness of the rest of the palace was one of the reasons she and the other two girls felt vulnerable. However, Father now had so many guests that the empty rooms were often used for hospitality. Serena shuddered again when she recalled the reason for Father's elevation in Caliphate society—his help in creating the tsunami the previous October.

Tiphanie's sobs faded. Serena reflected how she'd comforted Liliana when they'd first been kidnapped from Italy. But over the months, Liliana had stabilised and found a role for herself. Her blonde hair lightened in colour in the constant heat and light of the latitude on which they lived, and her limbs fleshed back out to what they had been when Serena had met her. And then, Tiphanie arrived. The French girl had a stronger determination not to show her suffering, so her journey was the inverse of Liliana's: as time passed, Tiphanie's strength ebbed and the frequency of breakdowns like this increased.

Tiphanie sniffed and pulled back from Serena's embrace. The young woman said, "Thank you, sister. Tomorrow is the Feast of Sacrifice and I sometimes wonder if they will decide to sacrifice us."

Serena smiled and replied: "The house will be very busy, but the only sacrifice will be many lambs. You know this feast day is when the rich among them are supposed to go out and feed the poor in their communities?"

Tiphanie scoffed and her eyes flashed with indignation. She said, "I am certain they do not."

"Sister, there will be much cooking, serving and cleaning."

"Kasra will threaten me again. I know he will."

"When he does, you must come and tell me."

"I would feel like a coward."

"No, sister. We must help each other. You must promise you will tell me if any of them try to abuse you, yes?"

The girl let out a sigh and answered, "Yes, sister. If you will not think me weak for doing so."

Serena repeated, "I speak their tongue now and I have Father's ear. You have nothing to fear."

A brave grimace formed on Tiphanie's face. "Thank you," she whispered. She stood, cleared her throat, and walked away.

Serena watched Tiphanie enter the ensuite bathroom. When the door closed, Serena whispered, "And if Kasra does do anything? Well, the knives in the kitchen are very sharp, and I will drive one of them through his skinny ribcage and into his black heart before any of them will be aware of what has happened."

Her head tilted in consideration and she added: "Of course, child, I would rather wait for a more justified target, but if that is the work the good Lord sent me here to do, then so be it. At least one of these vile savages will die by my hand, and God Himself shall guide it."

Chapter 28

00.23 Wednesday 2 May 2063

Pip Clarke couldn't sleep. The heat of the English spring was something she needed to get used to once again at the end of every 'winter'. There were no real winters anymore, of course, just autumns that dragged through the change of the year and slowly evolved into the next spring.

She got out of the uncomfortable bed and stood, her thoughts drifting to Forward Observer Phillips and doubting if she'd handled the situation as well as she might have. It probably didn't matter now. Mark was a good-looking guy and would not have a great deal of trouble finding a replacement for her. To Pip, emotional and physical needs were dampened by the practicalities of being a captain in the British Army. This meant that, more than anything, a decent night's sleep was her first and most important need. And on this night, the growing heat prevented that.

She went over to the only window in her quarters and pulled the thin, lank curtain to one side. Dull orange lights placed around the airfield on posts that seemed to be needlessly high ensured the minimum visibility to those on the ground, and gave little away to anything flying above. Pip wondered again why those lights had to be that height; certainly, she'd never agree to such a thing when designing new barracks, but it hadn't been her choice. On arriving, Squonk had adjusted and amended her plans to increase the capacity of Rochester airfield so that it would hold thousands of more troops; so many, in fact, it would be redesignated as Rochester barracks—more than simply a base for NATO's ACAs.

She decided to get some exercise in the hope that it might help her sleep later. She threw on a dark green top and army fatigue trousers. She left the single-storey building that contained her quarters and began a fast jog around the perimeter.

The super AI's interference had irked her. It was supposed to assist, to recommend and advise her, not dominate the whole process. However, beyond a sense of irritation, the super AI's behaviour also aroused her curiosity. From the day she arrived in February, nearly three months ago, one of the construction requirements had been an unidentified building. In that location, the replicators had put up a basic, windowless, medium-sized hangar. In itself, this was not suspicious, for barracks that would house thousands of troops often needed locations for storing arms and other sensitive material, and Brass might not want every squaddie knowing what heavy-duty kit might be right under their noses.

A strong breeze carried the tang of muddy river water, and the cloud cover prevented any starshine from adding some illumination to her surroundings. Pip accelerated her pace to burn through her frustration. She followed the road as it turned north and ran parallel with the M2 motorway. She reached the edge of the airfield and slowed to a walk. A hundred metres in front of her, she could just make out the windowless hangar.

"You're out late, captain," a voice said.

Pip spun round to see Major Pickard striding towards her. Two others flanked him, a man and a woman. Pip said, "Good evening," as affably as she could.

Pickard tutted and said, "It is night, not the evening, captain."

"So it is," Pip said, hackles rising at the tone of his voice and the blank looks on the faces of the others. In the dimness, Pip could not make out any insignia on their uniforms.

Pickard said: "Captain, I order you to retire to your quarters at once."

Pip's senses urged caution but she answered: "Excuse me? With respect, Major Pickard, I am seconded here and am not directly under your com—"

"Nevertheless," he broke in, "I outrank you and order you to return to your quarters without delay."

Pip was nonplussed. Until tonight, Pickard had been reserved but accommodating, his handsomeness not compensating for his standoffishness. While she'd directed the expansion of the airfield, he'd not been either excessively helpful or awkward.

Pickard's eye twitched and he muttered, "Shit."

Pip saw the faces of the other two fall. All three of them swapped worried glances that only heightened Pip's suspicion.

The young man behind Pickard murmured: "Thirty seconds."

Pickard looked at Pip and barked: "Captain Clarke, I order you to sign the Official Secrets Act, now."

Through her lens came a red-level comms notification. Pip's skin chilled in the night air. She reacted as quickly as she could, confirming acceptance of being bound by the English government's universal gagging law.

"Good," Pickard said. "Breathe a word of anything you see or hear on this airfield tonight and you'll be on a court martial before you can blink. Now, captain, piss off back to your quarters."

Before Pip could issue an appropriate rejoinder, Pickard trotted off, his two little helpers in tow. Pip slowly retreated and muttered: "Fuck you, sir." She kept walking backwards until she noticed large, wheeled shadows approach the hangar. She twitched her eye to call up a local map and realised that opposite from her position, on the other side of the hangar, ran the M2 motorway. Thus, whatever had arrived must have travelled on that road.

Pip watched while the large shadows trundled inside the hangar. Abruptly, she understood. The whole base had heard the rumours. Gossip among the ranks and in the mess halls revelled in the same generalisation: Brass had developed new ACAs. The prototype tests had been completed and the new ACAs had gone into production. Certain, specially selected locations would receive production models that would undergo field testing.

Pip turned and began jogging back to her quarters. The fresh air and the flash of drama had wearied her limbs. Only one question remained in her mind: why deploy, for their vitally important field tests, these state-of-the-art autonomous combat aircraft to a horrible little dump like Rochester?

Chapter 29

09.56 Saturday 5 May 2063

Journalist Geoffrey Kenneth Morrow lifted his head off of his pillow and waited for the hangover to hit him fully. He shuddered when the increase in blood pressure aggravated his headache. He forced his legs out from under the warm duvet and his feet touched the cold floor. He leaned forward, put his head in his hands, and felt the grease in his unwashed curly hair.

"You're a bastard, Geoff Morrow."

Lisa's voice chided him as it did every morning when he awoke. It didn't matter how much he drank; it didn't matter how much he cried or apologised or how much the regret burned the back of his throat.

Lisa's voice spoke from behind his headache again, "You're a bastard, Geoff Morrow."

"I know, darling," he whispered with a sob as the tears welled in his eyes.

He sat, sniffed, and wiped his face with the palm of his hand. He checked the time in his lens and tried to remember if he had food in the fridge or if he'd have to visit the food bank on the high street and scrounge a slice of replicated pizza.

A comms signal arrived. He groaned and twitched his eye.

"All right, Geoff?" asked Alan, his editor and former line manager at *The Guardian* media outlet.

"No, not really. You?"

"Great," Alan said in a tone that conveyed a complete lack of concern. "I've got a freelance job—if you want it."

Geoff wanted to tell Alan where he could shove his freelance job, but his stomach rumbled as it waited for some breakfast. The pain in his head increased. "Yeah, what is it?"

"There's a lot of guff on the platforms about ACAs flying around the countryside."

"Yeah, it's what they do. I thought you knew there's a war on. Makes sense to—"

"Don't get cute with me, Geoff. Check the platforms and then get your lazy fat arse somewhere where the shit's going on. We've got the MOD saying it's normal defensive patrols but witnesses are saying they're new ACAs. Tiptop secret."

"So, either the MOD or Downing Street will put an R-notice and you'll not be able to use anything I find."

"Maybe and maybe not."

"What?"

"Wake up, Geoffrey," Alan admonished in a louder voice. "Tiptop secrecy is one thing, but right now this island is heaving under the weight of nearly three million soldiers with no-one to fight. It wouldn't hurt to give them a little titbit of the direction the war effort could be going in—"

"Can't you put me back on the payroll, Alan?" Geoff asked, hearing the pleading tone in his voice but no longer caring.

"Sorry, fella," Alan replied, for once his voice carrying no outward sarcasm. "Look, you got some really good content last year when you went to the continent—"

"And nearly died in the process."

"Yeah, I know all that. And that's why I'm contacting you now. Give me something to use and I'll see you get weighed out whether or not Downing Street sticks an R-notice on the new ACA story. That's the best I can do for now."

"Okay, yeah," Geoff said, rancour fading with his headache. "I'll see what I can do. Thanks."

Chapter 30

14.15 Sunday 7 May 2063

Terry Tidbury pulled open the door to his office and said, "Welcome to the War Rooms, general."

General Hastings nodded and entered. "Thank you for seeing me on a Sunday."

Terry pushed the door closed. "Every day is pretty much like all the others down here. Have you been offered something to drink?" he asked, conscious of Hastings' hospitality at Kendrew barracks a few weeks earlier.

"Yes, and I declined. Field marshal, time is short. I would like to bring you up to date and have your permission to proceed."

"I appreciate your forthrightness. Let's sit." Terry indicated a functional chair on one side of his desk and then sat in his own chair.

"If I may?" Hastings asked, holding a small data-pod between his thumb and forefinger.

"Of course. Squonk? Display both on my personal desk screen and the wall screen."

"Confirmed," the super AI answered.

Hastings placed the data-pod in the port on the desk.

Terry said, "You could've given me this briefing via comms. There was no need for you to come down to London."

"I believe," Hastings said, "that you and I both harbour a certain mistrust of our computers. Personally, I regard their abject failure to warn us of the approaching disaster in February last year as unforgivable, and I prefer to keep them at arm's length whenever possible."

"That's not a bad idea."

"In addition, this mission must be subject to the utmost secrecy."

Terry caught the look in Hastings' eyes. The man stroked his moustache in the same manner as when Terry had met him previously.

The pause lengthened.

Terry ordered: "Squonk, the information contained in the data-pod and all subsequent discussion in this room is not to be recorded or stored. By my order, field marshal, Terry Tidbury."

"Confirmed."

A look of relief crossed Hastings' face as he said: "Thank you, sir."

"Summary records will still be kept. Proceed please, general."

Hastings nodded. "Computer, show map one and follow my directions."

A map of North Africa resolved on both the wall screen behind Terry and his personal screen in his desk. A fragment of the coast was highlighted along with the location of Tazirbu in the interior.

Hastings spoke: "Firstly, the infiltration team shall require transport to and drop off at an appropriate point on the northern coast of Africa, in an approximate line directly north of Tazirbu. This would best be done by submarine."

"Uh-huh," Terry murmured.

"Any attempt to insert the team by air would be certain to be exposed and defeated. In addition, we will require dropping off with a substantial weight in kit. The team will travel to Tazirbu and back again by motorbike."

"Motorbike?" Terry echoed in surprise.

Hastings nodded. "Yes. My research suggests a machine called a Bonneville T–140 would be the most suitable, originally manufactured by a company called Triumph nearly a century ago."

A diagram of the motorbike replaced the map. The image rotated on a horizontal plane through three hundred and sixty degrees as the general explained, "We've made some refinements that will improve performance but will still keep us safe from detection. The machine contains an internal combustion engine typical for the era, and we've managed to increase the efficiency of its performance so we will have to carry substantially less fuel for each of them than would have been the case according to the engine's original specification."

"How many of these things do you plan to take?"

"The idea is that, due to the weight of the other equipment we will carry, each team member will have his own motorbike. However, each machine is able to carry two people. So, if for example one of the motorbikes breaks down on or before the return part of the journey, by that point we will have used up enough of our fuel and water that a team member will be able to ride pillion. In this way, up to two out of the five motorbikes can fail and the mission can still succeed."

Terry nodded in approval. "Good."

"Thus," Hastings said, "the submarine drops us off. We motor down to Tazirbu, destroy the weapons' production facility, and return to be picked up by the submarine."

Terry sighed. "No, no, wait a moment. Before we get to how you intend to neutralise the target, you need to cover nearly six hundred kilometres of desert. Are you sure those motorbikes will ride properly on sand?"

"Oh, yes," Hastings said. "There is of course some method to be learned to control them on sand, but in any case, we're using detailed maps prepared before the Caliphate dominated North Africa, and the computers have allowed for drift and things like that. But, for a large part of the journey, we will traverse rock, shale and other hard surfaces."

"Okay," Terry said, deciding to accept that detail. "Next question: you are going to be travelling across enemy territory. As we know, more than a few intrepid fools have gone in, but precisely none has ever come out. What makes this mission any different, general?"

"At the risk of repeating myself, sir, primarily the fact that we will carry no modern technology in our equipment will ensure our anonymity."

"But you're still going to be rolling across open desert sitting on internal combustion engines that, I assume, will be belting out heat. If a passing enemy patrol ACA decides to scan its surrounding using heat-signature, you will be discovered."

Hastings nodded. "We can hardly eliminate every risk from this mission. According to intelligence, the primary detection method employed by the enemy's ACAs is signals—digital comms traffic, end points on the vast networks that run everything in a typical military or society. After that, the enemy identifies the signature presence of 3-D ultra-Graphene in equipment and munitions. Only after that does the enemy consider using old-fashioned scanning and tracking techniques like heat-signature. Provided we can maintain secrecy and the enemy won't actually be looking for us, the chances of discovery are actually slim."

"The enemy will certainly be looking for you if the mission is a success," Terry observed.

"Indeed, field marshal. But what, exactly, will he be looking for? One of his main weapons' production facilities will have been levelled and the enemy will not know how or by whom. The scale of the destruction will point to a substantial attacking force, yet he will find no traces of one. In addition, the return trip will be staggered to give each team member the best chance of escape."

Terry's eyebrows rose. "That's quite a boast, general. So how do you intend to destroy their facility?"

"Computer," Hastings called, "show the image for 'sonic mine'."

In the screens, a nondescript, black oblong slab resolved, including indicated measurements of fifty centimetres long by fifteen wide, with a thickness of ten centimetres.

"A 'sonic mine'?" Terry repeated, a note of incredulity in his voice.

"Yes, it's really rather simple. Each of these modest units contains a rotating shaft loaded with nanobots. Each end of the unit contains the raw amplification catalyst. To detonate the mine, the shaft must reach a critical minimum rotational speed. When it does, the catalyst is released to penetrate the nanobots. Each nanobot then expands in a fashion not dissimilar to nuclear fission—"

"But—"

"No, no, field marshal, this is most assuredly not a nuclear device. What happens is that when the mine detonates, it emits ultra-low sound waves. When these waves penetrate solid structures like metal and stone, they cause a molecular shift in the materials' composition, the practical upshot of which is to make them collapse."

Terry couldn't keep the shock from his face or voice. "Are you seriously suggesting you're going to demolish an ACA production plant with nothing more than sound waves?"

Hastings' face creased in offence, "Certainly not, sir. These mines generate ultra-low sound waves. Field marshal, there is nothing scientifically new here, merely something science has forgotten about and moved on from. And, I should like to point out, these sonic mines are not some kind of miracle weapon. They will require precise placement among the buildings we intend to destroy to be effective, and a coordinated, uniform detonation. This will be no simple task."

"What's in the catalyst?"

"A refined type of dysprosium."

"But these mines are not nuclear weapons?"

"No, sir. They do, however, employ the principle of fission to generate and amplify ultra-low sound waves that can and will destroy everything inside their effective radius."

"How many will you need to take?"

"Fifty should be enough to do the job. We are waiting on further intel concerning Tazirbu, the facility, and its adjoining city."

Terry shook his head, lost for words.

The look on Hastings' face returned to one of absolute martial professionalism. He said, "I do hope this plan meets with your approval, sir. With your permission and given the nature of the mission, I would like to suggest the codename 'Operation Thunderclap'."

Terry nodded and whispered, "Sounds good."

"Thank you," Hastings said.

"I have one more question, general."

"Yes, sir?"

"I've been thinking about your intention to lead this operation. Is it strictly necessary? Surely you must have many competent officers in your regiment?" He let a pause hang before adding: "Who are, perhaps, closer in age to the troops in the team?"

Hastings nodded and a wry smile formed on his face "Field marshal, you are doubtlessly correct. However, I do believe it is important for a commanding officer to lead by example, and the other competent men and women under my command will have many more obligations when Repulse kicks off. I do my best to look after myself and I would rather prefer to ensure Thunderclap succeeds in person."

"Very well," Terry conceded.

"Sir, this mission can and will succeed. I only need your permission to proceed with acquiring and training the personnel I will take with me, and producing the sonic mines and other equipment the mission requires."

Terry still fought against a wave of incredulity at the sheer audaciousness of Hastings' plan. He drew in a breath, looked Hastings in the eye, and said: "Permission granted."

Chapter 31

20.33 Monday 8 May 2063

Crispin Webb looked on in dismay as the faces around the conference table in the COBRA meeting room seemed to fall even further. His eyes flicked from one to the other and he wondered again why the boss had COBRAs late in the evening, when everyone was invariably tired and irritable.

The narrow, pointed face of David Perkins, the head of MI5, spoke from the screen on the wall. He was making some kind of qualification of intel, "…and therefore we need to treat this information with some scepticism."

The boss, sitting between Liam Burton and Charles Blackwood, leaned forward and said: "So what is your anticipation of future information? Do you think the mole will send actual evidence or will it remain just hearsay he or she seems to pick up?"

Perkins tilted his head in consideration and replied: "It is difficult to say. The contact began sending data-pods in March, and since then, I have conducted a dialogue with them pressing for something more definitive. But as I said at the beginning, the proposition is a tricky one to prove: if elements of the Chinese secret service—which, let us not forget, is a vast and byzantine organisation employing many thousands—have picked up signs or other intelligence that NATO is planning a counterattack, it is certain that such information would find its way back to our enemies."

From another screen on the side wall, Terry Tidbury spoke: "PM, Mr Perkins and I discussed this issue a few days ago. I think it's very important we take such intel into account, although so far it doesn't change anything from the military perspective."

"Very well. As usual, Mr Perkins, please keep us informed of any and all developments. Now, before we move on to political developments, Terry will update us on the new weapons."

Crispin saw all of the heads around the table perk up, and he wondered if subjects like this should be discussed at meetings that included heads of civil departments such as England's police force.

Terry spoke, "Field tests are progressing as planned. The new weapons are in production and have been deployed to several airfields around southern England for advanced field tests."

There came a pause.

Napier tucked a strand of auburn hair behind her ear and said, "Is that all?"

Terry seemed unfazed. "Yes, PM. For now."

Crispin smiled at the Field Marshal's brevity, silently congratulating the wily old soldier on keeping his cards close to his chest.

"Apart from my usual reminder that, although these weapons are in production, they still require extensive field testing to calibrate and refine the software governing their manoeuvrability. Everything about them is top secret, and as

Mr Perkins will attest, the last thing we need is the Chinese gaining more knowledge of what we are planning."

"Thank you, Terry," Napier said.

Crispin noted most of the attendees' faces seemed to display a mildly confused kind of awe.

"Good," the boss went on. "Given the events of the last few days, about which Mr Perkins has just updated us, and with acknowledgment to Liam for what was originally his idea, today I had calls with both the Norwegian and Swedish prime ministers with a view to hosting a potential diversion that might assist in our military plans. Both women assured me that they would each consult their respective equivalent cabinets and their military advisers, and revert within forty-eight hours."

Foreign Secretary Charles Blackwood added: "We obviously pointed out the potential risk before they did. I'm sure no one needs reminding what happened to the United States last October and 'Allah's divine punishment' for aiding the infidel. So far, the Nordic countries have managed to remain pretty much neutral, apart obviously from the quite remarkable volumes of refugees they've taken in."

"But now," Napier went on, "I hope they will support us in a strictly passive capacity. This might be useful to muddy the intelligence waters and at least sow some confusion during the summer."

A dour man with a mane of straight black hair that obscured part of his face asked: "Will this 'passive' help occasion the need to draw on our limited civilian resources?"

Napier said, "No, Mike. Or at least nothing more than can easily be replicated onsite in those countries, and I think they are well supplied with replicators." She glanced around the table and continued: "Okay, next item. Latest crime situation. Tom, the press is reporting growing friction between groups of refugees of differing nationalities, and local populations. City centres, especially those that have been shored up, are seeing increasing disturbances. How are you and your area commanders managing the problems?"

As the police commissioner answered, Crispin stifled a yawn and began scrolling through various governmental feeds and those military comms' channels to which a civilian like him was permitted access. His concern focused on NATO's new weapons and their advanced tests. It seemed the sort of thing that, back in the old days before the war, some hack might want to latch on to, to find some kind of problem, and by publicising it and creating needless trouble, make a name for him or herself and embarrass the boss.

Chapter 32

08.37 Thursday 10 May 2063

Colour Sergeant Rory Moore looked at Heaton's craggy face across the mess table and asked: "But what does a general want with me? And a general in the Anglians at that?"

Heaton shrugged his shoulders, drained the tea from his mug and let out a short and deep-throated belch. "I have no bloody idea," he said. "But you best not be late seeing him. Come on, your transport's here." Heaton stood.

"Yeah," Rory agreed, also finishing his tea.

They left the rickety table and deposited their mugs at the canteen window. They wove around other squaddies in the mess and exited the building into bright, hot sunshine. Beyond the rows of barracks, sunlight glinted off assorted autonomous air transports that dotted the field.

Rory said, "You don't think it's got anything to do with that misunderstanding last year with Doyle, do you?"

"Nay, laddie. That's all water under the bridge now, isn't it?"

Rory recalled the near court-martial over his drunkenness the previous year. "God, I hope so. I've still got the nanobots in my system, you know. One lousy swig of real beer and those little bastards will put me to sleep."

"Aye, and that's a good thing, too."

"You would say that, grandad; you can still drink the real stuff."

"And hold it as well, which is more than you could, laddie."

Rory looked down at the grass. "I had my reasons."

"Aye," Heaton replied with a hint of sympathy in his voice.

Rory changed the subject, "You think the rumours are true?"

"There's probably something behind them. Brass would want to keep the squaddies gossiping. Besides, it's been a while and the ragheads aren't coming at us with anything new."

"Yet," Rory qualified. "We knew they weren't likely to have a go in winter since we know they don't like the cold."

Heaton shook his head. "When we were pulling back across Europe last year, there's no way I would've thought we'd still be around a year later."

Rory grunted his agreement.

"Okay, I got to run," Heaton said abruptly. "Looks like another blob has passed out during an exercise."

"Seriously?" Rory exclaimed. "Are they still coming through basic training so overweight?"

"Aye. Have fun with your general."

"I won't, thanks."

"And don't forget: if he asks you for a blowjob and you refuse, that's a court martial offence, laddie."

"Piss off, grandad."

Rory watched with a smile as Heaton trotted off the way they'd come. He turned and strode towards the AAT indicated in his lens. The low door on the small vehicle slid up and he ducked to enter. Alone inside the fuselage and without kit or a weapon to stow, he pulled down a seat and strapped himself in. The door closed and he felt claustrophobic. The row of small windows opposite offered only glimpses of the field and barracks. The bright daylight darkened the drab and functional interior.

The engines gave a slight whine and the AAT rose. Rory closed his eyes and the picture of Georgina's smiling face formed again in his mind's eye. A ripple of melancholy ran through him when he realised he hadn't thought about her for days or maybe even weeks, time seemed to be passing so quickly.

The aircraft accelerated and increased altitude.

After an uneventful cruise in a blue sky, twelve minutes later it descended into a brown, open space surrounded by low buildings. Rory forced his jawbone in every direction to free the pressure in his ears. The AAT landed with a gentle bump, the door slid up, and his hearing returned fully.

Rory exited the aircraft and his lens guided him to a building on the right, a single-storey block finished in grey stone. He pushed open the indicated double doors and at once a guard moved towards him.

"Welcome to Kendrew barracks, Colour Sergeant Rory Moore," the soldier said, saluting.

Rory returned the salute, a little nonplussed at the level of formality. In the air next to the severe-looking man appeared the words, 'Lieutenant Alexander Fincastle'. "Thank you," Rory said. "Can I go straight through?"

"Yes, sir. He's expecting you. Can I fetch you some refreshment, sir?"

Rory shook his head. "No, thanks."

"Very good, sir."

Following the directions in his lens, Rory left the guard and turned right into a long corridor with black and white floor tiles on which his boots squeaked with disconcerting loudness. What the hell did a general want with him?

He reached the door and rapped his knuckles on it. At once, he heard a faint, "Come," from within. Rory grasped the handle and entered. When he stepped through, he felt as though he'd walked into a museum. The general's office had a huge Persian rug on the floor and the walls were adorned with portraits of soldiers wearing antique uniforms. On his left was a fireplace above which two elegant sabres hung, blades crossed. Rory's first reaction was that the antique weapons must be worth a small fortune.

A thin, lithe figure stood up from behind the wide—and also very antique—desk. "Welcome, Colour Sergeant Moore. Thank you for coming all this way."

Discombobulation grew inside Rory. The atmosphere in this office could best be described as eccentric, but it was even more unnerving that a soldier of such a rank should thank a mere sergeant for anything at all, let alone simply following an order, albeit couched as a request, to appear before him. Rory stammered, "Er, my pleasure, General Hastings."

"Good," Hastings replied with a half-smile. "Take a seat."

Rory advanced to the chair at the desk and sat, struck by the general's affability and the ridiculous little moustache he had, like a black worm over his upper lip.

"I shan't beat about the bush, sergeant," Hastings said. "I am putting together a team for a very particular mission. And I think you would be a good fit."

Rory smothered the foulest curse his mind could throw up. Of course, why would any general want to meet a lowly sergeant, if not to involve him in something probably very bloody dangerous? Rory felt suddenly furious with himself for not guessing something like this would happen, before a more reasonable voice pointed out that, whether he guessed or not, he would never have been able to avoid this meeting. His heart began thumping harder in his chest. He mumbled: "Thank you, sir."

"However," Hastings said, "I'm afraid I am obliged to put you in a difficult, perhaps even invidious, position."

Rory wanted very much to swear out loud, but held himself in check. He heaved in a breath and replied: "That's quite all right, sir. There is a war on, after all."

Hastings nodded in approval. "Indeed there is. Let me start by saying that everything we discuss—in particular, everything I tell you—is subject to the utmost secrecy. The very future of Europe depends on it. Is that clear?"

Rory involuntarily swallowed. His throat tightened and he wished he'd asked the guard for something to drink. He croaked, "Yes, sir."

"Good. Now, before I give you some more details, could you give me an idea of what the lower ranks are chatting about these days at your barracks? How would you describe morale, for example?"

Rory felt nonplussed again and asked himself why the general would want to go on such a fishing expedition. He replied, "I would describe morale as good overall, sir. There are some points of friction and I often have to deal with minor complaints. We have the occasional dust-up among the lower ranks, but that's only to be expected in a barracks that's swelled so much and now has well over ten thousand troops. Tensions sometimes run high if certain squads or battalions are perceived to be getting better treatment, for example more fresh fruit and veg."

"But on the whole, you'd say morale is holding up, yes?"

The more Rory thought about the question, the more doubts arose. He said, "To clarify, I think a lot of ordinary squaddies are starting to feel at a bit of a loose end, in a way."

"Oh, how?"

"They've done their basic training, they're working on their specialisations, and they're doing their fitness. The whole thing runs like a modern army should, sir. But some troops can be pretty vocal about the future. There are rumours flying around that Brass—er, senior commanders—"

"Using the term 'Brass' is quite acceptable," Hastings said with a reassuring nod.

"Right, thank you, sir. Well, rumours are going about that plans are being made, and now, over the last couple of weeks, a lot of squaddies are talking about new ACAs, apparently faster and better armed. If I were to suggest one thing, general, it would be that Brass might be a bit more forthcoming with what's going to happen next."

"But you'd agree that mission secrecy is vitally important. The element of surprise and all that?"

"Absolutely, but, well, you asked me how things were among the lower ranks." While Rory had been talking, he'd noted the general staring at him with narrow eyes. Rory didn't want to rock any boats, but then considered that some honesty wouldn't hurt, either. He'd decided he was in all kinds of trouble anyway, it was now only a question of how bad it would get.

Hastings tipped his head back and said, "There are plans. Advanced plans."

"Oh, right."

"However, these plans depend upon that very specific mission I mentioned."

Rory decided to take the bait. He asked, "Can you tell me what it entails, sir?"

"Before you decide whether to accept or refuse my proposal, I can only repeat that the future of Europe depends on its success. I offer you the chance to take part in something historically unprecedented; something that, afterwards, will offer you opportunities for professional and personal fulfilment beyond your wildest dreams."

"Right," Rory muttered, expletives shrieking in his brain, his senses alive with excitement and the promise of danger.

There came a pause. Hastings stroked his ridiculous moustache with the knuckle of his index finger.

Rory decided to push. "Why me, sir?" he asked. "What kind of special skills do I have that this mission needs?"

Hastings gave a slight shrug. "One, your combat history. You are one of the most—if not *the* most—experienced soldiers of this conflict. Your action in Spain at the outset, the first NATO soldier to take on a Caliphate Spider and beat it; your endurance in escaping from behind enemy lines and successfully rendezvousing with the *Spiteful*; the role you played in capturing the first wounded enemy warrior; the action you saw in the retreat of NATO forces across Europe last year. The team I'm putting together will benefit invaluably from that experience."

Rory nodded in sombre acknowledgement of his extensive combat record. Sometimes he forgot just how much shit this war had put him through.

"Two, and if you'll forgive my bluntness, sergeant, I need a strongman. You are well over six foot and I fancy you would make a pretty formidable prop-forward for England if you felt like it. The mission will involve notable heavy lifting and we will likely have to do some digging in. I need a man I can rely on not to shirk at a little hard labour."

Rory nodded again, his spirit accepting that the general was talking him into agreeing to be part of this mission in the softest, most complimentary way possible.

"Indeed," Hastings went on, "another fact that made me choose you was your, shall we say, deep clean at the Advanced Medical Research Establishment last year. This means you're in perfect health and therefore you fit the bill very well."

"I see."

Hastings stood and walked to a window that looked out on a copse of scraggly silver birches outside. He turned back to Rory. "Ordinarily, I should like to give you a period of time to think about it, but I'm afraid things are such that I cannot. If you wish to decline, Sergeant Moore, you may do so rest assured that your career in the British Army will not suffer in any way—it hardly could, given what you've already achieved in this war.

"If you accept, then you will join a mission that will make history, and you will be able to enjoy all the benefits of that. However, I must have your decision now. If it is no, I will need to continue looking; if it is yes, you will need to join us at once." He put his hands behind his back and made for the door, saying: "I will return in a few moments."

When the door closed behind the general, Rory exhaled and whispered, "Oh my sweet Christ Jesus, what the hell am I involved in?" He stood and paced around the room. He peered at the sabres over the fireplace. He stared at the portraits of the military men and wondered who they were and what they'd done to be remembered in oil on canvas. He speculated if any of them had had to face the kind of decision he now had to make—and if those men had died knowing they'd made the right or wrong choice.

Rory wanted very much to call Heaton and ask him for his opinion, or any one of a dozen guys he worked with in his regiment. But he realised he couldn't; and if he did, Hastings would know and probably question his trustworthiness.

His thoughts drifted to Colonel Doyle, whom he hadn't seen since that unfortunate business the previous September. But then, Hastings was a general, and he spoke as though he could do whatever he liked, regarding this mission at least. So, Doyle wouldn't have much to say either way.

A chiming came from an ornate clock on the mantle, below the crossed sabres. It pinged an annoying metallic sound to announce that it was nine o'clock, and as Rory expected, the door to the office clicked open.

Hastings re-entered the office and closed the door. He spoke as he walked back to his desk, "As I mentioned, Sergeant Moore, there is no obligation upon you. You have done more than enough in support of the war effort. But I must now ask you if you accept my proposal."

The air seemed to evaporate out of Rory's lungs. From all of the critical moments in his life since his four-soldier squad had been deployed to the Sierra Nevada mountains of Spain the previous year, there came the impression that this carried more importance than all of them; that, incredibly, the stakes had increased further. A part of him wanted to decline, politely. General Hastings was an eccentric, and whatever the mission involved, Rory suspected it would also include much eccentricity. The young boy inside him shook his head and insisted this was not a good idea—there was too much danger, too much risk. But the proud Royal Engineer shot back that General Hastings had paid him an unparalleled compliment by inviting him to join this mission, and these sad, sorry Royal Anglian types would be doomed to failure without a proper soldier in their team.

Rory heaved in a breath. "General Hastings, I accept your invitation. And I would like to thank you for considering me. I will do my best not to let you down."

Hastings strode across the floor with his hand outstretched and a warm smile on his face.

Rory grasped and shook the general's hand. As he did so, he felt the direction of his life change irrevocably. Something fell away, like an old, wrinkled skin. In its place appeared a vast, blurred vista, challenging in its potential, exciting in its uniqueness, and full of unknown danger.

"Excellent," Hastings said. He let go of Rory's hand and called: "Squonk? Colour Sergeant Moore is, as of this moment, transferred to the Royal Anglian Corps for an indefinite period. Arrange for his belongings to be collected and transported from his current billet to this location."

"Confirmed."

Rory's limbs began to tremble. He forced himself to remain calm, at least for as long as he stood in front of Hastings.

The general strode back to his desk. He opened a drawer out of Rory's sight. He hefted a bottle and asked: "A brandy to mark your joining our enterprise?"

"Ah," Rory said, suddenly feeling awkward. "I'm afraid I cannot partake, general."

"Whyever not?"

"Well," Rory said, deciding he could now be as open as he liked, "I almost got court martialled for drunkenness last year. Now, I have nanobots in my body that will knock me out if I so much as take a sip of proper booze. Sorry."

Hastings looked crestfallen for a moment. Then he asked: "Tell me, sergeant, was the cause a female?"

Rory nodded. "Yes, sir. A young lady I'd met and of whom I'd grown rather fond. She passed away suddenly."

"Perfectly understandable and nothing for which you should reproach yourself."

"Thank you, sir."

"Thank you for your candour, young man."

"If I may, sir. Could you now give me an idea of the mission?"

Hastings poured the translucent brown liquid into the snifter. "Very well," he said, screwing the cap back on the bottle. "It is quite straightforward, actually."

"Oh?"

He lifted his glass. "Yes. We're going to infiltrate six hundred kilometres into enemy territory, destroy his largest ACA production plant, and then escape without being detected. Should be a piece of cake. Cheers."

As Hastings drank, Rory's mouth fell open.

Chapter 33

06.05 Sunday 13 May 2063

Mark Phillips watched his sector of the English Channel with less than half of his available attention. In the last month, the enemy had made fewer than five sorties, all of them in sectors other than his, and all of them identified by the new local operators and stopped easily with batteries of Falaretes.

In the seven months since the Cumbre Vieja ridge had fallen into the Atlantic Ocean, Mark Phillips had searched in vain for proof that the enemy had caused the collapse and resulting tsunami. The objective still consumed much of his free time. The enemy must have brought the ridge down with explosives, so there must be evidence of how those weapons were transported or flown to the island.

He'd rowed with Cho about what she called his 'obsession'; he'd spoken to Simon as recently as a couple of weeks ago, and Simon had told him to reconsider his objective. But he'd made his intention clear that he would never stop seeking the proof. However, as time passed, he found himself merely revisiting the same records, scanning the same satellite imagery, making the same requests for other data streams that might shed light on what happened in the Canary Islands on that night the previous October.

In the meantime, 3rd Airspace Defence had also changed. Monitoring stations around the English coast had been built and staffed, so instead of just one central command in the heart of London, local operators also oversaw smaller sectors of the southern coast, acting as an extra layer of security. Fears that the enemy would deploy more advanced weapons were acknowledged and discussed at every review and update the unit had. So far, the fears remained unrealised.

A burst of white noise erupted over the Normandy coast, the sign that the enemy had decided to attack again. Mark's attention increased. He waited for the SHF burners to burn through the jamming. Would the oncoming machines be the same, or would this be an assault by something new and better?

In seconds, a corridor appeared and Squonk confirmed the signatures of the approaching ACAs indicated a core of twenty-seven thousand Blackswans screened by three thousand Lapwings. The force flew in at altitudes from ten thousand to forty thousand metres in a rotating geometric sequence that offered the best protection in the event of external attack.

"Okay," Mark said aloud, "why not dump another few thousand tons of scrap metal in the English Channel?"

The lead enemy machines streaked northwards high over the Channel, and Mark wondered if their target might be Essex or points further up the English coast. But as he watched, they suddenly veered to the west, and then turned further, bringing them onto a south-westerly heading towards north Kent. The bulk of the force followed the leading machines, looking like the paw of a huge bear turning to swipe angrily at the Thames and Medway estuaries. The enemy ACAs began their familiar, rapid descent.

Mark scoffed. "Oh, come on. Dudes, you are going to have to get up a lot earlier in the morning to catch us out like that. Dumbasses."

Squonk identified the most likely targets as numerous points along the coast of northern Kent, but Mark waited to see if the ACAs would ease to the right and make a beeline for the Thames estuary. They continued to plummet, thus revealing their intentions. As Mark followed them down in his view, they splayed out to attempt to attack locations from Gravesend in the west to Herne Bay in the east.

Mark said, "Squonk, open red-level comms to all local operators in the most likely target areas."

"Confirmed."

A distant voice inside Mark marvelled at how easy it was to follow the protocol Cho and Captain Shithead had trained him in. Any hesitation or nervousness simply didn't occur to Mark; he performed his role automatically.

Squonk said, "Open."

"Attention, operators. Tracking thirty thousand inbound. Standard signatures and approaches. Squonk will ready defences. Ensure notifications to local civil fire and rescue units. Allhallows, Grain, Sheerness and Sheppey, you are the first in line. Good luck, everyone."

Mark still thought his obligatory pep talk was mostly redundant—the computers would handle the defences better than any humans could, anyway—but Lieutenant Cho had explained that local civil defence operators were volunteers who'd only had the minimum of training, and having proper soldiers in support would reassure them. In addition, even if not wholly required at first glance, civil defence networks played a vital role at the local community level in helping people to cope. Mark thought that was rubbish, at best.

The lead Blackswans came within range and the copious Falarete batteries opened fire. Mark zoomed his view closer to ground level to see for himself, still bemused that the enemy came at them with the same weapons and the same tactics. One little Falarete would smash into a Blackswan to force its fifty Spiders to eject the frame, whereupon clouds of Falaretes would fall on the exposed Spiders. To Mark, the whole exercise seemed like a pointless turkey-shoo—

"Shit, I've got a problem," announced a nervous male voice edged in shrillness.

With deft flicks of his wrists and fingers, Mark zoomed to the speaker's location and opened a link: "Operator Rattenburg, what's the issue?"

"Er, sir, I've got refusal to fire on my Falarete batteries. It's never ha—"

"Okay, okay," Mark said in an effort to calm the man, who sounded older than himself. "Let's take a look at it. Squonk, why are the Falarete batteries in Sector 878 not engaging the enemy?"

Squonk replied, "There is a malfunction in the propulsion activation system."

"So fix it, now," Mark uttered, holding his temper.

"Negative. Diagnosis confirms a hardware issue that cannot be resolved remotely."

Mark instructed: "Compensate by directing alternative batteries to cover the break."

Rattenburg whined, "Oh God, we're not going to be able to stop them, are we?"

Mark replied, "There are quite a lot of batteries at your location."

Squonk said, "Alternative cover is in place, however there is now a possibility that less than one hundred percent of attacking enemy aircraft will be destroyed."

"What?" Mark exclaimed.

"Oh, no," Rattenburg said.

Mark reacted as quickly as he could. He saw that Operator Rattenburg was located at Rochester Cathedral. He instructed: "Squonk, comms to the duty officer at Rochester airfield, now."

"Confirmed. Stand by."

Mark watched the numbers drop: enemy machines flew into wave after wave of Falaretes and were destroyed. As he expected, some Blackswans and Lapwings climbed out of the kill zone, but this was a pointless tactic because as soon as they tried to attack again, the defences would get them.

Squonk said, "Open."

"Attention. This is 3rd Airspace Defence. You need to roll out replacement Falaretes to cover a gap in the screen. Your inventory shows you have over a thousand in hangar 7B. You need to get them unpacked now."

"Er, right," came a distracted voice. "You do know it's 6.30 on a Sunday morning, yeah?"

Mark held his temper. "Second Lieutenant Temple, you will certainly have inbound Blackswans in the next ninety seconds—"

In the background of Mark's audio, Lieutenant Rose Cho said, "Keep going, Mark. I'm getting Squonk to redirect mobile units."

Second Lieutenant Temple said, "There must be other batteries, right?"

With a swipe of his arm, Mark zoomed to the Medway Towns themselves to see the malfunctions involved all of the Falarete batteries stationed to defend Rochester, Chatham and Gillingham. From the streams of text data on his right, he noted they had all been produced by the same replicator. Somehow a glitch must have got in and gone unnoticed. Mark had never known something like this to happen before. Then again, his reason argued that millions of Falaretes had been produced, so the odds were that—

"Danger," Squonk announced. "The probability of Blackswans breaching the defences is now a certainty."

Mark swore and wondered how bad the damage would be.

Chapter 34

06.31 Sunday 13 May 2063

Pip raced for the armoury, adrenalin giving her legs a fleetness she didn't notice. She'd woken minutes earlier with an odd premonition and had activated her Squitch for her planned morning run. But when it informed her an attack was in progress, she knew the run would have to wait.

The view in her lens guided her to the building. She wished Squonk would shut off the surging two-tone alarm, as every soldier in Rochester barracks already knew what was happening.

She arrived at the armoury and slowed to a trot. The duty officer at the entrance gave a nervous salute and said, "Are you sure you need a weapon, ma'am?"

She pushed past him with, "Get out of my way, lieutenant." Her Squitch guided her to her weapon. She unclipped it, hurried to the racks of ammunition, grabbed six magazines and signed for them with a wink of her eye.

Knowing that the attack had begun with thirty thousand enemy ACAs approaching the north coast of Kent, she asked, raising her voice above the alarm: "How many have breached the defences?"

Her Squitch answered: "The battlespace is too dynamic to sustain a re—"

"So speculate," she hissed.

"From five to twenty enemy ACAs are anticipated to survive the defences."

"ETA?"

"Twenty-five to forty seconds."

"Christ, what about countermeasures?"

"Rim 214 missiles are standing by."

"They'll make no difference. Pulsars?"

"The nearest BSLs have insufficient elevation."

"So why don't you send up the protypes?"

"That information is classified."

Fury burned inside Pip. The windowless hangar at the northern edge of the airfield housed the new prototype ACAs. Everyone on the base knew, whether or not they'd seen them with their own eyes. Rumours had been swirling for days in the mess halls on the barracks that advanced tests were either planned or were being carried out in the dead of night.

The alarm shut off.

Pip stomped along the road cradling her Pickup. A hiss of air whooshed overhead and she shuddered on seeing a Blackswan so close. A dozen RIM 214 missiles streaked out from her left in pursuit.

"How many?" she asked.

"Fifteen enemy ACAs have survived the defences."

She stopped walking. "Comms to Major Pickard, now."

Pickard's terse voice spoke at once: "And what do you want, captain?"

"Why don't you send up the prototypes, sir?"

"Because it's already too late, not that it's any of your business."

She twitched her eye to end the connection and choked down an expletive. Her anger did not subside. Distant pops echoed on the air and thumps reverberated through the ground as the Blackswans delivered their lethal cargoes. Pip strode on, eventually reaching the hangar that housed NATO's new ACAs.

She stared at the building in frustration. Even a mere fifteen Blackswans carried seven hundred and fifty Spiders, every one of which could reduce several residential houses to rubble.

"Current status of attack?"

Her Squitch replied: "The attack is over; all enemy munitions have detonated."

"So, where's the invasion?"

"The highest probability is that this was a speculative attack not expected to succeed."

"Current status of defences?"

"The breach has been closed."

"With what?"

"One thousand PeaceMakers from Cox Heath airfield; two thousand, three hundred PeaceMakers from Maidstone barracks; seven hundred mobile Falarete batteries from—"

"That's enough." She looked into the hot, blue sky to see familiar dirty, black plumes of smoke rising from the south, and the air carried the distant wailing of emergency vehicles. She muttered, "This is total bullshit," as she turned to return her Pickup to the armoury.

Chapter 35

21.56 Monday 14 May 2063

Journalist Geoffrey Kenneth Morrow sat on the bar stool and listened to the technician talk. Geoff used to think he missed the part of his job that involved digging and having to work to find the story. But the last few hours had disabused him of this feeling.

Roland concluded his story with an affable smile, "Anyway, that's when she finally had enough. She packed her stuff and left me."

"Typical woman," Geoff sympathised, thinking that in her position, he would've left Roland far sooner.

"Yeah," Roland said, and drained his bottle. "Anyway, I best be on my way."

"Have another?" Geoff suggested. "My shout."

"Go on, then," Roland said with a shrug, his weathered face lifting in approval. He scratched the stubble on his cheek.

Geoff leaned around to catch the barman's eye. He called, "Another two beers over here, mate, yeah?" and received a nod of acknowledgment. He turned back to Roland

and finally made his pitch: "Listen, it's been great to chat. Like I said, I like meeting people, seeing as I'm new to the area."

"Yeah, you mentioned that."

"But I've got to admit, since my missus chucked me out, I've been struggling a bit for work. You know, I've been doing a lot on construction sites, but it's been months and the replicators are catching up now. And it's a bit heavy on my back, if I'm honest."

"You tried the military?" Roland asked.

"Leave off," Geoff said as the barman plonked two open bottles down on the bar in front of the men. "Do I look like a wannabe squaddie?"

Roland took the new bottle and waved it as he spoke, "No, no. I'm talking about civilian support roles. There's all kinds of work if you need some dough."

"Yeah?"

Roland swigged from his bottle and confirmed, "Sure. Listen, I work over the road at Rochester barracks—"

"Really?" Geoff broke in, feigning surprise. "I had no idea."

"Yeah, I'm a civilian techie. And I'm telling you, they're always looking for civies to do a bit of heavy lifting."

"Yeah, I heard that Rochester is a really big barracks now," Geoff said, wondering when he should really push, and how far he could do so without Roland getting suspicious.

"Bloody massive, now," Roland confirmed.

"So what do you do there? Anything interesting?"

Roland shook his head and replied: "Can't say. Official Secrets Act and all that, you know."

"Oh, right," Geoff said as his mind calculated. He asked himself if Roland had consumed enough beer or if Roland was simply the kind of man who took his obligations seriously. Then again, given what had happened with his wife—

"You know what?" Roland suddenly said, pointing a finger at Geoff.

"What?"

"I could tell you what I do, but then the SAS would have to kill you." Roland began chuckling and slapped his hand on the bar in celebration of his wit.

Geoff decided that it was now or never. "Go on, then. I'll take the risk of the SAS killing me."

Roland's lined face took on a look of secrecy between mates. Geoff's spirit soared in anticipation.

Roland said, "I'm a techie on the next-gen ACAs."

"No way," Geoff exclaimed, feigning amazement.

Roland took another swig from the bottle and Geoff saw more light reflect from the surface of the techie's eyes. Good.

Roland went on, "Yup. Seriously, I'd get in big trouble just for telling you, if it got back to my bosses."

"Nah," Geoff said, "you're all right with me, Roland. Like I said, I'm just looking for some work. Mind you, Rochester barracks seems a bit dodgy after what happened yesterday."

"Yeah, I know," Roland agreed. "But that was the army's fault."

"That's not what I heard, mate," Geoff said with an intentional, measured note of confrontation.

"Oh yeah?" Roland responded, his expression showing Geoff that he'd taken the bait.

"You bet," Geoff said. "Those Falaretes broke down. Nothing could be done. Heart-breaking to see Gillingham and Chatham suffer, but there really was nothing that could've helped them."

"Bollocks," Roland spat, and Geoff knew he had his man.

"You're just a techie. What do you know?" Geoff goaded.

"Plenty."

"Leave off."

"I'm telling you, Kenny, they could've stopped that attack yesterday morning."

"No, they couldn't," Geoff said dismissively. "I think you've had enough to drink, young Roland." Geoff lifted his own bottle and drank, closing his eyes and praying that Roland wouldn't suspect.

Roland declared: "I ain't a liar, mate."

Geoff knew what to do next. "Of course not. I didn't mean anything, fella. Look, let's call it a night, eh? It's happened and that's that. I tell you what. I'm going to go to the barracks first thing tomorrow morning, and if I can get a berth, I'll buy the drinks tomorrow after work. How does that sound?"

Mollified, Roland said: "Yeah, that sounds all right. But I meant what I said, you know. They could've stopped yesterday, stopped it happening all together."

The need to find out burned inside Geoff, but he had to dangle the pilchard just a little longer. He said: "I believe you, but come on, I don't want you getting in any trouble. Best let's just call it a night, eh?"

"Yeah, you're right, Kenny," Roland said, standing and draining his bottle.

Geoff did the same, silently thanking the man for the reminder that Geoff had used his middle name for this sting.

Geoff followed Roland around tables and out of the pub. The door clanged shut. Outside on the pavement in the warm evening air, Geoff said, "Anyway, I'm just glad we've finally got some new weapons, that's the main thing."

"Which way you going?" Roland asked.

Geoff shook his head. "I dunno. I fancy walk. I can go your way."

"Okay, I've got digs up on the hill. You can see two of the smashed bridges from there."

Geoff smiled and they began walking.

"Yeah," Roland said, "but they could've stopped it."

"Really?"

"Yeah, wankers. We had four X–7s powered up."

"You're joking?"

"Nah, wankers," Roland repeated.

Geoff stayed silent.

Roland went on: "We had advanced field testing due to start at exactly 6.30, just when those Falaretes failed."

"Maybe the X–7s weren't armed, so there would've been no point?"

Roland gave Geoff a sideways look. "They've got a massive new Pulsar in their bodies. They were armed all right."

"Wow," Geoff said. "I never would've guessed." Geoff's amazement was genuine: he'd been hoping to get confirmation only that the next-gen weapons were on the base. He did not expect that they had actually been ready to go.

They walked on in silence for a while. They reached the river Medway and Roland pointed at the destruction there, "See?" he said.

The road and rail bridges that had run parallel across the river now lay slumped like sleeping drunks with their bodies in the dark water.

"Where's the construction replicators?" Geoff asked.

"Probably still busy elsewhere, I expect."

"Yeah, the hospitals took a pounding, I heard."

Roland sighed. "Anyway, I shouldn't have told you that. You'll keep it to yourself, won't you? I'd be in real trouble otherwise."

"Yeah," Geoff said in feigned friendliness. "Don't worry, buddy. I'll get some work there and the drinks will be on me tomorrow. Deal?"

Roland smiled the same affable smile and stuck out his hand. "Deal."

Geoff shook it. "Listen, I really appreciate your help."

"Ah, come on. Just go to the barracks in the morning and ask."

"I will," Geoff said. "Take care of yourself, fella."

"You too, Kenny."

Geoff turned and walked away as quickly as he could. In his lens, he called up transport options to get him back to London, but there were none. With the bridges over the Medway down, he'd have to return via Maidstone, and nothing was free until the morning. He flicked through options and booked a hostel close by. With instant acceptance and directions, he crossed the street and turned left into another residential area.

He then called up the recording of the evening's conversation with Roland and edited it as he walked, cutting all of the earlier guff about how Roland's put-upon wife had finally seen sense and left him, and then trimming down the rest of it to make it as incriminating as possible.

He turned right into another bland street of terraced houses. He called Alan.

"What's up, Geoff?"

Geoff couldn't help himself: "I have got the scoop of the year. Do you want me to write it, or do you want to see the recording and have the AI or a staffer write up the copy?"

"Piss off with the histrionics, Geoff. You sound like my wife when she forgets to update the menopause bots in her system."

"Alan, let's have a little respect, yeah? I've got a recording of a techie at Rochester barracks admitting that the new ACAs were there yesterday morning and ready to go. The army could've stopped that attack yesterday if they'd wanted to."

There came a pause. Geoff turned into the next residential street, irrationally beginning to hate the uniformity of the houses. He felt as though he were stuck in an endless warren of clichéd suburbia.

"Well?" he asked.

Alan said, "Okay, send it over. If it's as hot as you say, I'll write the copy myself."

"Good," Geoff said, sending the recording at the same time he terminated the connection.

Geoff reached the local hostel he'd found to stay the night before heading back to London in the morning. He reconsidered: perhaps the old-fashioned ways of getting the story weren't so bad after all?

Chapter 36

10.12 Tuesday 15 May 2063

Dahra Napier closed her eyes in concentration. She spoke softly: "Thank you, Terry, for coming here."

Terry Tidbury replied: "It's no trouble, PM."

She opened her eyes and looked into the field marshal's face. On purpose, she sat behind the desk in her main Downing Street office, instead of using the living area in the flat for a more informal atmosphere. For the first time since the war had begun, she did not want the atmosphere between her and her commander-in-chief to be informal.

Terry stood on the other side of the desk in his combat fatigues. Even now, over a year into this godawful war, Terry appeared indomitable. His face carried an expression of professional patience, and standing there with his legs slightly apart and hands behind his back in the military fashion, she thought he could have been hewn from granite.

She said, "You probably know the reason why I asked you here."

"Things are a little... hectic? right now, PM. We have many logistical and other—"

"Sorry," Dahra broke in, not at all sorry. "I'll make the question plain: do you know why I asked you here this morning?"

Terry remained unfazed. "My best guess is the enemy's successful attack on the Medway Towns two days ago."

"Yes, at least obliquely."

Terry said nothing.

"I know you have much to deal with, field marshal. But, then again, so have I."

"Yes, PM."

"My office had to put an R-notice on a story dug up by some hack journalist supposedly working for *The Guardian*. When that outlet wouldn't run it, he hawked it about until, surprise, surprise, those vultures at *The Mail* picked it up and tried to run it. Crispin became quite agitated until we spiked it for them. But of course, by then it was too late. We've managed to limit the damage; officially, the Scythes were there but not ready to fly, so they couldn't've helped, even though that's not the truth."

Terry's head dipped and he said, "I'm sorry, PM, but I don't see what this has to do with me or military matters in general. As far as I recall, I also have a press officer but my adjutant deals with him as I do not have the time."

"The story centred on a technician at Rochester barracks who was recorded saying that the new Scythe ACAs were present on the airfield and could have been used to stop the fifteen Blackswans that managed to break through the defences on Sunday morning, and which proceeded to cause over eighteen thousand casualties."

"That claim is true," Terry said.

"What?" Dahra exclaimed, not expecting such a blunt admission, at least until a voice in her head pointed out that Terry was not a politician. "You mean we could've stopped that attack?"

"Yes," Terry said flatly. "Although, I suspect the Scythes might not have been quick enough to destroy all of them."

Dahra fought to control her anger. "So why didn't they, field marshal?"

"Op-sec."

"What the hell is that?" she asked, furious that he should try to gain an edge by using one of his military terms.

Terry's face betrayed no emotion. He replied: "It is a portmanteau, made from 'operational' and 'security'. And what that means, PM, is that the Scythe ACAs will not be deployed in any live combat situation until the commencement of Operation Repulse—in any circumstances."

Dahra felt the breath escape her lungs but needed some seconds before she could draw more air in. "But," she protested, shaking her head, "over six thousand people were killed on Sunday, and twice as many again were injured."

The expression on Terry's face did not change.

"Did you see any of the feeds?" she asked in exasperation. "All of the residential nurses' blocks at Medway hospital were brought down; entire streets were levelled. And because it was all so sudden, the people had almost no warning."

"PM, those people died due to a malfunction in the Falarete defences. Given that since last July, we have replicated and deployed millions of those lifesaving defences, I think something like this was bound to happen the longer the defence of these islands continued."

Dahra put her index finger to her temple and repeated: "But you could have stopped it. And you didn't."

"Not quite, PM."

"'Not quite'?" Dahra echoed.

"Firstly, it was a remarkable coincidence that the enemy commenced such an attack at all, at that location. The Channel has been relatively quiet, with only nuisance missions to probe our defences. Like the invasions last August, I'm tempted to speculate that what we would regard as the enemy's normal chain of command was not followed or was bypassed on Sunday morning. Secondly, it did not matter where this happened, PM. Those Blackswans might have been about to deliver a Spider in through my own front door, and I can assure you, I would not have allowed the Scythes to launch."

"Really?"

"Yes, because of op-sec. The enemy must not have any advance notice of what we will attack them with a few months from now. We are already walking the tightest of tightropes given that the enemy may yet surprise us with his own next-generation ACAs. The very last thing we can afford is to give him the slightest clue of what we have. If I had approved the launch of those Scythes on Sunday morning, then before they destroyed their targets, those targets would have relayed the Scythes' design, their flight characteristics, and the power of the weapon attacking them, back to the enemy's computers. Thus informed, the enemy would have ample time to develop countermeasures in advance of Repulse's start date in October."

"So, you thought those civilians were expendable, yes?"

"I don't judge the value of any life, PM. My superiors—which include you—have tasked me first with defending England and the Home Countries, and second with recovering Europe from the enemy. I must therefore decide how best to do that. An important part of any campaign is op-sec. Choices are not always straightforward; compromises must be struck. Operation Repulse will involve over two million NATO troops—just to begin with—recovering what is currently enemy-held territory, and I intend to lose as few of those troops as possible. This is for two main reasons. The first is, obviously, humanitarian. But the second is strategic.

Even if Repulse succeeds, which remains a vast unknown, I foresee the potential for further confrontation. And in that case, we need to preserve as much of our armies as we can."

Dahra sighed. Unable to fault her field marshal's logic, her anger and frustration at the loss of life, after so many lives had been lost in this bloody war, melted into melancholy. She said, "I see."

"I hope you do, PM. This is not about some lives being worth more than others; it's about strategy. And a good strategy has to be constructed as dispassionately as possible. Once we allow raw emotion to control our decisions, our success rate in every endeavour will invariably plummet. If I, as you seem to wish, had authorised those Scythes to intercede in that battle, that would've set in motion a sequence of events that would certainly cost us more troops when battle is joined. I'm afraid the cold truth is that that does not make strategic sense."

"Terry," she began, tucking her hair behind her ear, "I am the leader of this country. After more than a year of this vicious war that no one asked for, and after so many tragedies, I find even one more death that might have been avoided to be, somehow, an even worse tragedy. Yes, yes, you're a soldier doing your job—and what a 'job' you have, I know that. But I am the one who must look ordinary people in the eye, people who've suffered, and tell them that the loved one they've lost did not die in vain.

"I have to convince them that their country will continue the fight, that we will never surrender. Tomorrow, I'm going to visit Medway hospital. They lost over three hundred nurses in those accommodation blocks, young men and women with their whole lives in front of them. And the rumours that the British Army could've stopped it are already out there, over all of the platforms, despite the R-notice. What do you suggest I tell their parents, their sibling, their friends?"

Terry drew in a deep breath. "I don't really know, PM, but my best guess would be to tell them what you've just told me. We will continue; we will persevere. But the true cause of the pain of their loss is not any failure to deploy the Scythes. It is, and will always remain, the enemy. Those people were killed by enemy Spiders, like tens of thousands before them since last year."

Dahra watched Terry and the notion came to her that, perhaps, there were greater considerations under his hard, military exterior. She said, "So I must be the velvet glove around your iron fist, field marshal, yes?"

She saw confusion crease his forehead.

He said: "I'm not sure what you mean, PM. I'm a soldier, trying to execute my orders to the best of my ability, and the abilities of those under my command."

Dahra felt the moment vanish like the scent of a blooming rose on a breezy day. Not wishing to cause any awkwardness, she said: "Of course, and I value your skill and counsel, and always will do."

"That's good of you to say so."

"Thank you again for coming over, Terry. There's one more thing before you go."

"Yes, PM?"

"I had a catch-up with the American ambassador yesterday, and he said there is growing momentum among the American military to bring the commencement date for Operation Repulse forward by some time."

"Oh?" Terry said.

"Yes, I thought you should know. Goodbye for now, field marshal."

"Right. Yes, that's not the first I've heard of it. But thank you, PM."

Terry turned and left Dahra's office. The door clicked closed and she exhaled for several seconds. Her thoughts roamed over the conversation as she tried to see what had happened in the Medway Towns as Terry might see it—

"Boss?" Crispin said, throwing the door open. "I saw the field marshal go. We've got a lot of ground to cover. Loads of platforms are claiming—"

Dahra stopped Crispin with a wave of her hand. "Listen to me. I want you, or someone else we can trust in this building, to take every single step possible to eliminate every bloody trace of the fact that what happened to the Medway Towns two days ago could or might or would have been stopped or avoided by those new ACAs that are still subject to tests. Understood?"

"Er, okay. If that's what you want, boss."

"Yes, that is precisely what I want," Dahra said.

Crispin nodded and made to leave, but Dahra stopped him with: "Come in and close the door."

He did so.

An observation struck her and she asked: "Is your hairline receding, Crispin?"

A look of irony crossed her director of communications' hurried face. "We're none of us getting any younger, boss."

"Quite. Anyway, I also want you to use all of your skills to ensure a 'nothing could really be done' narrative."

"Right."

"I don't want any negative press against Terry, as much as you can influence, okay?"

"I'll do my best, boss."

Chapter 37

07.53 Friday 25 May 2063

Terry accepted the mug of tea absentmindedly and said, "Thank you, Simms." He glanced up at the screen in the wall of his office in the War Rooms, lost in concentration at how to best deliver the information he would shortly divulge.

"Would you like me to remain here, sir, in case you need anything?"

"I'm not sure. How's the workload out there?" Terry asked, indicating the main operations area outside his office.

"Manageable," Simms replied with a reassuring nod.

"I'm still irked at the way the Americans have behaved in this case."

"It was an intense meeting on Tuesday, sir. I believe you made the correct choice."

Terry looked up at his adjutant in surprise. "They gave me no choice," he protested. "The way they dropped the data was intentionally designed to leave me no other options. Really, Simms, that woman in Downing Street and that other woman in the White House have been playing some silly game of one-upmanship—or perhaps I should say 'one-up-womanship' that placed me in a wholly invidious position."

"Sir, you are SACEUR. You do have the final say on military matters."

"Hmm," Terry scoffed. "Easy to say. Not so easy to pull rank on European generals who've seen their countries destroyed, who do not know anything that has happened in those countries for the better part of a year, and who are straining at the leash to get back and avenge that loss."

"Indeed," Simms agreed.

"And that master sergeant in the USAF, what was his name, Carter? He was a wily fox to pull that stunt."

"Perhaps the Americans felt that simply asking you would not have been successful?"

"And they would've been right," Terry confirmed.

Simms said nothing.

"Anyway, here we go. You double-checked the attendance list?"

"Yes, sir. All permitted ranks have been notified and confirmed, as we might expect."

"And with more personnel finding out, so the risk of a breach of security increases."

Simms again kept quiet, and Terry appreciated once more how his adjutant knew just when to offer as much counsel as Terry needed, and no more.

In the screen, thumbnails of the authorised attendees resolved. In a moment, layers in the screen held hundreds of faces of all outlines, features, hairstyles and skin tones, but each of which shared one thing: an expression of professionalism. Looking from the generals Terry had briefed in March, to each colonel and lieutenant colonel, a wave of pride rippled through him. He considered that, given the increase in average sizes of battalions and regiments, most of the colonels in the screen would in peacetime expect to be at the rank of general.

"Good morning, everyone," Terry began. "As you might have heard over the last few months, we have been putting together a plan to hopefully give the enemy an unpleasant little shock. As we all know, the enemy has for some time now regarded Europe as defeated. To a degree, he is of course correct. However, you will be pleased to hear that we do indeed have a plan to eject him from our home and regain Europe. This was presented to senior ranks in its initial form last year, and the next, more detailed version, was presented to them in March. Now, I will describe to you precisely what this plan, called Operation Repulse, means for your regiments and battalions."

Over the next twenty minutes, Terry set out an enhanced description of the same information he had given his generals in the previous March, including the key regiments, battalions and specialist units that would constitute Attack Group East and Attack Group South.

On completing this briefing, Terry announced: "Originally, the start date for Operation Repulse had been 1 October this year. However, due to several factors, including the efficiency of the United States Navy, deliveries of supplies from other NATO allies, and the high level of England and the Home Countries' production facilities, at a sitrep meeting two days ago, the decision was taken to bring this start date forward to 1 August, a little over nine weeks from today."

Terry kept his face blank. He would still have preferred to keep the start date where it was, but political and diplomatic necessity forced him to accede to the Americans' demand. Repulse could not succeed without them, and the state of Coll's and Napier's failing relationship meant he could not rely on any leverage from that direction. So, for the sake of NATO unity and effectiveness once battle commenced, he compromised. But that didn't mean he was happy about it.

Terry went on: "Given this, each of you can expect to see increases in both supply deliveries and movement of kit and personnel. I need hardly remind you of the need for opsec. In particular, all details of the Scythes must remain top secret. You may not begin briefing your subordinates on the details of Repulse until Squonk gives you authorisation. While we remain confident that knowledge of Repulse has not escaped to our enemies, we cannot be certain. I believe it is important not to forget that this war began last year with a massive, unprecedented failure of intel.

"Finally, I once again urge all of you to continue performing your vital roles in this crisis to the outstandingly high level you have been to date. Any army is only as good as its commanders—at all levels. Morale, discipline and comradeship are the three pillars on which we will build our ability to return to the battlefield with confidence. I have shown you what Operation Repulse entails. The way forward. The way to take back that which was taken from us. You too can now see how we can achieve this.

"The next nine weeks will pass quickly. We will have regular updates and I will appraise you of the key strategic developments as the start date approaches. Your corps and other commanders are ready to assist you with any concerns you might have at battalion level. In the meantime, please maintain the morale, discipline and comradeship of the troops under your commands at the high level we need if Repulse is to succeed. Thank you. That's all for now."

The screen went blank and Terry sighed. He sipped his tea, glanced at Simms, and asked: "Not too clichéd?"

Simms shook his head and replied: "Not at all, sir. I think the strongest emotion will be relief. Finally, they have something to go at, as it were."

"I would've preferred more of the operation to take place in the colder months. It's going to be bloody hot on the continent in August, in more ways than one, and I think that will better suit the enemy."

"On the other hand," Simms offered, "given that our logistics' capabilities will support the earlier start date, it may work in our favour."

"Because it will increase the element of surprise?"

"Precisely, sir."

Terry finished his tea and put the mug down on his desk. He made for the door, saying, "As long as we can keep that, and those blasted Chinese don't get wind of this."

Terry entered the main War Room and glanced at the various situation screens. They displayed standard statistics and no unusual enemy movement from the mainland. Terry realised that he had to contact General Hastings and discuss the new date for Repulse. Hastings thought he had until the end of September to train his team. Thunderclap was due to be executed the day before Repulse began. Now, that would have to change—

Simms broke into his thoughts, "Sir, your next appointment is with Adjutant-General Sir William Chase. I believe you asked me to organise a discreet table in the mess hall."

"Bill Chase? Good, I like him. He has a much better grasp of the detail than I. When is it?"

"At nine o-clock, sir."

"Very well. What else have I got today?"

"COBRA at ten; generals' conference at eleven; your next private meeting with the PM at midday. Then, at fourteen-hundred, there's a tech presentation on the latest SkyMaster performance results. Shall I cancel your attendance for that?"

"No, I want to know the differences between the SkyWatcher and the SkyMaster. It has to be able to manage the Scythes on the battlefield, and I want to know how it's going to do that."

"Very good, sir. Then, from sixteen-hundred is your Q&A with the mid-level ranks you just addressed, before a meeting with the generals of surviving European forces—"

"How many issues has Pakla raised so far?"

"Six."

Terry shook his head. "I sometimes wonder where we'd be without soldiers like Pakla, but he can be demanding."

"And then, from nineteen-hundred, you will be free to deal with business that arises during the day."

"Anything from Hastings?"

"Not since his update on Monday, no sir."

"Hmm. I need to talk to him soon, Simms. He and his team no longer have the time we thought they had."

Chapter 38

14.45 Wednesday 6 June 2063

The powerful, burning sun of an English summer afternoon bore down on the group of five men. Sitting out in the heat constituted part of their training for Operation Thunderclap. Beyond the spindly trees that struggled to grow leaves, a long, wide lake reflected the light.

Rory Moore looked into Captain Harry Dixon's blue eyes and asked: "Have you ever been inside a real submarine?"

"No. Not yet, anyway," Harry replied.

"I have, and it's bloody awful."

"Really?"

"The bunks are miniscule and the metal latrines have literally zero room for manoeuvre."

"Yes, but you are quite a large fellow, aren't you?"

"No," Rory said, shaking his head. "I'm normal; everyone else is small. I live in a world designed by, built for, and full of, pygmies."

"Very droll. So when were you on a sub?"

"Last year. Me and a pal managed to get out of Spain on the *Spiteful*."

"Nick mentioned that," Harry said, nodding to the edge of the lake where the other three men stood, deep in discussion. "Said you've been in this war since the whole thing kicked off."

Harry's voice irritated Rory. The 'off' came out as 'orf' which made the man sound like a snob.

A new voice spoke: "All right, lads? I think the guvnor is about ready for us all to get soakin' wet again."

Rory turned and smiled at Nick Bird, the team's navigator, as he came bounding up to the table. Wide cheekbones and a light voice made Nick come across as the easiest-going of the whole team. "Christ," Rory complained, "have we got to do that again?"

Harry said, "It'll be a few more times yet, old boy. The general's got the wind in his sails, especially now the start date's been brought forward."

"Come on," Nick encouraged, "it's really hot out in the sun anyway. We'll cool off in the water."

Rory smiled at Nick's pronunciation, where 'water' sounded like 'ward-er'. "Yeah, come on," Rory said with a trace of sarcasm, "let's go and do the same bloody thing we've already done twenty times, yet again."

Rory and Harry stood and followed Nick down to the water. At the edge of the lake stood the slender, upright General Hastings, hands clasped behind his back. He addressed a short, wiry figure next to him. All of the four younger men wore only swimming trunks with wide belts around their stomachs, while Hastings observed them in his fatigues and a military green T-shirt. Rory felt like pointing out that on the mission, the general would have to swim with the rest of them, so he might as well get his trunks on too, but decided against it.

Hastings was talking, "…packaging should be more than sufficient to keep everything dry."

The young, wiry man next to Hastings, called Declan Gardner, said in an Irish brogue, "Buoyancy will be a key issue as well. It's a lot of weight to be taking ashore."

Hastings turned to the arrivals. "Good, that's your sauna break over. Now, we do it all over again. And this time, do try to be quicker. The submarine will not be able to stay on the surface for more than a few minutes. We will need to get out of it and tow our kit away sharply. Off you go."

Rory waded into the water. Its warmth caressed his lower legs before he pushed on to the cooler water further out. He swam towards a pontoon anchored thirty or more metres from the shore, hearing the splashes made by the others following. After a few minutes of pulling himself through the water with a powerful breaststroke, he reached the pontoon and heaved himself up on it with ease, appreciating this effect of his body's deep clean at the Advanced Medical Research Establishment the previous year, which in turn provoked an image of Georgina's smile and her smooth skin—

"Oi, fella," Nick called from the water. "Give us an 'and up, will yer?"

Rory leaned down, grasped Nick's forearm, and pulled him up. Next to him, Declan climbed out with a roll of his hair-covered body. Last was Harry Dixon, whom Rory also helped from the water. From the other side of the pontoon came the sound of wood rubbing on crutch as four large rowing boats withdrew, having returned the kit from the shore to the pontoon. Rory looked at the kit and let out a heavy sigh. Eight cylindrical equipment tubes as tall as him stood pointing upwards on the slats of the pontoon, dripping water.

"Okay, chaps," Harry began with a clap of his hands. "Let's do this again. This is one of the trickiest parts of the whole mission. We will exit the submarine with the kit through the aft hatch." As he spoke, he leaned down and retrieved a heavy coiled rope from which hung further strips of material that ended in carabiner clips. He went on: "Once out of the sub but before we get in the water, we attach the lanyards on the cable to the nose of each cylinder, and then the belt around our trunks. We'll only have moments." He hurried to the far end of the row of cylinders.

Rory followed him, taking up position in front of his own pair of cylinders. He turned to his right to see Nick next to him and then Declan's hairy torso and legs at the far end of the row of cylinders, each man responsible for two cylinders.

From the shore, Hastings shouted: "Stand by. Give me your mark, Dixon."

"Ready?" Harry called. "Now!" he yelled, and slung the coiled rope over to Rory. Rory caught it deftly, turned and threw it to Nick, who caught and tossed it on to Declan at the end.

"Clip on," Harry yelled.

Rory grabbed two of the three carabiner clips and snapped them onto the rings protruding from the nose of each cylinder.

"Lay the cylinders down," Harry ordered.

Rory took care but worked quickly to lay his two cylinders on the pontoon, noting the others do the same. As they rested parallel with the slats from which the pontoon was made, the cylinders did not roll.

"At the rear, push off."

Rory stepped backwards, and from the rear pushed the first cylinder into the water and then the other.

"And get to the shore, now!" Harry shouted, leaping into the water.

Rory threw himself off the pontoon and into the cooling water. He broke the surface ahead of his two cylinders, located the third lanyard with its carabiner clip and snapped it closed on one of the loops on the wide belt around his trunks. Then he turned for the shore and swam, one part of a four-man line splashing frantically to tow the eight cylinders through the water.

Six minutes later, Rory lay on his back on the warm grass heaving for breath. The others lay to his left and right, while silhouetted by the bright blue sky, Hastings paced back and forth. The general said: "A modest improvement; fifteen seconds faster than last time. Any more thoughts, men?"

Rory sat up and said, "Sir?"

"Yes?"

"I really do not think it is realistic enough to make these timings useful. We have those slats on the pontoons that stop the cylinders rolling."

Nick pitched in, "And if there's even a slight swell on the sea, we won't be able to link anything to anything on the hull of a sub."

Hastings nodded and said, "Yes, your observations are relevant. The purpose today is to see if this method itself is doable. We still have time to refine, gentlemen, although not a great deal since our departure date has been brought forward."

Harry pushed himself up onto his elbows and offered: "Can't the damn sub just shoot the things out through its torpedo tubes?"

Hastings shook his head. "Unfortunately not, due to the increased risk of detection. We have to be as silent as possible."

"So," Harry persevered, "can't they not fire them out as such, but just give them a gentle shove?"

"Yeah," Nick said, "they can open the outer hatch while a rating pushes them out from the inside of the sub."

A wave of good-natured chuckles floated off the water.

"Another thing," Declan said, "is that even if we could be getting the kit out through the tubes, we'd have the devil's own job getting them cylinders back to the shore. A sub is not exactly a small thing. Are you with me?"

Hastings said, "There's no question, the kit has to come up through the hatch and we have to come off the sub's hull with it and tow it to shore. And we must do so under our own steam, as it were."

"I wish we could use inflatables to tow the cylinders to shore," Rory said.

"Not possible due to the need for motors on the back of them," Hastings said.

"So at the very least," Harry said, "we need something on those cylinders that will stop them rolling us flat like pastry under a rolling pin if there's a swell, but which will still let us pull them off the hull cleanly."

"Acknowledged. Very good. Time for another sauna. Thirty minutes sitting in the sun. If anyone starts burning, put your T-shirt on."

With the others, Rory got to his feet and walked up the incline to the bench. He found himself alongside Declan, and said to the wiry Irishman, "Bet you can't wait to get back to assembling the bikes."

Declan flicked Rory a disinterested look. "It's all the same to me. This whole mission is gonna be a beast."

"Yeah, you're probably right. So why are you here, then?"

Declan's eyes widened. "Not for the same reason as you, no? Did the general over there not make you an offer you couldn't refuse?"

"Something like that."

"I'm sure, Rory. He gets me in his nice, plush office and says he needs an expert in old types of transport. I tells him, aye, I'm a right enthusiast. I got the permits and can even get petrol and oil when I need it. But my first love is a Harley Davidson. Do you know what that is?"

Rory shook his head and offered, "An old type of car?"

Declan scoffed. "Be off, fella. It's a great motorbike, the greatest. And what does the general get me on his team to do? Put together a lousy Triumph." Declan spat the name out as though he'd never ordinarily lower himself to touching one.

"What's up, then? Are they no good?"

They reached the bench next to the table and sat. Declan conceded, "It's true they're lighter than the Harleys—although I'd never have one of the things in my garage, mind you."

Nick also reached the table and sat. "Stone me, don't set him off on the bikes thing again."

Rory shrugged, confused, "Again? First time he's mentioned it to me."

Nick said, "There ain't a lot wrong with those Triumphs—"

"But not much right, either, it has to be said," Declan broke in.

"As long as you can get us to the job, Nick, right?" Rory said.

"You betcha," Nick replied with confidence. "I can navigate by the stars if I have to."

Harry Dixon came up to the table and announced: "The general has decided to reward you for your efforts today, chaps."

Nick said, "What's the guvnor decided we're worth?"

"Well," Harry replied, "in keeping with our intensive training programme prior to our deployment, he wants me to let you know you've earned an extra twenty-five millilitres of water to drink today, which I think is very generous of him."

Rory watched as Nick's face fell in a manner reflecting his own disappointment.

Chapter 39

19.45 Monday 11 June 2063

Crispin Webb could not recall the last time he had been so shocked, so wholly stunned, that he'd nearly forgotten to breathe. A distant memory recalled the heart attack he'd suffered the previous year, but his reaction then had been surprise rather than shock.

On this remarkable evening, in the last forty-five minutes, he'd sat through a presentation which he thought would've made a fabulous—not to mention hilarious—comedy routine delivered by one of those hip young things in a dark London club of the kind in which Crispin used to go cruising before the war.

He stood at the back of the living area of the flat in Ten Downing Street. The boss reposed on the soft couch in front of him. Charles Blackwood, looking as gorgeous as ever in a smooth, grey suit, and Liam Burton, were the only others present, given the utmost security attached to the mission.

Crispin wondered if the need for such secrecy was driven by a desire to protect the safety of those involved, or to save embarrassment at the fact that the British Army could or would undertake such an insane objective.

In front of the three most important politicians in England, one of Terry Tidbury's generals had described a ludicrous plan to invade, almost singlehandedly, the mighty, undefeated New Persian Caliphate, and attack one of its huge weapons' manufacturing plants, destroying it to prevent the enemy reinforcing when Operation Repulse began, and thus assisting the many hundreds of thousands of NATO troops who, in a few weeks, would try to turn the tide in this awful war.

The soldier, called Hastings, had sounded professional enough, and unlike many people who had to present to the boss, he had no problem delivering his message in the most succinct way. He'd suffered no trembling nerves or dry throat. But to Crispin, that erudition had been the cause of such overwhelming disbelief.

The image in the screen above the fireplace faded out to be replaced with the portcullis placeholder of the English government.

Hastings, thin and straight-backed and sporting a little, pencil-thin moustache, glanced at each of the politicians and asked: "Does anyone have a question regarding Operation Thunderclap?"

Crispin had to stop himself from asking why 'Thunderclap' and not 'Pointless Suicide' instead?

The boss leaned forward. "How long will *Spiteful* wait before concluding that your unit, or certain members of your unit, are not going to return, and will then leave the North African coast and return to England?"

Hastings replied, "A maximum of five days after the team is due back, irrespective of whether Thunderclap succeeds or fails."

The youthful defence minister, Liam Burton, said, "But the sub won't know if the mission succeeds or fails, will it?"

Hastings replied: "That is correct. sir. As I mentioned during my presentation, if the sonic mines perform as designed and as we expect them to, then seismic monitoring stations within a few thousand kilometres should easily detect the resulting destruction of the weapons' production facility, so the world will know if the mission is a success. Regarding the submarine, it need only wait until the time limit means that our water has run out."

Liam said, "I think those masks you're taking—what did you call them, moisturisers?—that's a smart thing."

"Thank you, minister," Hastings replied. "The moisturisers can extend our water supply, albeit nowhere near as effectively as a water replicator would. In any case, five days is the upper limit. If any team members have not reached the rendezvous by then, they will certainly not be able to."

"I must say," Charles said, tugging on his cufflinked shirtsleeve, "you do seem to have thought of everything."

Hastings' face creased. "We endeavour to do so. Not only must Operation Thunderclap succeed, but, I can assure you, we'd all quite like to make it back home afterwards."

Crispin smiled along with the others at the mad general's lame attempt at humour.

Terry said, "If that's all, PM?"

Napier stood. "General Hastings, thank you for your presentation." She stepped forward to shake his hand. "On behalf of the whole country, I want to wish you and your team the very best of luck, a successful mission, and a safe return."

Hastings' face reddened in a blush. He tipped his head forward and mumbled, "Thank you, prime minister. I shall convey your kind words to my team."

"Please do so," she replied.

Charles and Liam also stood, shook the general's hand, and wished him and the mission luck.

Terry nodded to the room and steered Hastings out through the heavy oak door. When it clicked shut behind the two military men, everyone exhaled.

Liam said, "Rather him than me. Pretty sure I wouldn't sign up for a mission like that."

"Nonsense," Charles admonished, "we need men like him to do deeds like that if we're ever going to succeed."

The boss said, "I think it's incredibly brave of them. Don't you agree, Crispin?"

Caught off guard, Crispin stammered, "What? Er, yes, of course. Very brave."

Liam said, "Do you really think that tech will work? I mean, it looks good in the screen like that, but it does seem to be asking a great deal to reduce a huge production facility to rubble, doesn't it?"

Charles tutted. "The science behind it is good. The key issue is if those mines will work once they've been knocking around in a sub for ten days, and then spend a further twelve hours bouncing around on the back of a motorbike. The design of the mine looks a little delicate to me, somehow."

Liam said, "I think their kit will work fine. Trust me, a soldier always makes sure his kit is in the best possible shape, especially if there's any special risk attached to the mission. My concern is the distance and the heat involved. The Sahara is like a furnace. Those moisturisers look all right if they can really extend the water they'll carry by as much as he claims, but I see a real risk there. If any of them end up dehydrating, they'll be finished pretty smartly."

The boss said, "As General Hastings mentioned, they only have six weeks before they embark on the submarine, and before then they need to test the mines and all of their other equipment thoroughly. But you know, I actually think they can pull it off."

Charles said, "If Operation Repulse is to succeed, so must they. That much is certain."

Crispin looked from the boss to the foreign secretary and then to the defence secretary, staggered that otherwise rational people could delude themselves in such a fashion. He hoped, wished and prayed that NATO forces would go crashing back into Europe and give those 'warriors' a taste of their own medicine, but it would mean those new ACAs doing the job ahead of the soldiers. Crispin shook his head, convinced Hastings and his madcap plan were destined to end in soon-forgotten ignominy.

Chapter 40

00.34 Thursday 28 June 2063

The Englishman lay back on the soft bed with the most overwhelming sensation of fulfilment he could recall for many months. Qianfan had made him feel so incredibly complete. The Englishman kept as still as he could in the silent darkness and barely breathed. He waited for Qianfan's breathing to become more regular after their delightful nocturnal exertions.

The Englishman had been supplying Qianfan with narcotics for weeks. Along with Hu and Fen, the Englishman now had a fabulous bed of information to mine—not to mention three beds for recreation. Both Qianfan and Hu were slim and muscular, and he enjoyed each for his enthusiastic curiosity. Qianfan was quieter; Hu more boisterous. But both men were also typical of the lower ranks in Chinese intelligence: unimaginative and generally unsupervised because they owed their jobs to family connections, not merit.

Fen was different. The Englishman had never enjoyed the female body as much as the male, but inside Fen was a man, and she knew it. She also liked to spar, even to playfight to an extreme that the Englishman did not appreciate. Since the torture he'd endured the previous year, he'd done everything to avoid unnecessary pain. Besides which, he could not afford to carry fresh physical marks on his body, because the most satisfying aspect of the entire situation was that Qianfan, Hu and Fen had no idea the other two existed. All three were young, low-level Chinese intel 'operatives' in the loosest sense of the word. They had some useful access to restricted information, and pleasuring them first with drugs and then physically invariably created a sense of gratitude that he could exploit.

Qianfan made a short little snore and turned further away from the Englishman. Good. His thoughts drifted to how his luck had changed since the maintenance team had cleaned the bots in his body the previous August. The most important defence he'd taken was to report back to London via data-pods. He recalled the maintenance guy's ludicrous protocol about mentioning the weather if he'd been compromised. Instead, all of his live 'reports' now consisted of whatever made up rubbish he could think of. At first, the strain to come up with false intel annoyed him immeasurably; then, he decided to enjoy the challenge of letting the MSS think he was sending London stale or bad intel. And all the time since last August, he'd kept the MSS at bay, he had developed his three 'habituals' and had still been able to enjoy living in the biggest, richest capital city in the most powerful country on Earth. And in certain districts in that city, if you knew where to look, there were pretty young things like his habituals, all looking for some exciting relief from the boredom their spoilt lives engendered.

He snuggled into the soft mattress and let the pillow caress the back of his head and neck. Now, with data-pods he could supply London with the genuine intel, and over the last few days, new developments had come to light with potentially far-reaching ramifications. Of course, as nearly all of the world's largest countries were dictatorships in one form or another, intel became something to treat with suspicion. New intel suggesting novel developments needed to be cross-referenced; one source simply could not be judged reliable.

And that was the true beauty of these three pretty young things he'd ensnared. A broad smile formed on the Englishman's face as the effects of the narcotics and alcohol began to wane in his body. Qianfan was an idle analyst in the sub-Asia department; Hu had a role in reviewing African deployments of Chinese operatives, while Fen, the girl that thought she was a boy, had a position that gave her access to nearly all of the intel that leaked from the sieve that was the Brazilian intelligence service.

The Englishman felt sleep descending and closed his eyes. Tomorrow morning, he would prepare the next data-pod for London, and its contents would cause more than a few ripples. And for the first time in this war—a war for the most part forgotten in China—the news would be helpful to his beloved England's cause.

Chapter 41

14.38 Tuesday 3 July 2063

Rory Moore stretched his arms high and heaved in deep breaths in preparation for the next practice run. He glanced to his left and looked along the row of this motley crew. Harry Dixon stood next to him, blond mane flapping in the breeze as he lolled his head back and forth and around in circles to limber up. Next to Harry, Nick Bird stood with his arms stretched out behind his back, half-whistling an unclear tune that sounded more like he was simply blowing air through his teeth. Finally, the wiry Irishman Declan Gardner stood immobile.

Above them, the hot summer sun baked the dusty earth and brittle concrete on the ground. Behind them stood the annoyingly familiar tall cylinders they would have to tow through the water to the north African coast when they left the claustrophobic safety of the submarine.

General Hastings stood in front of them, making eye contact with each team member in turn. "Right, chaps," he said, "unpacking and assembling the kit is going to be the most demanding part of the mission, in relation to the journey at least. It's one thing to get these equipment tubes off the sub and swim them to the shore, but when we reach enemy territory, we will have to unpack, assemble, and then bury the packaging. And, as with everything else, we will have to do it as quickly as possible."

"We thought you might say that, sir," Nick said in a light voice.

"Hmm," Hastings replied. "I'm glad to hear it, Bird. Now, we drag the cylinders up onto the beach. Then we need to: one, unpack the gear; two, assemble the five Triumph motorbikes; three, load our other supplies, including the sonic mines, water, food and fuel; four, use the portable shovels to dig enough to cover the evidence; and, five, get ourselves to Tazirbu."

"Simples," Nick muttered.

Hastings said, "You all know your own roles as well as each other's. Let's begin with cylinder one. Positions."

Rory took up his assigned position. Harry approached the first cylinder. He inserted a special metal key close to the tip of the nose cone and twisted it. A lever popped out of the housing. Harry grasped and turned it, and the nosecone broke open in two halves. Harry pulled out the first package. A thin cord connected it to all of the packages of kit further inside the cylinder. When Harry had pulled the first package a couple of metres clear, Rory and the other two moved in and also grabbed the line. With a team shout of encouragement, the cylinder's entire contents emerged into the sunlight.

Hastings called: "Separate the bike parts from the rest and assemble. Come on, look lively."

Rory gripped the package for which he had responsibility—the engine—and began ripping Velcro straps open. The noise multiplied as the others did the same. In quick succession, Declan stood the frame and offered it to Nick, who had uncovered the front fork and handlebar assembly. Harry had unpacked the seat and fuel tank, and finally the wheels, whose diameter allowed them to fit just inside the cylinder.

"Come on, big guy," Declan called.

Rory heaved the engine block, which weighed over sixty kilos, and placed it with care into the middle of the frame.

"Right, lads," Declan said, "give me the tools. Wrench first."

Over the next two minutes, Rory worked with his mates to put the Triumph Bonneville together. Declan talked as he worked, explaining the differences between this replicated version and the original design from eighty years earlier; how simple engineering advances since then allowed parts to be fixed together easily and more strongly than on the original. Rory listened as Declan described to all of them how the original carburettor functioned and how the sparkplug ignited the fuel. The super AI had improved the design and performance of the bike in ways that, obviously, would not compromise mission safety.

Once the team had put together the first bike, they moved on to the next cylinder and repeated the unpacking and assembly process. By the time all five bikes had been put together, and the water, fuel, mines, and other kit loaded, Rory's arms, legs and back ached. Hastings had not been joking about needing a strongman: Harry, Nick and Declan were barely troubling to hide their own fatigue, while Rory enjoyed the advantage of being in near-perfect health.

Hastings announced: "We'll go to the mess now and have a bite to eat. And then we'll come back and disassemble the kit and put it all back in the cylinders. Any questions?"

Declan said in a tone of complaint, "Excuse me, sir, but what is the point in having us put all the stuff back in. Are you expecting us, after the job, to clean up our mess and bring everything back? Is that it?"

"Not at all," Hastings replied. "But you are going to learn how this kit goes together inside and out, backwards and forwards. Once inserted, we need to be able to do this work on autopilot, in moonlight. And the best way to learn that, Gardner, is training. We've only got three weeks before we depart, and we still have a lot of ground to cover, both literally and metaphorically. Any more questions?"

A sudden, shocking idea formed in Rory's head. He blurted out, "Sir, you know that last year, I went through a deep clean?"

"Yes, that is one of the reasons I recruited you," Hasting replied with a trace of irritation.

"That involved the Advanced Medical Research Establishment strengthening my battlefield injures with 3-D ultra-Graphene, right inside my bones. Won't the enemy's ACAs be able to detect it? Wouldn't I be putting the whole mission at risk?" Rory noticed the attention of the others centre on Hastings.

But the general replied, "No, because you have merely strands that are too small to be detected."

"Oh, right," Rory said.

"Really, Sergeant Moore," Hastings added, "you are going to have to try a great deal harder than that to get out of going on this mission."

"Oh no, sir," Rory spluttered, "that's not what I meant..." before his words were lost under a wave of good-natured jeers from the others.

Chapter 42

08.34 Thursday 12 July 2063

David Perkins sipped his glass of cool apple juice and observed the drifting, broken cloud outside his office window. The day promised yet more withering heat and he hoped the ancient air-conditioning in the building would not break down again.

But the heat of the morning was not the only thing that made him sweat. The previous Friday, his best contact in Beijing had made a promise of significant news, and in the port on his desk sat the next data-pod.

He said, "Computer, scan the data-pod. And run SPI protocols."

"Confirmed. There is one sub-topic."

"Play sub-topic."

The familiar voice sounded in Perkins' office, "The Englishman, reporting from Beijing. The headline news is that the New Persian Caliphate might be preparing an incursion into India."

Perkins stopped musing and spun around to stare at his desk.

"I have two distinct and separate sources that confirm this. To keep this as brief as possible—"

"That would make a nice change," Perkins muttered.

"—I urge you to check the extent of Caliphate jamming. One of my contacts showed me a readout of increased levels. And no, I couldn't get a copy. He's not that stupid. This was backed up by a little snippet of Brazilian intel I got from a different and completely separate contact. Also, check things that might be below the intel radar. These include imports and exports between the Caliphate and China, and from India to China and vice versa. Get the super AI to run historical comparisons and you should see a pattern emerge which will back up the intel rumours. It could be good news for Europe if that maniac in Tehran decides to pick another fight."

Perkins exhaled and nodded in agreement.

"Also, I don't think this is any kind of decoy. The situation in Europe simply doesn't exist here. All the usual business that the most powerful countries engage in has been continuing since last year with barely a mention of the Third Caliph's unfinished business with Europe. Even now, if you ask any random Chinese person in the street, they'll probably be able to point Europe out on a map, but that would be about it."

"Stop rambling," Perkins admonished.

"Even last year's tsunami failed to cause the kind of outrage I might've expected to see even just a couple of years ago. That's partly why I think you need to act on this intel and am as convinced as I can be that it's genuine. Sub-topic ends."

"Computer? Do as he says. Analyse historical import and export patterns between those countries, identify unusual recent changes, if any, and hypothesise their causes and speculate the reasons."

"Confirmed."

"How long will it take?"

"Up to five minutes."

"I think you must be slowing down."

"Current performance lev—"

"Not now," Perkins broke in with a wave of his hand. "Give me red-level comms to Field Marshal Sir Terry Tidbury."

"He is currently engaged."

"I'll wait. Put him in the wall screen."

"Confirmed."

Perkins sipped his apple juice, the liquid having lost its coolness. He paced around his office, holding onto his patience.

A moment later, the field marshal's curious face appeared in Perkins' screen. The soldier asked: "Mr Perkins, can you make it quick?"

"Sir Terry, I have some information that may be of use to us."

"Summarise for me now, please."

"There are indications the New Persian Caliphate is massing forces on its eastern borders. This might be a prelude to a potential assault on India."

Sir Terry's head leaned out of view and Perkins caught some indistinct muttering. He came back into view and said, "What indications?"

Perkins repeated what the Englishman's data-pod contained.

Sir Terry asked: "What do you think we should do with this intel?"

Perkins was surprised at the question. He tilted his head. "My reaction would be to disseminate it. I assume that having the world's attention on a new and potentially terrible crisis would benefit Operation Repulse, yes?"

"It would," the field marshal replied. "Let me know how you get on, please."

Perkins nodded and Sir Terry's face vanished. Perkins said: "Computer? What about my request?"

"Results are ready."

"Summarise."

"An analysis of over fifty thousand publicly available data units suggests a pattern, based on movements of international trade in non-replicable materials and other goods in the last two months, that the New Persian Caliphate has taken steps that would facilitate an attempt to invade northern India."

"What about Pakistan?"

"Insufficient data."

"Show me a map of the area and explain."

A map of the region resolved in the screen, showing what was left of Pakistan after the wars that ended in the formation of the Caliphate twenty-one years earlier in 2042, and the Caliphate's border with India, which included a sizable demilitarised zone.

The super AI said, "The Caliphate has intensified jamming over eighty percent of the border zones. In addition to the international trade changes, cross-referencing this data with global currency movements further supports the hypothesis that the Caliphate is taking a more belligerent stance."

"What is the Indian military's state of readiness?"

There came a moment's silence while the super AI did its research. It reported: "All available indications show no increase in its state of readiness."

"Really?" Perkins said with a smile. "Well, let's see if we can't do something about that. Computer? Comms now to Vivek Singh, Intelligence Bureau of India. And put him in the wall screen."

The map of the subcontinent vanished and a face resolved. The man had a heavy complexion the colour of burnt chestnut. Suspicious eyes peered out from a fleshy face. Singh said, "Good day, sir..." his coarse voice trailed off as recognition dawned. He said, "Is that really you, David?"

Perkins allowed himself the rare luxury of a smile. "Yes, it is," he replied. "How long has it been, Vivek?"

The man also smiled, his jowls lifting, and he exclaimed: "Goodness, it must be at least ten—no, wait twelve years, since you came here to learn how to do proper intelligence work."

"I'm head of MI5 now," Perkins said, keeping the pride from his voice.

"That is marvellous indeed. You were the very wily one, now I remember."

"Vivek, it would be good to catch up, but first I wanted to let you know that we've come across some intel you might be interested in."

Vivek's face creased in curiosity. "I am all ears," he said.

Chapter 43

19.01 Tuesday 17 July 2063

Colonel Trudy Pearce stared at the map of Crowhurst barracks in the screen on her office wall. "Marta, I never thought we'd get as big as this."

Her adjutant, Marta Woodward, replied: "When I was posted here last September, the plan was to increase the barracks' capacity to twenty thousand."

"And now it's thirty thousand, plus equipment."

"I think you're running a good base, ma'am."

Trudy smiled. "Less of the mutual appreciation society, young lady. If I were in charge of this many troops in peacetime, I'd be a general."

Marta's eye twitched and she said, "We've just received confirmation of tomorrow's deliveries of stores."

"Any fresh fruit and veg?"

"Only the minimum tonnage, ma'am, I'm afraid. How do you want the kitchens to allocate those supplies?"

"Let me think." Trudy's thoughts drifted as her eyes roamed the plan of the huge base. Her base. Today was three-hundred-and-seven days since she'd last had a drink. She counted every day. She still missed the deep, physical calm she distantly recalled suffusing her limbs and mind by the third vodka and tonic. She wondered if the need for alcohol would ever recede. She doubted it and a part of her accepted that she would always have to live with the dissatisfied need, the ever-unquenched thirst. But she had far more to live for today than she ever thought possible. If only Dan could've lived to see it.

"Squonk?" she called. "Update current status for Operation Repulse."

The British Army's super AI replied, "Preparations for Operation Repulse are proceeding according to plan. The operation is due to commence in fourteen days, six hours—"

"That's enough," she broke in. "How many infantry brigades stationed at these barracks are assigned to go in with the first wave?"

"Three, totalling approximately six thousand troops."

Trudy glanced at Marta with an eyebrow raised in question.

Marta said, "I don't recommend it, ma'am."

"Why not?" Trudy inquired.

"Unless… I suppose you could bring the briefing forward?"

Trudy repeated, "Why not?" in a rhetorical tone. "All new leave is cancelled from tonight, anyway. And comms are secure."

"How about at this evening's sitrep?"

"That would at least give us some justification for favouritism regarding the fruit and veg."

"Good idea. Start notifying the ranks. Let's gather all the captains, majors and lieutenant colonels in the central conference room—"

"Maybe the new hangar, W4, on the west side would be better, ma'am? We're talking about more than sixty officers going over in the first wave. Also, that hanger is housing three hundred X–7s and over a hundred X–9s."

Trudy considered before replying, "I had wanted a screen to explain their objectives."

Marta said, "Perhaps give them just an outline for now? Details can follow closer to the day."

"Okay. If it's that many officers, use Squonk to arrange it."

"Yes, ma'am."

"Dismissed."

Marta nodded and left Trudy's office.

Once alone, Trudy asked: "Squonk, any notifications from HQ?"

"Only the daily intel package."

"What's in it?"

"New data on warrior training methods and more detailed estimated tolerances of the personal shielding that protects members of the enemy's elite corp."

"Okay. Don't disseminate that yet, I will do so at the sitrep later."

"Confirmed."

She sauntered over to the large window that looked north over one of the four huge training grounds. "What is the current status of this base?"

"Operating as normal."

"Specify today's current automated actions."

"Construction replicators AR–14 and AR–76 are sinking the piles on which hanger N6 will stand. The stores replicator has today issued three hundred and ten replacement combat uniforms or parts thereof, plus forty-eight replacement pairs of boots and ninety-three sets of webbing. Arms and other lethal munitions are on their arranged supply schedule. Hangar N6 will be erected by 13.00 tomorrow. Thirty minutes after then, four hundred Scythe X–7s will begin to arrive on autonomous cargo transports, requiring two hours for the delivery to be completed. Commencing at seventeen hundred, a convoy of ACTs carrying small arms will begin to arrive."

"I thought we had a full inventory of small arms."

"Affirmative. These are for support waves in the second week after Operation Repulse commences."

"Good. What about the new ATTs?"

"Increased deliveries of autonomous troop transports will begin next Wednesday, followed by sufficient Boeing 828 autonomous air transports to commence Operation Repulse."

"Are all ATTs fitted with Falaretes for self-defence?"

"Affirmative."

"Good," Trudy repeated, staring at platoons of troops running across the baked field. A wave of pride ran through her for all that she'd achieved since the enemy's failed invasions. As Crowhurst expanded, Trudy had placed a huge emphasis on physical fitness, training new recruits hard to burn off the excess bodyfat with which so many of them arrived. The troops' days were always full, with physical exercise as well as combat training. She encouraged her commissioned subordinates to interact with the squads and platoons they commanded to foster comradeship. Discipline remained good and any problematic squaddies could be reassigned by the super AI to positions better suited for their personal shortcomings.

She asked: "Has Marta notified all of the relevant commanders?"

"Affirmative."

Trudy decided to walk to the new hangar. She left her office, spoke briefly to Master Sergeant Pierre LaRue about the state of health among the most recent arrivals and approved a request for additional GenoFluid packs from the base's onsite doctor.

She exited the building and began the half-hour walk to hangar W4. The orange sun hung low and hot over the westward horizon, and as she strode on it finally dipped below a building. She marvelled at the level of organisation she'd never expected England to survive long enough to see. Super artificial intelligence managed almost all logistical issues. Although the food replicators for the most part produced shit, other machines were able to churn out uniforms and boots, while buildings could be put up without human effort. And on top of all that, the computers organised the provisioning and movements of an army now over three million strong. Trudy reflected that for all the pride she felt in having overseen so much expansion at Crowhurst, there were many other bases scattered the length and breadth of England that could boast more impressive stats than hers.

The walk to the hangar stretched tendons and muscles that had become stiff and lazy from another day of the relative inactivity of discussing, clarifying, encouraging, extoling and listening to superiors and subordinates. She entered hangar W4 and the coolness of the air allowed her to draw in a light and easy breath free from humidity and heat. The grey metal crossbeams above her ran parallel for more than fifty metres.

Protected from the outside heat and bright sun, two rows of the new Scythe X–7 ACAs lined the external walls. She strolled to the nearest machine and appreciated the smoothness of its lines that remained partially hidden by its translucent protective covering. It looked nothing like the awkward, bulky PeaceMaker. The Scythe X–7 had leaner curves with a body shaped as though it had been designed to cut through the air with effortless ease. Trudy stared at the hidden central portion that housed the Pulsar.

The slight whine of a vehicle arriving came to her ears. She turned back to see figures enter through the large hangar doors. She greeted each one by their first names: men and women with whom she'd been working for months. More vehicles arrived and discharged captains, majors and two lieutenant colonels. Trudy's spirit rose when she spoke to them. Some of the captains had known no other base: they had arrived from basic training, developed and had been commissioned. Soon, these young men and women would lead their own companies into battle.

Trudy disseminated the day's intel report and held a brief discussion on its contents. She moved on to describe their place in Attack Group South, noting the serious expressions. She curtailed the briefing so as not spend too much time on the minutiae, because there would be many occasions in the next two weeks for detailed planning for each company of infantry and the role they would play in the overall strategy. Trudy made the briefing just long and detailed enough to justify giving the base's meagre fruit and veg delivery to those troops who would go over in the first wave, as per Marta's unspoken suggestion earlier. None of her subordinates dissented when she made the decision.

Night had fallen by the time the briefing ended. The air outside the hangar held onto the day's heat like she held onto her memories of Dan. She boarded one of the vehicles with the others to return to her quarters. Trudy peered through the window, looking at the stars. She could hardly contain her enthusiasm for Operation Repulse, and counted each day until it began. She dreamed of all the enemy warriors she would kill.

Chapter 44

14.02 Tuesday 24 July 2063

Rory Moore finally realised the full extent of the trouble he'd got himself into now that Operation Thunderclap was about to begin. He stood on the quayside at the Royal Navy base in Faslane, Scotland. The huge, black bulk of *HMS Spiteful* lay in the water, immobile yet somehow menacing. His chest heaved after the exertion of helping to load the supplies for the operation, even though a quayside crane had done most of the heavy lifting.

From next to him, Nick Bird gave Rory a friendly nudge. "Beginning to wish I'd said 'no' to the guvnor now. How about you?"

Rory glanced down at the affable Londoner, his normally chirpy voice subdued. He nodded to the *Spiteful*. "Eighteen days cramped inside that thing are going to be the worst for me. I hated it last year and I am not expecting it to be any more pleasant this time around. Completing the mission on the bikes will be a piece of cake by comparison."

The large equipment loading hatch in the aft section of the submarine clunked shut, and the hard edges of the submarine were uniform once more.

Nick said, "You reckon those bikes are gonna stay the distance?"

Rory shrugged. "They should do, but we've got redundancy."

"I ain't sure. It'll be bloody baking out in that desert."

Rory gave Nick a withering look. "Do you reckon?"

"What if three of them break down?"

"Then you'll have a long walk back, won't you? Look, Declan's happy enough, so just relax."

"Relax? We were supposed to have had seven more weeks to get ready for this mission, and then they say it's changed and we have to go sooner, when the bloody desert will be at its hottest. And you, you big, lumbering giant, tell me to 'relax'. Yeah, okay then."

A new voice spoke: "Loading all complete, chaps?"

Rory turned, recognising Harry Dixon's upper-class accent. "Seems like it," he said. "Declan's in that thing now, making sure the kit is stowed securely."

"Excellent," Harry said, the sun flashing off of his blond hair. "I've had a chat with some of the bridge crew. They haven't been told a great deal more than their route and timings, and the general thinks we should keep it like that."

"Where is he?" Rory asked. "Don't we finally have to get on that bloody thing soon?"

"In good time, old boy," Harry replied.

Rory glanced at Nick and they both rolled their eyes at Harry's accent.

"Besides which," Harry went on, "we need to wait for the leaving party."

"Sounds great," Nick said. "Will we have some booze, then?"

Rory smirked.

Harry said: "It's not that kind of party, you pill."

Declan Gardner emerged on the hull of the submarine and paced with care along the narrow gangway that led from the vessel's hull to the quayside. He reached them, pointed back at the gangway, and observed, "That thing is a death-trap, I'm telling you."

Harry nodded back to the *Spiteful*. "Is everything secure?"

"It is. Mind you, there's no spare room at all."

Nick said, "Just as long as the kit works when we get there, that's all that matters."

Rory said, "Being scrunched won't cause it any grief, but when we leap off that bloody thing and into the Med, well, that might."

Nick indicated further along the quayside. "Look sharp, lads, guvnor's here."

The four young men turned and Rory noticed Hastings' unusual gait, as though one of his legs were shorter than the other. The general approached, dressed in his uniform with a cap dipping stylishly over the right side of his hair.

Harry announced, "All the kit is stowed, sir."

"Good," Hastings replied. He stood in front of Rory and the others, and said: "Right, chaps. We've got a leaving party due here and I think the captain will get us below decks and on our way."

Rory noticed the bulky form of an autonomous troop transport rolling along the expansive quayside towards them. It arrived and stopped. The main doors opened and four figures stepped out. Rory's mouth fell open when he recognised Field Marshal Sir Terry Tidbury, Supreme Allied Commander, Europe. He glanced to his right to see similar shocked looks on the faces of Nick and Declan, while at the other end of their short line, Harry's face beamed with pride.

Rory turned his head forward again to confirm he wasn't hallucinating. The field marshal stood shorter than Rory had imagined. His round, bald pate was supported by an extra roll of flesh around his neck. His chest protruded in a manner that suggested an artillery shell would not dent it. Rory recognised the commander standing next to Terry as Commadore Young, acting head of the Royal Navy. He thought that did not mean a great deal, given that the entire Royal Navy now consisted of just four submarines. The two commanders were accompanied by their adjutants.

Hastings addressed the field marshal: "Thank you for taking the time out of your busy schedule to travel here, Sir Terry. This is the specialist team I briefed you on."

"Good to be here, General Hastings," the Field Marshal replied.

Hastings guided the field marshal along the line: "This is Captain Harry Dixon, Royal Anglian."

Sir Terry saluted and said, "Good luck on your mission, captain."

Harry saluted. "Thank you, field marshal."

Hastings then indicated Declan. "This is Second Lieutenant Gardner, formerly of the Royal Irish, now on secondment."

The field marshal saluted and repeated his wishes.

Hastings said, "This is Bombardier Nicolas Bird formerly of the London Regiment, now on secondment."

And then the field marshal stood in front of Rory.

Hastings said, "And this is Colour Sergeant Rory Moore, formerly of the 21 Royal Engineers, now on secondment."

Rory stared dumbfounded as the field marshal saluted him.

"21 Engineers? How is Colonel Doyle these days?"

"Er, very well, sir. The last time I saw him, at any rate."

Terry stepped back and asked Hastings, "May I, general?"

Hastings smiled and indicated with a wave of his arm.

Terry said, "Men, due to the importance of this mission, you've already been briefed on what our forces are going to begin next week. I would like to offer you my apologies for the truncated training time, although your CO assures me you are ready. Our allies have been champing at the bit, which is why the start date was brought forward. Nevertheless, Operation Repulse cannot succeed unless you do. It really is that simple. What you achieve when you are inside enemy territory will make all the difference to the future of Europe. You take with you the hopes and best wishes not only of everyone at SHAPE, but also of all NATO forces. Good luck." Terry turned to Hastings. "I think the *Spiteful*'s captain might be getting impatient to get underway."

Hastings smiled. "Quite so, field marshal. I look forward to debriefing you on our return. Perhaps, if you wouldn't mind, one of your assistants might book a table at my club, the Twenty-nine in Kensington? I think that might be a more agreeable location for our debrief."

Terry nodded. "Indeed. I expect Repulse will be done and dusted by the time you get back, for the most part."

Hastings nodded his agreement. The field marshal and his party reboarded the ATV. The door slid closed and the vehicle rolled away.

Hastings turned to his team. "Let's embark. Come along."

Rory followed the general along with the rest of the team. He stopped at the narrow gangplank to let the others go first.

Declan said, "Thanks, fella. And don't go starting to cross this rickety thing until I'm safely off the other side, will you?"

Rory nodded in acceptance and fought down an overwhelming urge to leap onto the gangplank and jump up and down on it when Declan was halfway. Instead, he looked at the broken cloud scudding past above them, the choppy water that sloshed at the sides of the black submarine, and wondered how long it would be before he would again be able to stand out in the open like this in safety.

Memories resurfaced in his mind's eye, of fearing for how long his luck might last, of the instants of disorientation when shrapnel hit him, of panic when he believed he'd reached the end. A strong breeze blew into his face suddenly. Declan jumped off the far end of the gangway. The memories faded in realisation that his war was not yet over. Rory hurried onto the hull of the submarine, eager to catch up with his teammates.

Chapter 45

14.01 Monday 30 July 2063

Anger and frustration burned inside Captain Pip Clarke. The heat suffocated her, like the air itself had turned to soup. She stomped across the airfield towards her quarters at Rochester barracks. Every time she inhaled, her blood seemed to obtain less oxygen. This aggravated her mood further. The sun bore down on the shrivelled grass, hot like a blowtorch. She tried to identify the real source of her emotion, but too many causes offered themselves up for the first prize.

She loathed still being stuck at Rochester after nearly two months. She'd done everything she'd been sent here to do. She'd also helped with the reconstruction after the successful enemy attack in May. Perhaps, she considered, that was where it had all gone wrong: ever since what the media and everyone else now called the 'Medway Incident', friction between the military and the locals had boiled over into fights in Rochester, Chatham and Gillingham, at least until Major Pickard, now the base's commander, had confined all troops to barracks.

But while this allowed local civilian issues to cool, it had made the barracks themselves a hotbed of rumour and pent-up resentment towards the local populations that had caused the thousands of newly trained recruits—from all over England—to be hemmed in. In addition, to placate the locals and diffuse the media attention, Brass had announced an investigation into the incident, and despite her not being involved at all, she sensed it might turn into a witch hunt that required victims to be burned at the stake.

Suddenly, a red-level comms flashed in her view. Finally, it was her recall to her own barracks. She jogged across the airfield, reached her quarters, and packed her kitbag. She activated her Squitch to confirm her orders. Hauling the kitbag and Bergan, she hurried to the armoury and collected her Pickup. As she expected, her Squitch told her to return her six magazines of ammunition. She did so and exited the armoury. Pip found a quiet spot close to where her Squitch told her the AAT would arrive. She waited with a mix of patience, relief, and happiness at finally escaping the awful Medway Towns, a mass of concrete and sad, bland little hovels no one in their right mind would choose to live in.

After ten minutes, a distant black dot in the sky grew in definition. The small Airbus touched down on the apron. When her Squitch instructed her, she approached the AAT and entered it. She stowed her kit and secured her Pickup. She was surprised to find the fuselage empty. She asked: "Do I get my very own transport all the way back to Catterick?"

Squonk replied: "Negative. Your Squitch will now display this flight's itinerary."

In her lens, the list included twelve stops. The AAT would fly west parallel to the south coast before turning northeast. Pip was the only passenger scheduled for the entire flight. But her mood lifted as soon as the aircraft rose fifty or so metres above the airfield, banked to the west, and accelerated.

Over the next three hours, Pip felt the claustrophobia of Rochester dissipate through conversations with strangers. At a base near Tonbridge, a four-man squad boarded. She chatted with them and found out they were left behind from a regiment-level relocation of troops to close to Pip's battles on the south coast. A larger group of non-coms from the Guards then boarded and also mentioned troop movements. Finally, she shared the final leg of the flight with two Royal Engineers who were returning from western England after having attended a course on the Scythes' propulsion systems.

The AAT finally set down at Catterick and Pip's spirit filled with relief that she'd returned to her home base. Lugging her kit with her Pickup slung muzzle up behind her, Pip followed the directions as her Squitch guided her to the temporary accommodation block. The afternoon air smelled fresh and the wind blew cooler this far north. The entire garrison seemed far busier than she remembered, but then, as with all the other bases, the ranks must have also swollen here.

Two hours later, refreshed and rested, Pip headed for the assembly room, a large hall on the ground floor of the main red-bricked Georgian building around which the base was centred. She filed in with many other officers, from second lieutenants up to lieutenant colonels. She glanced at the other figures; their names, ranks and commands resolved next to them but she recognised none. She took up a position to one side. She noticed there were no chairs. This boded well: whatever information was about to be delivered shouldn't take very long. As more people entered, the swell of additional bodies forced her further along the wall. Abruptly she realised chairs hadn't been put out because there were too many people.

At length, a certain quietness descended. Coughs and shuffles and muted whispers floated around the hall and echoed off the high windows and ceiling. There came a click and a creak from the main door and Colonel Doyle entered, appearing exactly the same as he had when Pip last saw him. She recalled being in his office with Rory after they'd escaped Spain, leaving Pratty and Crimble behind from their squad.

Doyle mounted a low, wooden stage, cleared his throat and said: "Good evening, ladies and gentlemen. I will try to keep this as succinct as possible. I have very important information to impart to you."

Pip was taken aback. She looked at the dozens of other faces in the packed hall and their expressions ranged from trepidation to delighted enthusiasm. Suddenly, the conversations she'd had on the AAT earlier in the day took on a new meaning. Of course, there'd been rumours; all the troops were guessing and second—

"In a little over twenty-four hours," Doyle said, "NATO forces will launch an invasion of Europe. This invasion will be carried out by two thrusts. In northern Europe, Attack Group East will disable enemy forces in the Netherlands and Belgium before advancing into Germany. Attack Group South will invade France. Please raise the highest feed in your visions now to see the maps of the invasion plan for the first ten days."

Every eye in the hall twitched. Pip looked on in shock as the plans for the retaking of the European mainland resolved in her vision.

Doyle went on, "You will no doubt be pleased to hear that I managed to reserve some of the most important objectives for we Royal Engineers."

A vast cheer went up in the room. Pip smiled. Whooping and clapping rang out but quickly subsided when Doyle raised his hand.

"All of you will shortly receive orders for the specific objectives of the troops under your command. You are not at liberty to discuss those objectives until two hours before you go in. In the meantime, I suggest you refer to 'special manoeuvres' or a 'special night training exercise'."

Doyle paused and looked around the hall. "I shan't try to deceive you, troops. I have too much respect for you to do that. Operation Repulse is well planned and very well equipped. The new Scythe ACAs will really take the fight to the enemy. But there is every possibility we will be obliged to suffer casualties, although we anticipate only the minimum number. Therefore, I remind each of you that you represent one thousand years of history of providing service to the British, now the English, crown. Take a moment to reflect on all that the Royal Engineers have achieved down the centuries, and understand that what you will embark upon tomorrow is the next step in our on-going and illustrious history. Dismissed."

The double doors clicked open. Pip looked at the detailed plans that her Squitch revealed to her of her small role in the operation. A memory came to Pip of the regiment's first deployment to Spain the previous year. Doyle had given a similar speech about defending Europe; and now, eighteen months later, she would be in the first wave to claim it back.

The other troops filed out of the hall. Pip made her way out of the front of the building and into the cool evening air. Away from any other people, she still spoke quietly to ensure she wouldn't be overheard: "Contact Colour Sergeant Rory Moore, Royal Engineers."

The super AI replied: "Communication with Sergeant Moore is not possible at this time."

"Why not?" Pip asked, shocked.

"That information is restricted."

Pip's shock turned to concern. "Is he still alive?"

"Affirmative."

"Can you tell me anything else about him or his whereabouts?"

"Negative."

Chapter 46

10.09 Tuesday 31 July 2063

Maria Phillips readied herself for what she would find on the dilapidated small pleasure boat that had drifted into the Port of Dover during the night. Two of the onsite techies had secured a rope and dragged it to the quayside.

Her friend Nabou gave her a smile of encouragement, her brilliant white teeth complimenting her onyx skin. She said, "Relax, Maz. It is not going to be anything worse than we have dealt with fifty times before."

"But we're qualified field surgeons now," Maria complained, raising her hand to shade her eyes from the bright morning sun.

"There has been no action for months and months," Nabou said.

"Yeah," Maria conceded, "can't say I'm disappointed about that."

"Besides, the techies that brought it in said it felt light."

"I can't believe they didn't check it themselves."

"Look, it has a lower deck. They probably did not feel like it."

"And you do?"

Nabou smiled again and shrugged. "It is our job. Stay here. I will go."

"That's it. Make me feel guilty, why don't you?"

Nabou said nothing as she leaned forward and stepped on the broken and faded white plastic of the rear footplate. She climbed into the small pleasure craft. Two padded benches lined the main area and the wheel had glass and wood housing to protect it.

Maria followed her friend and shivered at the state of the interior. Some kind of plastic hung from the benches and the wood colour had been sun-bleached a sickly yellow.

Nabou turned back. "Stay here. I will do this one."

Maria nodded, placing her legs apart as an arriving wave rocked the little boat.

Nabou disappeared into the forward compartment and emerged again. "It is empty, Maz. Have a look."

Maria did so and felt relieved that for once there were no decayed, rotted or shrivelled corpses to collect and try to identify. She followed Nabou and climbed back onto the quay. They began trudging back towards their hospital close to the main port building.

"Have you seen Felix lately?" Maria asked referring to the harbourmaster.

"Not since his last check-in. The nanobots in the pack flagged one or two problems. Ranny asked me for advice."

"And?"

Nabou's head tilted up in consideration, "I do not think I am qualified, Maz. I suggested to Ranny that he refer the harbourmaster to an expert."

"He's always struck me as—" Maria broke off when a red-level comms notification arrived in her lens. She glanced at Nabou and asked: "You've got it too?"

"Yes."

"Rats," she exclaimed. "We've been transferred. I can't believe it."

"I am surprised, I think," Nabou said, her voice lacking its usual enthusiasm.

"You think you're surprised?" Maria questioned.

"Yes, we have been here for nearly a year, Maz. After all that happened before that, I am... happy here?"

They stopped walking. Seagulls cawed over the sea, the shore, and in front of the cliffs from the base of which they had collected more than a few bodies.

Maria said, "I am as well, mate. But this is war. The order says we've been attached to First Corps for further operations. And actually, we don't have much time before the transport will arrive to take us to Crowhurst barracks."

Nabou strode off and Maria followed. She caught up with her athletic Senegalese friend.

"It must mean something," Nabou said. "Doctor Miller and Ranny will not be able to manage everything by themselves."

"They might have to," Maria said, skipping every third step to keep up.

"Did Mark say anything? When did you speak to him last?"

"A few days ago," Maria said. "But whenever he's hinted at something, he said it wouldn't be for months yet."

"The order says we must go to the barracks where we will receive a further briefing."

Maria said, "What if they were planning something and brought the date forward?"

Nabou replied: "Hmm. So perhaps we will get a chance soon to use our skills as surgeons?"

Maria's heart beat faster, and not only because of the exertion of keeping up with Nabou.

Her friend urged: "Come on. We have less than fifteen minutes to pack and say goodbye to everyone."

"I know, but don't run. Please don't..." Maria's words trailed off as Nabou broke into her elegant running stride and effortlessly pulled away. Maria sighed and did not try to pursue, her mind flooding with questions and a strange excitement that a change had finally arrived.

Chapter 47

13.09 Tuesday 31 July 2063

With one hand, Professor Duncan Seekings held onto the side of the small sink in his kitchenette. With his free hand, he flipped the lid off of the small metal container in which he kept his tea bags.

"Oh, blast. Last one," he muttered to himself. He tipped it into the mug on the work surface. The kettle chimed. He lifted it and wondered if he hadn't poured too much water in it, for it was extremely heavy. He filled the mug and some water splashed over the rim and onto the work surface.

"Damn," he said, and decided not to try and wipe up the spillage as it wasn't such a mess anyway. He added the milk and his free hand trembled. He paused, regulated his breathing, and wondered why even the simplest tasks seemed to demand greater effort. He lifted the mug of hot tea and held on to the available fixtures as he made his way through the doorway and back to the couch. He placed the mug on the coffee table, but as soon as he let go of the handle, it toppled over and hit the carpeted floor. The brown tea splashed out and quickly formed a large stain on the tan rug.

Duncan sighed and flopped down into the couch. "That was the last tea bag," he said with a trace of the mildest annoyance. He reached across for the small GenoFluid pack the doctor had given him two days earlier. Or had it been three days? Never mind. He lifted the pack and rested it in the crook between his shoulder and neck.

A moment later, an alert flashed in his lens. He read it but, oddly, did not understand the words. A wave of pain swept from the top of his head down his spine. He read the alert again and said, "What a bore." His strength abruptly left him, but he did not know if it was because of tiredness or for a different reason.

Squonk announced: "Information. The nanobots in the GenoFluid pack have identified increasing numbers of super-cancer strands in the upper thalamus. Appropriate corrective measures have commenced."

Duncan thought about the words but struggled to comprehend them. Was something wrong? He decided to speak to his friend. "Comms," he said, and then waited.

Squonk said, "Specify contact."

"What? Oh, what's his name, you know… English. Graham English."

His friend's face appeared in the bottom-left of his vision. "Ah, old chap. How are you doing over there?"

Something happened and Duncan did not understand the words. The pain in his head worsened. He couldn't speak and only stared at a face he recognised but could no longer place.

"I said," Graham repeated, "how are you?"

"What?" Duncan replied, the words suddenly making sense. "Yes, well, sort of, I suppose. But you fouled the black so that's seven points to me. And a free ball because I can't see both sides of a red."

"Are you feeling quite all right, professor?"

"Of course I am," Duncan protested, not at all sure how he felt. "I found the snags," he announced. "All of the little blighters. Every single one of them."

"Er, what snags, old chap?"

"The sonic mines," Duncan said, wondering if the man, which he now remembered was his friend, was being deliberately obtuse. "For that odd, thin, little fellow—what's his name? General Hastings, yes, and his jaunt to the snooker world championships. Although I must say," Duncan added on reflection, "it really is bit rum for a solider like that to take my sonic mines to watch the snooker."

"Are you quite sure—?"

"Really, Mr English. What is the matter with you? Have you been practising without telling me again? I know, I know, your flying hairnet was jolly clever, but my sonic mines are better—why, I do believe they might even—ah, right. Yes, I probably shouldn't be talking about sonic mines."

The tone of Graham's voice changed. He said, "Professor, I am contacting the medical facility at Porton Down and telling them you need urgent assistance."

"How odd," Duncan said, full lucidity returning, along with a vast and punishing pain in his neck and across his shoulders. "There's no need for that, old man," he said with a sigh. "It's already too late, you see? I just, well, I just wanted to say thank you, Mr English. And goodbye. Yes, I wanted to say goodbye. I think I must leave now. You see, they first warned me months ago."

"Oh, Lord. Surely not?"

"I'm afraid so, yes. And if the super-cancer cells inside my brain mutate in certain ways, you'll need three snookers to win the frame. And, really, Mr English, is either of us capable of coming back in a frame when needing three snookers?"

"You don't need the snookers, professor. I fouled the black. Seven points to you and a free ball. You haven't lost the frame. Please, professor, I implore you. You can win and we can enjoy one more game."

Duncan's vision filled with flashing red indicators, but he did not know what they signified. Didn't red mean danger? No, a red was only worth one point. So, therefore, they could not mean a great deal.

"Professor? Professor, please."

Duncan's head lolled back on the couch and his hearing and sight failed. The super-cancer strands in his brain accelerated, multiplying far faster than the nanobots in the GenoFluid pack could keep up with. Finally, they smothered the neurons inside the medulla oblongata, which controlled Duncan's breathing, and his brain stopped telling his lungs to inhale.

Chapter 48

21.53 Tuesday 31 July 2063

Terry looked at Dahra Napier's face and a feeling of discomfort made him lean back a little. He had much to deal with this night, and the PM seemed overly concerned.

They stood in front of the elegant marble fireplace in the flat at Ten Downing Street. The screen on the wall displayed a map of the coastal areas of northern Europe, with locations indicated as 'R-plus-one' objectives.

"But, realistically," she said, thin eyebrows coming together in worry, "we are going to have casualties, yes?"

"In my opinion, we will suffer some, PM. But that is the nature of warfare. As much as is possible, the ACAs will clear the ground before the air transports go in. In the last two months, we've run thousands of training approaches to typical enemy positions, and we know what we intend to do. Tonight, my only real concern is if the enemy has developed new weapons of which we are not aware, and tomorrow morning will introduce them to destroy our forces. Since we repelled the two attempted invasions last year, we've been in a race to develop and deploy new machines. At least, NATO has."

Napier nodded and half-smiled. "I know. All this tension over whether the Caliphate will invade India has been a useful distraction."

"More than just useful. I was not inclined to believe he had given up on the British Isles. But as time has passed, it seems the enemy has indeed considered us defeated and that we no longer presented a threat. But the increasing potential for conflict between the enemy and India may possibly represent the only evidence of that we might ever have."

"Although," Napier said, "I did not appreciate Dasgupta's assertion that his country would not yield as quickly or as completely as Europe."

Terry did not understand what she meant, and did not wish to find out. He went on: "Operation Cloud Cover will, I hope, also send misinformation, again if the enemy wishes to look. Thank you for your political work on that, PM."

"You hardly have to thank me, Terry."

"If you don't mind, I'd better get on."

"Of course, yes."

Terry nodded and turned to his adjutant, Simms. With a nod to the map on the wall over the fireplace, he instructed: "Deactivate that and let's get to the War Rooms."

Simms gave him a curt nod. The map vanished. Terry avoided looking at the PM's face before he left. He exited through the door that led to the lift. The PM's aide, Webb, gave Terry a sombre nod as he held the door open for him and Simms. Once outside in the corridor, Terry asked: "Any developments?"

"No, sir," Simms replied. "Squonk is managing base readiness across the country. It reports that the SkyMasters are ready to launch. Hundreds of wings of Scythes are ready to be brought into position."

"How long will that take, precisely?"

"A little under five hours from when you give the command to go."

They reached the lift and entered. The doors closed and Terry rocked on the balls of his feet as it descended. "Latest weather?"

"No change from the twenty-hundred forecast, sir. Atmospheric conditions are well within acceptable parameters."

"Any outstanding requests for new intel while I was talking to the PM?"

"Not at your level, sir."

Terry glanced at Simms out of the corner of his eye. "So, what have I been missing?"

The lift doors opened. Terry exited and strode with purpose down the long, grey corridor that led to the War Room complex.

Simms gave his usual tight smile. "Minor adjustments to the order of battle, effected by Squonk at corps and battalion level, requiring those commanders to sign off."

"For example?"

Terry saw Simms's eye twitch and wondered for the hundredth time if he shouldn't have one of those confounded things in his eye. Then again, his slate remained sufficient for most duties, and he preferred having Simms inform him.

His adjutant answered, "Elements of REME have been reassigned to Attack Group East as their construction replicators will more speedily help with rebuilding the Delta Works in the Netherlands. The elements remaining in Attack Group South will only require a further two hours to rebuild the expected damage at Caen."

"Very well. There's no question I would not have authorised that. Were there many other similar issues?"

"All at lower organisational levels," Simms replied. "I believe this is more a question of the computers refining and tweaking as greater or fewer assets become available. It seems, for example, a delay in the manufacture of Pulsar units caused one battalion to be lowered to the second wave of the invasion."

They reached the main War Room. Without looking at any of the operatives at the comms stations, Terry waved a hand and said, "As you were." He reached the central display console. "Squonk? Let's see NATO readiness levels, now."

In the large, empty space above the console, there resolved a holographic image of the British Isles. Indicators flashed all over England containing regiment and corps codes and a single percentage figure that denoted that element's readiness.

He glanced back to the NATO comms station to see, on the larger screen above the operator, more digital representations of hundreds of bases, barracks, airfields, and remote monitoring stations at which the commanders were watching and listening. At the next comms, Home Countries, those civilians who had security clearance were also able to attend.

"Sir, you are receiving a large number of messages of support," Simms said. "I have taken the liberty of archiving them for your later consideration, if you wish."

"Thank you, Simms," Terry replied. He stared at the map. "Squonk? Show the 'R-plus-one' objectives, how they will be obtained and by whom."

"Confirmed."

The image withdrew to bring northern Europe into view. Red lines resolved that began at points in southern England and crossed the English Channel in two directions: east and south. Many more lines appeared, splaying out at points in Belgium and the Netherlands, and to the south around Caen and the Cherbourg peninsula.

"Simms," Terry said, "is there any change or any imminently expected change in current geopolitical tensions?"

"Not that we can discern at the moment, sir."

Terry's voice dropped, and he let a trace of anger escape, "Do you think they know we're about to come for them?"

Simms appeared to consider his answer, although Terry knew it could not be known. "I believe not, sir."

"Indeed," Terry said. He ordered, "Open general comms now."

"Open, sir," called the flaxen-haired operator.

"Attention, all ranks. We have reached a moment in this conflict where, after months of determination, ingenuity and phenomenal hard work by many thousands of us, I must now decide whether to proceed." Terry paused and collected his thoughts. He went on: "When this enemy exploded on us some eighteen months ago, it quickly became apparent that the Europe we knew would in all probability be completely destroyed. We faced a cataclysm equal to any of those down the centuries that have seen entire peoples and nations removed from history by more powerful foes.

"Although the enemy caught us unawares, a year ago he made the mistake of allowing us a mere forty-eight hours to deploy a new weapon in defence of these islands. He has made another mistake by leaving us for dead and turning his attention to more attractive prey. Now, we are about to show him how much these mistakes will cost. For eighteen months, we have been fighting for our survival. In a few hours, we will begin fighting for victory, to reclaim that which has been stolen from us. Now, we will take the fight to the enemy. I thank each of you for your resolve and your courage."

Terry felt that he wanted to say more, but in his mind, he saw all of the innumerable thousands of NATO troops readying themselves and their weapons, waiting to board the aircraft that would take them to reclaim Europe. He pictured the SkyMaster battle management ACAs and the wings of Scythes, all standing by in airfields and hangars, waiting on his command. Terry felt his role diminish, somehow. He was the leader, but he knew that those he led would be the ones to fight and the ones to suffer.

He drew in a measured breath. "Squonk: by my order, field marshal, Terry Tidbury. Commence Operation Repulse."

The super AI answered, "Confirmed."

THE END

Coming from Chris James in 2023

The Repulse Chronicles
Book Six

Operation Repulse

For the latest news and releases, follow Chris James on Amazon

In the US, at:
https://www.amazon.com/Chris-James/e/B005ATW34C/

In the UK, at:
https://www.amazon.co.uk/Chris-James/e/B005ATW34C/

You can also follow his blog, at:
https://chrisjamesauthor.wordpress.com/